Dan Wells has a Bachelors in English from Brigham Young University where he was the editor of *The Leading Edge* magazine. He now runs *www.timewastersguide.com*.

By Dan Wells

I Am Not A Serial Killer
Mr Monster
I Don't Want to Kill You

I DON'T WANT TO KILL YOU

DAN WELLS

headline

First published in Great Britain in 2011 by
HEADLINE PUBLISHING GROUP

1

Cataloguing in Publication Data is available from the British Library

ISBN 978 0 7553 4883 1

Typeset in Goudy by Ellipsis Books Limited, Glasgow

Printed and bound in the UK by
CPI Mackays, Chatham ME5 8TD

Headline's policy is to use papers that are natural, renewable
and recyclable products and made from wood grown in sustainable forests.
The logging and manufacturing processes are expected to conform
to the environmental regulations of the country of origin.

HEADLINE PUBLISHING GROUP
An Hachette UK Company
338 Euston Road
London NW1 3BH

www.headline.co.uk
www.hachette.co.uk

This book is dedicated to my teachers,
who taught me how to read, and to my parents,
who taught me why.

Acknowledgements

I love writing acknowledgements, because I get to sit back and remember all the awesome people who believe in me and in my book, and who helped to make it a reality. We'll start with the professional crew: my agent, Sara Crowe, my editors, Moshe Feder and Hannah Sheppard, and the whole UK team of publicists and editors: Maura Brickell, Sam Eades, Celine Kelly, and everyone else at Headline. You guys are awesome. Next comes my writing group, the fabled Rats with Swords: Karla Bennion, Drew Olds, Ben Olsen, Janci Patterson, Brandon Sanderson, Emily Sanderson, Isaac Stewart, Eric James Stone, Heidi Summers, and Rachel Whitaker. This is such a better book thanks to their input, I can't even tell you. Many other friends and family gave their support and encouragement as well, including Martha Andelin, Dave Bird, Steve Diamond, Nick Dianatkhah, Eric Ehlers, Dawn Wells, Rob Wells, and of course my parents, Robert and Patty, whom I already mentioned in the dedication. They're going to get big heads.

Special consideration goes to Allison Hill and Jennifer Zeller, who wanted to be in my book and were intensely excited to learn of their own grisly deaths. Last but not least, a shout-out to my future son-in-law Thorfinneas Olsen: here's looking at you, big guy. Consider this the dowry.

where
always
    it's
        Spring and everyone's
in love and flowers pick themselves

'who knows if the moon's'
e. e. cummings

Prologue

I didn't know Jenny Zeller very well. Nobody did, really. I guess that's why she killed herself.

I know she used to have friends, and I know she did a lot of stuff at school. When we were kids she used to play unicorns with her friend on the playground at recess, which I remember only because I used to think her friend was cute. By middle school her friend had moved away, and Jenny ran for student government – not President, just one of the weird little ones like Secretary or Treasurer. Her campaign posters had cats on them, so I guess she liked cats. She didn't win. By high school she'd gone off my radar completely. According to her obituary, she was fluent in American Sign Language, but that's not the kind of thing that makes people remember who you are. That's the kind of thing you read in an obituary and say, 'Oh. Huh.'

Her suicide, in early July, came as a shock to everyone. She didn't leave a note – she just went to bed one night, apparently a little more melancholy than usual, and the next morning her mom found her on the floor of her bathroom with her wrists slit wide open. And the thing is, I've seen a lot of death: over the past year I've watched my neighbour across the street sprout claws and gut three people; I dragged my nearly-headless therapist from a car (oh, the irony); and I spent three days chained in a psycho's basement while he tortured and killed a parade of helpless women. I've seen a lot of sick, gory stuff, and I've even done some of it myself. I've been through a lot, to put it simply, but Jenny Zeller's death was different. Somehow, this one, simple suicide – that I didn't even witness – was the hardest to deal with.

You see, I didn't want to kill those people. I did it to save my town from a pair of vicious killers, but in doing so I had to break every rule I'd ever set for myself. In some ways I risked my life for Jenny Zeller.

But what's the point of saving someone's life if she's just going to kill herself anyway?

Chapter 1

The phone rang four times before someone picked up.

'Hello?'

A woman. Perfect.

'Hello,' I said, speaking clearly. I'd muffled the receiver with a sweater to mask my voice, and I wanted to make sure she could understand me. 'Is this Mrs Julie Andelin?'

'I'm sorry, who is this?'

I smiled. *Right to the point.* Some of them babbled on forever, and I could barely get a word in edgewise. So many mothers were like that, I'd learned: home alone all day, desperate for a conversation with anyone over the age of three. The last one I'd called had thought I was from the PTA, and talked to me for nearly a minute until I had to shout something shocking just to get her attention. This one was playing along.

Of course, what I had to say was pretty shocking regardless.

'I saw your son today.' I paused. 'He's always such a happy kid.'

Silence.

How will she react?

'What do you want?'

Once again, right to the point. Almost too practical, perhaps. *Is she scared? Is she taking this too calmly? I need to say more.*

'You'll be pleased to know little Jordan walked straight home from daycare – past the drugstore, down the street to the old red house, then around the corner and past the apartments and straight home to you. He looked both ways at every street, and he never talked to strangers.'

'Who are you?' Her breathing was heavier now; more scared, more angry. I couldn't read people very well over the phone, but Mrs Andelin had been kind enough to answer hers in the living room, and I could see her through the window. She looked out now, wide eyes peering into the darkness, then quickly wrenched the curtains closed. I smiled. I listened to the air go in and out of her nose – in and out, in and out. 'Who are you?' she demanded again.

Her fear was real. She wasn't faking – she was legitimately terrified for her son. *Does that mean she's innocent? Or just a really good liar?*

Julie Andelin had worked in the bank for nearly fifteen years, her entire adult life, and last week she had quit. That wasn't suspicious in itself – people quit jobs all the time, and it didn't mean anything except that they wanted a new job – but I couldn't afford to ignore even the smallest lead. I didn't know what the demons could do, but I'd seen at least one who could kill a person and take its place, and who's to say that this one couldn't do the same? Maybe Julie Andelin was bored with the bank, but maybe – just maybe – she was dead and gone, and had been replaced by something that couldn't keep up the same routines. A sudden change of lifestyle might be, from a certain point of view, the most suspicious thing in the world.

'What do you want with my son?'

She seemed genuine, just like every other mother I'd talked to over the last two months. *Sixty-three days, and nothing.* I knew a demon was coming because I'd called her myself – I'd literally called her, on a cellphone. Her name was Nobody. I'd told her I'd killed her friends, that they'd terrorised my town long enough and now I was taking the fight to them. My plan was to take them all like that, one by one, until finally we would all be safe. No one would have to live in fear.

'Leave us alone!' Mrs Andelin screamed.

I lowered my voice a bit. 'I have a key to your house.' It wasn't true, but it sounded great on the phone. 'I love what you've done with Jordan's room.'

She hung up, and I clicked off the phone. I wasn't sure whose it was; it was amazing the kind of stuff people dropped in a movie theatre. I'd used this one for five calls now, so it was probably time to get rid of it. I walked away, cutting through an apartment parking lot, popping open the phone and taking out the batteries and the SIM card. I dropped each piece into a separate metal garbage can, wiped my gloves clean, and slipped through a gap in the back fence.

My bike was half a block away, stashed behind a dumpster, and while I walked I scrolled through my mental list, checking off Julie Andelin's name. She was definitely the real mother, and not a demonic impostor; it had been a long shot anyway. At least I hadn't spent much time on this one; I'd 'stalked' her son for barely five minutes, but that's all it took if you knew the right things to say. Tell a mother something creepy like, 'Your daughter looks good in blue,' and the maternal instinct will kick in instantly. She'll believe the worst without any extra work on your part. It doesn't matter if her daughter has never worn blue in her entire life. As soon as you get that intense, honest fear reaction, you've got your answer and you move on to the next woman with a secret.

I was starting to realise that everyone had a secret. But in sixty-three days I still hadn't found the secret I was looking for.

I pulled out my bike, shoved my gloves into my pocket, and pushed off into the street. It was late, but it was August, and the night air was warm. It was almost time for school to start again, and I was beginning to get almost unbearably nervous. Where was Nobody? Why hadn't she done anything yet?

Finding a killer was easy; aside from all the physical evidence he or she left behind, like fingerprints and footprints and DNA, there was a mountain of psychological evidence as well. Why did they kill this person instead of that one? Why did they do it here instead of there – and why now instead of earlier or later? What weapon did they use, if any, and *how* did they use it? Piece it all together and you had a psychological profile, like an Impressionist portrait, that could lead you straight to the killer. And if only Nobody would just come out and kill someone, I'd finally be able to track her down.

Yes, finding a killer was easy. Finding someone *before* they killed was almost impossible. And the worst part about that was the way it made me, John Wayne Cleaver, so much easier to find than the demon herself. I'd already killed two people – Bill Crowley and Clark Forman, both demons in human form – so if she knew where to look and took her time, Nobody could find me so much more easily than I could find her. Every day I grew more tense, more desperate. She could be around any corner.

I had to find her first.

I pedalled towards home, silently noting the houses I had already 'cleared'. *That one's having an affair. That one's an alcoholic. That one turned out to have a massive gambling debt – Internet poker. As far as I know, she still hasn't told her family that their savings are gone . . .*

I'd started watching people, going through their trash, seeing who was out late and who was meeting whom and who had something to hide. I was shocked to find that it was almost everybody. It was like the whole town was festering in corruption, tearing itself apart before the demons had a chance to do it for them. Did people like that deserve to be saved? Did they even *want* to be saved? If they were really that self-destructive, then the demon was helping them more than I was, speeding them along in their goal of complete self-annihilation. An entire town, an entire world, slitting its vast communal wrist and bleeding out while the universe ignored us.

No. I shook my head. *I can't think like that. I have to keep going.*

I have to find the demon, and I have to stop it.

The trouble is, that's a lot harder than it sounds. Sherlock Holmes summed up the essence of investigation in a simple soundbite: *when you remove the impossible, whatever remains, however improbable, must be the truth.* Great advice, Sherlock, but you never had to track down a demon. I've seen two and talked to a third, and everything they did was impossible; I've watched them rip out their own organs, jump up after a dozen gunshot wounds, assimilate other people's limbs, and even feel other people's emotions. I've watched them steal identities and faces and entire lives. For all I knew, they could do literally anything: how was I supposed to figure them out? If Nobody would just freaking kill someone already, then I'd have something to go on.

I was almost home, but I stopped halfway down my block to stare up at a tall beige house. Brooke's house. We'd gone on two dates, both cut short by the discovery of a dead body, and I'd really started to . . . like her? I didn't know if that was even possible. I'd been diagnosed with sociopathy, a psychological disorder that meant, among other things, that I couldn't feel empathy. I couldn't connect to Brooke, not really. Did I enjoy her company? Yes. Did I dream about her at night? Yes again. But the dreams were not good, and my company was worse. All the better, then, that she'd started to avoid me. It wasn't a break-up, because we'd never been 'together', but it was the platonic analogue of a break-up, whatever that's called. There's really no way to misinterpret 'you scare me and I don't want to see you any more'.

I suppose I could see her side of it. I came at her with a knife, after all, and that's a hard thing to get over, even if I did have a good reason. Save a girl's life by threatening it and she'll have just enough time to say 'thank you' before she says 'goodbye'.

Still, that didn't stop me from slowing down when I passed

her house, or from stopping – like tonight – and wondering what she was doing. So she'd left me; big deal. Everyone else had. The only person I really cared about was Nobody, and I was going to kill her.

Yay me.

I pushed off the kerb and rode two doors down, to the mortuary at the end of the street. It was a biggish building, with a chapel and some offices and an embalming room in the back. I lived upstairs with my mom in a little apartment; the mortuary was our family business, though we kept the part about me embalming people a secret. Bad for business. Would you let a sixteen year old embalm your grandmother? No? Neither would anyone else.

I tossed my bike against the wall in the parking lot and opened the side door. Inside was a little stairwell with two exits: a door at the bottom that led to the mortuary, and a door at the top that led into our apartment. The light bulb was burned out, and I trudged upstairs in the dark. The TV was on; that meant Mom was still up. I closed my eyes and rubbed them tiredly; I really didn't want to talk to her. I stood in silence a moment, bracing myself, and then a phrase from the TV caught my ear:

'. . . *found dead* . . .'

I smiled and threw open the door. There'd been another death. Nobody had finally killed someone! After sixty-three days, it was finally starting.

Day 1.

Chapter 2

The demon had killed a priest.

It was right there on the news – a pastor had been found dead on the lawn of the Throne of God Presbyterian Church. I closed the door and walked to the couch, sitting down next to Mom as we watched in silence. It was too good to be true. A reporter was interviewing Sheriff Meier as he described the scene: the pastor was sprawled flat on his face with two long poles sticking out of his back – a mop with the head broken off, and a flagpole stripped of its flag. They had been stabbed between his ribs just inside of his shoulderblades, one on each side. I leaned forward to get a better look at the TV, too surprised to hide my eagerness.

'Can you believe this?' asked Mom. 'I thought we were through with all this!'

'I know this killer,' I said softly. Recognition was dawning slowly, but it was definitely there.

'What?'

'This is a real killer.'

'Of course it's a real killer, John – the pastor is really dead.'

'No, I mean, this isn't just a local guy – I read about this exact crime scene a few years ago. Did he take the hands too?'

The news anchor looked grim. 'In addition to the poles in the back,' he said, 'the killer also cut off the pastor's hands and removed his tongue.'

'Ha!' I said, half-laughing.

'John!' said my mom sternly. 'What kind of reaction is that?'

'It's the Handyman,' I told her. 'He always does this to his victims: he cuts off their hands and tongue, and leaves them outside with sticks in their backs.' I stared at the blurred crime-scene photo, shaking my head in wonder. 'I had no idea he was a demon.'

'He might not be,' said Mom, standing up and carrying her dinner-plate into the kitchen. She'd seen the first demon, and she knew about the second, but she was still very uncomfortable discussing them.

'Of course he's a demon,' I said. 'Crowley was a demon, Forman was another demon who came looking for him, and now another demon has come looking for *him*.'

Mom was silent for a moment.

'You have no way of knowing that,' she said at last. I still hadn't told her about my phone call to Nobody; she'd only get in the way by trying to protect me.

'Do you have any idea of the odds against three unrelated serial killers in a town this size?' I asked, following her into the living room. 'And why on earth would the Handyman, whose attacks have all been in Georgia, show up in Clayton County North Dakota for no reason at all just two months after the last demon disappeared?'

'Because this town is *cursed*,' she said adamantly.

'I thought you didn't believe in supernatural stuff?'

'I don't mean literally cursed,' she said, turning back to me. 'I mean . . . oh, I don't know what I mean. They're demons, John! Or something just as bad. I don't know how much longer we can stay.'

'We can't leave,' I said quickly. Too quickly. Mom stared at me a second, then pointed at me angrily.

'Oh no,' she said. 'No no no no no. You are *not* going to chase after this one like you did with Bill Crowley. You are *not* going to play Superhero and risk your life like an idiot.'

'I'm not an idiot, Mom.'

'Well, you do some awfully stupid stuff for a genius,' she said. 'Crowley tried to kill you. Forman almost succeeded, *and* he almost got Brooke too. And Curt. This is not a game.'

'I didn't realise you were so worried about Curt's life.'

'I don't want him dead,' she shouted. 'I just want him out of our lives! He's an arrogant jerk, yes, but you can't just kill him.'

'Then it's a good thing I didn't,' I said, growing angry myself.

'No, but because of your obsession with these . . . whatever they are . . . somebody else almost did. How many people have to die before you back down?'

'How many more people will die if I *do* back down?' I countered.

'That's what police are for.'

'The Handyman's been killing for five years at least – probably centuries more, now that we know he's a demon. If the police are so awesome why haven't they stopped him yet?'

'You are *not* going after him,' Mom repeated.

'The police have no idea how to fight a demon,' I said, struggling to keep my voice calm. 'They have no idea what they're up against. I do. I've already stopped two of them, and if I can stop this one, I can save . . . I don't know, maybe hundreds of lives. Maybe thousands. Do you think it's just going to kill a couple of people and then go away forever? This is how these things live, Mom. It's going to kill and kill and kill until it doesn't have any victims left.'

'He,' said Mom firmly, locking my eyes with her gaze.

'What?'

'You called him "it",' she said, exerting all her authority. 'You know that you are not allowed to say "it". Say "he".'

I closed my eyes and took a breath. One of the hallmarks of a sociopath, particularly a serial killer, is that they stop thinking about people as people, and see them only as objects. When I wasn't thinking, or when I got excited, I started calling people 'it'. This was against my rules.

But the rules were designed for humans.

'It's a demon,' I said. 'It's not a person, it's not human. I can't dehumanise it if it's not human.'

'*He* is a living, thinking creature,' said Mom, 'human or demon or whatever. You don't know what he is, but you know who you are, and you will follow your rules.'

My rules. She was right. 'I'm sorry,' I said, calmer now. 'He – or she,' I added quickly. 'This might turn out to be a woman.'

'What makes you say that?'

Because the voice on the phone was female, I thought.

'Nothing,' I said. 'I'm just saying that we don't know.' I

13

put on a face of mock indignation. 'Are you implying that all psychopaths are men? Or that all men are psychopaths?'

'I'm not in the mood for jokes,' Mom said, turning off the TV. 'I'm going to bed. No more news, no more killers; we'll talk about this in the morning.'

I walked sullenly back to the kitchen and poured a bowl of cereal while Mom got ready for bed; I rarely went to sleep before 2 a.m., so there was still plenty of time to study the situation.

I'd read about the Handyman before. He was an unorthodox killer from Macon, Georgia – or at least, that's where his first and third known victims were found. He travelled all over Georgia killing every nine months or so, and every crime scene matched our new situation: the victims were killed inside, usually in their place of business or alone at home, and there the body's hands and tongue were removed. Then the body was carried outside, the poles were stuck into its back, and the killer disappeared.

The police had yet to find any real evidence of who the killer might be, though they could guess some things just by analysing the crimes themselves. First of all, everyone assumed it was a man, based on two things: the sheer physical strength involved in hacking off the hands, carrying the bodies outside, and driving the wooden poles into the victims' backs. Also for the simple fact that almost all serial killers were men anyway. Neither of these were especially strong bits of evidence, but psychological profiling is more of an art than a science. They took the information they had and went with the answers that made the most sense.

The other thing the police knew about him was that he

was very clean: the sites where the actual deaths took place were always full of plastic, including sheets and garbage bags and even disposable rain ponchos. This was not a person who wanted to get any blood on himself, and the lack of usable exterior blood evidence showed that he was very good at keeping himself clean. That penchant for neatness, plus the use of mops and brooms as poles in his victims' backs, had earned him the media nickname 'Handyman'. Well, that and the fact that he cut his victims' hands off.

I took another mouthful of cereal. The police and the FBI had been hunting the Handyman for years, but I knew they'd never catch him because they were working from flawed assumptions: namely, that he was human, and male. No matter what Mom said, he was most definitely a demon, and almost certainly female. I'd talked to her on the phone, for crying out loud – I think I could tell the difference. And that helped explain everything in vastly different ways.

To begin with, the strength: the demons had all revealed an array of bizarre supernatural powers, and it made perfect sense that the Handyman had above average strength, regardless of gender. Female serial killers were remarkably rare, but they did exist; so why not female demons as well? Assuming they had gender at all, they probably had representatives from both.

As for the cleanliness, a strong attention to detail suggested . . . what? That the demon was neurotic? Cautious? Scared of blood? If I could get on the computer I could look up some of the criminal-profiling websites I liked to read, but Mom kept the computer in her room and I didn't dare do this kind of research with her looking over my shoulder.

There was so much else this demon was telling us, if only I knew what it meant: things like why she displayed her victims outside, and why she shoved poles into their backs. These were messages directly from her to us – in fact, they might be messages directly to *me*, since I was the one she was here to find. But what did they say? I'd studied serial killers for years, as a hobby bordering on obsession, but most of my knowledge was trivia about who a killer was, how they did it, and so on. I knew why a killer did what he did, but only after the fact; I didn't know the steps the police had taken to decipher all of that information in the first place. I needed to do more study, which meant I needed the Internet or the library. I couldn't get either one until morning.

I finished my cereal and glanced at the clock: ten thirty. Morning was still hours away.

There was one other area where I had a definite leg up on the police, and I didn't need their studies to help me: the missing body parts. Most serial killers saved souvenirs from their kills because they liked to relive them, or in some cases because they simply wanted to eat them, but demons were different. Mr Crowley, the Clayton Killer, had stolen his victims' body parts because he needed them to regenerate his own failing limbs and organs. The Handyman – Handywoman? – might be doing the same thing, or something similarly supernatural. What could you do with hands? And what about tongues? What did *they* represent?

I stared at my own hands, looking for clues. Maybe she could absorb their fingerprints, or their identity, or something like that. It was hard enough to profile a regular killer who followed human rules; for a demon who broke those rules at will, I needed more information before I could say anything solid. I needed to see the demon in action.

Both of the demons I had met so far were completely different. They did different things, in different ways, for different reasons – but they had one similarity. Forman had said that the demons, or whatever they were, were defined by what they lacked: a face, a life, an emotion, an identity. Just like serial killers, the way they acted and reacted could be traced back to the holes in their lives that made them who they were. So, what did Nobody lack?

The phone rang, loud and strident in the silence. I grabbed it off the counter and glanced at the caller ID: Jensen. I carried it down the hall and handed it to Mom, who was washing off her make-up in the bathroom. It rang again.

'Officer Jensen,' I said, setting it on the sink. 'Probably something about the case.' I walked back to the living room while Mom answered.

'Hello? Oh!' She sounded surprised. 'Why, hello Marci, I thought it was your father.'

Marci Jensen was calling? Marci was one of the hottest girls in school. Even my friend Max, who'd go out with a chair leg if it asked him, harboured an impossible love for her. I'd probably talked to her three times in my entire life. Why was she calling my house at ten thirty at night?

'Don't worry,' said Mom, 'we're both still awake. He's right here, I'll get him.' She came out of the bathroom with one of those infuriating motherly smiles and handed me the phone. 'It's for you.'

I held it to my ear. 'Hello?'

'Hey John, it's Marci Jensen.' She sounded . . . I had no

17

idea how she sounded. I could read a face like an expert, but voices always threw me off.

'Yeah, I saw.' Pause. What should I say?

'I'm sorry to call you so late,' she went on. 'I've kinda been . . . well, I've been meaning to call all day and I just haven't.'

'Oh.' Why was she meaning to call?

'So anyway, I don't know if I'm supposed to say this or not, but my dad told me about you. About what you did, I mean. Saving all those people.'

Thanks to the 'protective silence' that kept my name out of the news, her dad was one of the only people who knew the real story. Well, the parts that didn't have demons in them. He'd been the first officer on the scene when we escaped from Forman's torture house in the forest.

'It's not really anything,' I said. 'I mean, it is, because they're all saved, but I didn't really do anything. I mean, I didn't do it alone. Brooke was there too; she helped get some of the women outside.'

'Yeaaaah,' said Marci, holding the vowel and dragging out the word for a few extra seconds. She paused, just slightly, and then said: 'I heard that you guys aren't really going out any more?'

'No,' I said, a little surprised. *Is this what I think it is?* 'We haven't really done anything for a couple of months, actually.'

'Yeah, I wish I'd known that sooner,' she said. 'So anyway, I thought if you're not dating anyone else, maybe we could go out sometime.'

Was that an observation or an invitation? Had she just

asked me out, or was I supposed to ask her? I had no idea what to do. After a pause I said, 'Sure. That sounds fun.'

'Sweet,' she said. 'I'm all tied up for the rest of this week, but how about one week from today? Monday afternoon?'

I had a brief mental image of Marci tied up, but I shoved it away. *Don't think like that*. 'Yeah, I should be free.'

'Sweet,' she said again. 'We can go to the lake. You have a bike?'

'Yeah.'

'Cool. You want to meet at my place? It's pretty close to the turn-off, and we can head out from there.'

'Sure,' I said.

'Three o'clock?'

'Sure.'

'Well, awesome,' she said. 'I'm glad I finally called.'

'I . . . so am I.'

'All right, I'll see you then. Bye.'

'Bye.'

She hung up, and I clicked off the phone. Mom was still standing there, watching. She always insisted that I try to be more social, and at the same time she always seemed to be terrified of what I would do.

'Did you just get asked out?'

'Apparently.'

She stared at me a moment longer, then nodded and turned back to the bathroom. 'Be careful,' she called out. 'And make sure to follow all your rules.'

I frowned and took another bite of cereal. Why had Marci asked me out? This was not the best time; I had a demon to catch, and this was a complication I didn't need. On the other hand, it was kind of funny: now there were two people in town who wanted to kill me – the Handyman, and Max, as soon as he found out I had a date with Marci. I laughed, and the sound was thin and hollow.

The game is afoot.

Chapter 3

When a person is murdered, the details of the case are kept secret, and thus it was with Pastor Olsen: we knew where he had died, and what the body looked like, but the police kept the rest of the details to themselves. Nobody was allowed to see the crime scene except the investigators, and no one was allowed to see the body except the forensic pathologist . . . and the morticians.

Thus it was that five days after the killing, when I'd analysed the news coverage a hundred times and run out of leads and was desperate for more information, the FBI delivered the corpse right to our very door.

I have the best job in the world.

My mom co-owns the mortuary with her twin sister, Margaret, and I'd been helping with funerals and general maintenance since I was seven years old. It was my dad who first showed me the embalming tools, back before he left, and it had been my passion ever since. My sister helped in the office, pushing papers and answering phones; she got a little creeped out by the dead bodies, or so she claimed, but I could never understand how that was even possible. Dead bodies are calm and silent; perfectly still, perfectly harmless.

A corpse will never move, it will never laugh, and it will never judge; a corpse will never shout at you, hit you, or leave you. Far from the zombies and junk that you see on TV, a corpse is actually the perfect friend. The perfect pet. I feel more comfortable with them than I do with real people.

Ron, the County Coroner, brought the pastor's body in his big government van, accompanied by a couple of policemen as escorts. I stayed upstairs until they were gone, watching through the window as they opened the van doors, pulled out the covered stretcher, released the wheels, and rolled him in through our back door. The police escorts paced aimlessly in the parking lot; they stared at the sky, or at the forest behind our house, or at the cracks in the asphalt below them. It was mid-August, and the cracks were full of ants scuttling back and forth on urgent, mysterious errands. One of the policemen stooped down to watch them, then stood again and dragged his foot across the crawling mass. The swarm scattered, reformed, and went on with their lives. The cop wandered away, his attention caught by something else.

When Ron left I went downstairs and joined Mom and Margaret in the embalming room, washing my hands and pulling on a medical apron and gloves.

'Hey, John,' said Margaret. With her face mask on she was almost indistinguishable from Mom.

The room was old, with faded blue-green tiles on the walls, but it was clean and bright, and the ventilator in the ceiling was almost new. The equipment was aging but serviceable, and the wheels on our carts and tables were well-oiled and silent.

We were the only mortuary in town, and our business was the deaths of our friends and neighbours. It's a different way to make a living, I'll admit, but not a morbid one. A funeral is a body's last hurrah before it is buried forever; an opportunity for the family to gather and remember all the best parts of their lives together.

I was taught to respect the dead, to treat them like honoured guests, and to think about death as a time to rejoice in life. I don't know how much of that I believed, but I do know that I loved embalming more than almost anything else in the world. It was time I could share with someone, even someone I didn't know, in a deeper and more personal way than I ever got to share it with the living. Small wonder, then, that I'd had so many dreams about embalming Brooke.

'Pastor Elijah Olsen,' said Margaret, reading from the sheaf of papers Ron had left us. The body bag sat peacefully on the table, still unopened. 'Deceased six days, give or take. Full autopsy, organs bagged, hands and tongue missing. Bullet wound in the back, exit wound in the chest, stab wounds in the back. Everything else is normal, assuming Ron did his job right.' She set down the papers with a small, humourless laugh.

Nobody moved.

'I'm really getting sick of this,' said Mom, staring at the body bag. 'Can someone please die of natural causes once in a while?'

'Think of it this way,' said Margaret, putting her hands on her hips. 'The Clayton Killer bought us a new ventilator, and Clark Forman bought us a new computer for the office.

If the Handyman hangs around long enough, we can buy a new sound system for the chapel.'

Mom laughed drily and shook her head. 'Then please let us never afford a new sound system.'

As hesitant as they were to get started, I was even more eager. 'Let's get this show rolling.'

'Let's hope the fan doesn't give out on us,' said Margaret. It was an old saying, from back in the days when our fan was worse and our chemicals more strident, but it had become a tradition. We couldn't start until she said it. We nodded and got to work.

I opened the bag and peeled it back, exposing the dead man inside. In a normal case we'd get the body about a day after it died, still in its clothes and stiff with rigor mortis, but rigor mortis only lasts a day or two, and post-autopsy murder victims arrived flexible, washed, and in several pieces. This body's chest was marked with a giant Y where the Coroner had cut it open, taken everything out, and then loosely stitched it back together. The organs that had been removed and examined were sealed in a bag and placed back inside. The body's arms ended in severed stubs where the killer had removed its hands, and the Coroner had bandaged them lightly to staunch the bleeding. Corpses don't bleed much, because the heart isn't putting any pressure on the circulation, but blood can still seep out, and it was cleaner to transport the body this way.

Mom and I lifted the body while Margaret pulled the body bag out from underneath it. We'd done this so many times that we worked without talking, each of us knowing exactly what had to be done and what our part would be: Mom

24

covered his groin with a sterile cloth, Margaret started loosening the stitches in his belly to take out the organ bag, and I pulled away the bandages on his wrists.

The severed wrists were perfect cross-sections of meat and bone and tendon, and I ran my gloved fingertip across one, trying to imagine what could have done it. My first guess was a bite. Mr Crowley had been able to distend his jaw and sprout dozens of long, needle-sharp teeth, and it was entirely possible that our new demon, Nobody, could do the same. But the wrist bore no teethmarks at all – no vertical lines where teeth had scraped down across the flesh, and no horizontal line where two rows of teeth had met in the middle. The stump was simply too clean. But what else could it be?

Mr Crowley had also been able to turn his hands into vicious claws, capable of cutting through almost anything, and I could see how a claw like that could have made this cut. A single slashing motion, severing flesh and bone and tendon in one swipe: it made sense. It was also further proof that the killer was strong, to swing a claw so powerfully and cut so cleanly. I filed it away in my mental folder and began helping Mom wash the corpse.

Margaret carried the bag of organs to a side table, preparing to clean each one individually and fill them with formaldehyde. That job would take her a few hours on her own, while Mom and I got to clean the body, set the features for the viewing, and pump preservatives through the remains of its circulatory system. A body in this condition was usually a huge hassle for a circulatory embalming, because the blood vessels were so perforated in so many places that the pump couldn't do its job. Instead of flowing through the entire corpse, the embalming fluid would seep into the chest cavity and out through the wounds. Fortunately (or not, if you asked my mom), we'd had so many mutilated corpses over the past year that we'd developed a fairly simply workaround: petroleum jelly. It took a whole jar, but if you slathered it all over wounds and then wrapped them in surgical tape, you could stop up most of the holes. When we finished washing the limbs, head and chest, Mom pulled out a fresh jar of Vaseline and we set to work sealing the wounds.

There were a lot of wounds to seal.

First were the wrists, of course, which got a pretty good layer of the stuff. After that I went to work on the presumed death wound: a large bullet-hole above the heart, presumably matched by a smaller one in the back. I wasn't stingy with the jelly, and packed it into the front bullet-hole pretty tightly. When I had finished with that, I opened the pastor's mouth and coated the tongue – or the tiny stub of what used to be a tongue – with another liberal glob. If the cut on the wrists was clean, the cut on the tongue was pristine; it had been severed with astonishing care and attention to detail. By another, smaller claw perhaps? Or a separate tool, like a scalpel? Whatever it was must have been as sharp as a razor, with a long blade and a fine point for precision work.

It was the very preciseness of it that got me thinking. We already knew that the demon was extremely cautious, bringing tarps and ponchos and goodness knows what else to keep herself clean of blood. That suggested a very meticulous killer, and the surgical removal of the tongue backed that up. I could see a bit of my own caution reflected in her, and that would make her very hard to trace. But there was more going on here, I guessed – something that both did and didn't fit with the rest of the attack. I puzzled over it and continued to work.

While I was covering the exterior wounds, Mom slathered Vaseline all over the inside of the chest cavity, coating it from top to bottom in a thick layer. She had to reach her whole arm inside to make sure she got it everywhere; the Coroner sawed open the breastbone during an autopsy, so he could fold out the ribs and work inside, but Mom hated doing that and thus left them where they were and tried to work around them.

'That's it for the inside,' she said after a moment.

I nodded. 'I'm done on the front. Let's roll him over.'

We set down our jar of Vaseline and stood on the body's left; I grabbed his shoulder while Mom grabbed him under the hips, and we rolled him up and over onto his face. Mom gasped out loud, and we both stared.

'I think we're going to need a second jar of Vaseline,' I said.

The back of the body was full of holes, presumably stab wounds – some long, some jagged, all deep and deadly. Any one of them could have been a killing blow. The two holes where the poles had been inserted were obvious, as they were slightly wider and rounder than the others, but the police had never said anything about any other wounds in the back. I touched one, lightly, trying to guess what had caused it – a single claw, or a whole hand of them? I glanced over the body quickly, looking for a pattern, but there didn't seem to be one.

The holes were ragged and messy, wet with dark black and purple blood like a liquid bruise. The entire surface had been mutilated and tenderised with almost animalistic ferocity. Nothing about the killer's clean, meticulous method had hinted that there might be anything like this.

'What on earth did he do?' Mom whispered. It was a brutal sight, even six days later in a sterilised room. Margaret stopped her work to come and stare as well. Mom looked up at me, eyebrows raised in a silent question.

'Holy . . .' said Margaret, touching the body gingerly. 'Did they talk about this on the news?'

'Not a word,' I said. 'I don't remember hearing about it from the other Handyman killings either.'

'It looks like he stabbed him thirty times,' said Margaret. 'Maybe forty.'

'What does it mean?' Mom demanded, still looking at me.

'What does it mean?' I echoed.

'You're the expert, right?' Her voice was hard to read – angry and curious and desperate all at once. I couldn't tell who the anger was aimed at. 'You're the one who studies this kind of stuff. What does it mean?'

I looked back at the body. 'The first thing it means is that the police are keeping it quiet – partly to avoid freaking people out, but mostly it's a marker. It's like a signature, that nobody knows but the killer, so they can always tell which is a real Handyman killing and which is a copycat. It can also help identify any letters that come in to the police or to the media. If the letter mentions the stuff the police haven't revealed yet, they know it's a real letter from the real killer.'

'Does that happen a lot?' asked Margaret.

'More often than you'd think,' I said. 'A lot of serial killers like to involve themselves in their own investigations.'

'But what does it mean about the killer?' asked Mom. She was still watching me, her eyes sharp and penetrating. 'What does this say about the person who did this?'

I looked back at her for moment, then down at the body. *Is she asking about the demon?*

'It means that she's angry about something,' I said.

'She?' asked Margaret.

'Or he,' I said quickly. 'He or she premeditates everything, and she's very meticulous about everything she does. But then after it's dead, and after she's done whatever else she needs to do, she just goes crazy on it.' I touched the back again. 'This is pure rage. Whatever else the killer wants, whatever other needs her killing serves, the base of the whole thing is anger.'

'At what?'

'I don't know,' I said slowly. 'Pastors? Men? Us?'

'Us?' asked Mom.

.I looked at her. *Is this what she wanted to know? If the demon is really on a vendetta?* I chose my words carefully.

'Whoever did this came halfway across the country to do it. He or she is very driven, and very careful, and very angry. Without more evidence, all it really tells us is that we're going to be getting more evidence soon. Probably very soon.'

We looked back at the body, watching half-congealed blood shine darkly in the harsh light. Now I had more pieces of the puzzle, and a better idea of how this demon was killing, and that was good. It was very good. But even as I learned more about the 'how', I was starting to doubt that I knew the real 'why'.

And that wasn't good at all.

Chapter 4

It was Sunday, and I was going to church.

I'm not a religious person, in any real sense, though I don't consider myself an anti-religious person either. The truth is I just don't really think about it that much; I didn't go to church because my parents never went to church. When I chose the word 'demon' to describe the monsters I'd seen, I honestly didn't even realise it was religious in origin. I used it because David Berkowitz, the Son of Sam, used it in a letter to the cops. Just because 'demon' was a cool word, it didn't mean that the Handyman was a fallen angel or anything goofy like that.

So no, I wasn't going to church in the sense that I was going to attend a meeting and sing and pray or whatever. I was going to a church building because that is where pastors hang out, and I was doing it on Sunday because that is the best day (I assumed) to find one. Specifically, I was going to St Mary's Catholic Church to talk to Father Erikson, who all the news programmes claimed was Pastor Olsen's best friend. St Mary's Catholic Church and the Throne of God Presbyterian Church were always working together on something or other, like soup kitchens and service projects, so I guess that made sense. A victim's friend was the best lead I'd had in two months, so I figured it was time to ask the priest some questions.

The parking lot was full, so I parked on the far side of the street and sat in the car until people started to file out: girls in floral dresses and men in white shirts and ties. There were more than I expected, but I sat quietly as they wandered to their cars, watching their faces intently. They talked and laughed. They smiled and scowled. They blinked in the light and stared at the world in sombre reflection. What were they guilty of? How far would they go if you pushed them?

Everyone was a suspect in my eyes, from the oldest man to the youngest child. Any one of them could be the demon.

They got in their cars and drove away. I climbed out of my seat and walked across the street and up into the church, ignoring the smiles of a group of old ladies who passed me in the foyer. Father Erikson was inside the chapel, walking up and down the pews and straightening a bunch of little red songbooks.

'Hello,' he said, seeing me and smiling. 'Can I help you?'

'I . . .' I'd never done this before and I wasn't sure what to say. It's not like I could just flash a badge and start asking questions. 'Do you have a minute?'

He cocked his head to the side, looking at me, then set down the songbook in his hand. 'Of course,' he said. 'What seems to be the problem?' He walked towards me, and I could see that his face was slightly frowning, his brow furrowed but his eyes wide. That was an 'I'm concerned about you' face.

I shook my head. 'No, no, it's not like that,' I said. 'I'm

not religiously troubled or anything, I just . . .' I really hadn't thought this through. Why would he answer some strange kid's questions about a dead priest? I needed a story, and I needed it quickly. He had almost reached me.

'Hi,' I said, 'I'm interning with the newspaper, and . . .' I looked him directly in the eyes. The question slipped out before I could stop myself. 'Do you believe in demons?'

He stopped short, smiling in surprise. 'Demons?'

'Like, real demons,' I said. 'That's a Catholic thing, right?'

'Well, yes,' he said slowly, 'the Bible does talk about demons and evil spirits, but it's not an especially big part of our faith. We teach people how to lead good lives and do good things, and if we're lucky we never have to worry about demons at all.'

'And if we're not lucky?'

He studied my face, looking different than before; concerned now in a worried rather than a caring way. 'Why do you ask?'

'Well, don't you think it's kind of important?' I said. 'If demons are real, and they can really attack people and stuff like they do in the Bible, shouldn't that be a big deal? You'd talk about it all the time, I'd think.'

He smiled again and gestured to a pew. 'Let me ask you something,' he said, sitting down. I sat as well, just across the aisle. 'You're not from my congregation, correct?'

'I'm not.'

'Do you belong to any of the other churches in town?'

'Not really.'

'There are a small handful of verses that talk about demons,' he said, 'and tens of thousands that talk about God. So if

God is real, and He can really help people and stuff, like He does in the Bible, shouldn't that be an even bigger deal than demons?'

I raised my eyebrows. 'This is why people don't like talking to priests.'

'Ouch,' he said, laughing. 'I'll admit that I came on a little strong there, but still – ouch.'

'Does the Bible say anything about what a demon looks like?' I asked.

'So you really just want to talk about demons,' he said, nodding. 'Okay. Demons. Well, the Bible teaches that demons are fallen angels who were cast out of heaven with Satan. So presumably a demon would look exactly like us. They're just regular people who made really, really, *really* bad choices.'

'So no horns or pitchforks or stuff like that?'

He chuckled. 'Not as far as I know.'

'I wanted to . . .' I paused. Now that the ice was broken I wanted to ask about Pastor Olsen, to see if there was anything Father Erikson knew that could help me find the demon. But there was something wrong with the things he was saying – something that bugged me. I had to ask him.

'How can you believe in something like demons and not worry about them?' I asked. 'It's like knowing there's a wolf outside that wants to kill you, and you don't care. That doesn't make any sense at all.'

'It's because I also believe in God, and I believe that God is stronger.'

'God didn't protect Pastor Olsen,' I said.

He paused, watching me closely.

'Bad things happen every day,' he said slowly. 'Every hour;

every minute. I had two hundred people in my congregation today, and I know that bad things are going to happen to each and every one of them. Statistics say that one of those two hundred will get into a car accident this month. Five of them will be unemployed by the end of the year, maybe more if the mill keeps losing business. Half of them will have cancer sometime in their lives. But even knowing all of that, I still gave them a sermon of hope this morning, and I still let them walk out that door to face the world.'

'But how could that possibly help?' I asked. 'You want to talk statistics, we've had three serial killers in town over the last year. At the rate they're killing, someone in your congregation is almost guaranteed to be killed by one – almost guaranteed. What's his family going to say? "The priest could have saved him, but instead he yakked about hope for a while. Thank goodness".'

'I'm a pastor, not a policeman,' he said. 'We all have different jobs, and we all help where we can. Now, I don't know the first thing about serial killers, or tracking down criminals, or anything like that; I don't even know first aid, if I were to find a victim on the street. But I'm a very good teacher, and a very good leader, and I can serve this community best by staying in that role.' He shifted, leaning forward. 'Do you have any idea how much our church attendance has increased over the last year? How many more people are donating to the poor, or volunteering for service projects? Trials bring people together. The killers come and go but the community will always be here, and people will always need to eat, and they'll always need homes and jobs and someone to rely on. There *is* a wolf out there, like you said, but some of us are hunters and some of us are shepherds. Working together is the only way to keep the sheep safe.'

He leaned back and folded his hands in his lap. 'I'm going to guess that you're a hunter.'

I stared back, suddenly nervous.

'That's fine,' he continue. 'We need hunters. We need protectors. But we need everyone else, too. No one can do it all on their own.'

We sat in silence a minute. I had no idea what to say next. I was thrown off, completely lost. I struggled for words.

'I'm hunting him right now,' I said, 'for an article in the paper, like I told you before, and I need your help. You were a friend of Pastor Olsen's. Can you tell me anything that might help catch his killer? Anything at all?'

He mumbled, tripping over his words. 'I-I'm not sure . . .'

'Anything you know will help,' I said quickly. 'What was he doing that day? Why was he in his church that night? Had he ever had any threatening phone calls or visits? The Handyman comes from Georgia – did Pastor Olsen have any ties there? There's got to be something we can use to find the one who did this.'

'I didn't mean for you to become a hunter literally,' said Erikson. 'I meant that you're obviously concerned and eager to help, and that's great, honestly – but you're just a kid. Don't do anything dangerous.'

'Oh, don't worry,' I said, feeling a lie spring easily to life. 'This is just a journalism thing – I get school credit. Anything you tell me will go straight back to the paper, and they're the ones who'll follow up on it.'

He watched me, saying nothing.

'I swear,' I said. 'I'm not going to do anything dangerous.'

'Give me your number,' he said at last. 'If I think of anything, I'll call you.'

Marci Jensen lived in an old yellow house in downtown Clayton, just a block off of Main Street. This was the oldest neighbourhood in town, and everything was tall – the houses bore high, gabled roofs, and the ancient trees stretched their branches even higher above that. The sidewalks were dark and cracked, and buckled in erratic peaks where the tree roots crept under and shoved them up. A police car sat along the kerb. I leaned my bike against the low wrought-iron fence and walked to her door, passing narrow strips of overgrown garden and rugged yellow grass that probably never saw much sun. It felt like a cottage in the woods, a place where life crept in and on and around until it was a part of everything else.

The porch was old and weathered, and the front door was open behind a loosely-latched screen. I knocked.

Footsteps pounded inside and a scruffy-looking kid, maybe twelve years old, emerged into the hall from a side room. The noise of a TV wafted out from the back of the house. I opened my mouth to say something, but instead he turned and shouted, 'Marci! Someone's here for you!' Before he'd even finished yelling he was gone, back into the recesses of the house.

There was an answering yell from upstairs, indistinct and feminine, and a vague clatter of doors and stairs. A pair of younger children, a boy and a girl who looked like twins, peeked out at me from another side door. I guessed they were four or five.

'Hi,' I said.

'Hi,' said the girl. The boy picked his nose.

'I'm here to see Marci,' I said, by way of explanation.

'You're not the guy that was here Saturday,' said the boy.

'Of course not,' said the girl. 'Marci has lots of boyfriends. She has more boyfriends than me, and I have five.'

I raised my eyebrows. 'Five boyfriends?'

'Tyson and Logan and Ethan and another boy from the bus who I don't know.'

'That's four,' I said, smiling.

'I'm four,' said the boy quickly, holding up four fingers.

'And Daddy,' said the girl. 'That's my other boyfriend. And Sheriff Meier. Is that five?'

'Close enough,' I said, nodding.

Footsteps crashed down the stairs and Marci came into the hall. She was wearing denim shorts, the really short kind that Mom called Daisy Dukes, and a short-sleeved flannel shirt. Her long black hair was tied up in a ponytail that bounced just slightly as she walked. She smiled, coming towards me with her thumbs hooked into her pockets, and suddenly the house that just seconds ago had been dark and old was now 'comfortable' and 'rustic'. It was something in the way she moved, and the way she carried herself. She made everything around her look better.

'Wow,' I said.

'You like it?' she asked, spreading her arms and looking down at her outfit. 'I got these shorts online: guess how much.'

'I'm the world's worst judge of clothing value,' I said, shaking my head. 'There's really no point in guessing.'

'Just give it a shot,' she said, opening the door and stepping onto the porch.

'Somewhere between five and five hundred dollars.'

She laughed. 'Yeah, I think maybe we scratch clothing value off the list of potential conversation topics.'

'I'm only bad with monetary value, though,' I said. 'I can still appreciate the look.'

'But the price is the whole point,' she said, walking around to the driveway and standing up a bike that leaned against the house. 'Anyone can buy nice clothes, but I was the one who found them for an unbelievable deal. Well,' she stopped, sticking out her hip and posing, 'I also make them look fabulous. You ready to go?'

'Yeah,' I said. 'My bike's out here. We're going to the lake?'

'I hope that's okay,' said Marci, walking her bike out to the street. 'I know we found a body there and everything, but the weather's great, and I want to get as much bike-riding done as I can before school starts again. And apparently all the dead bodies are at churches these days, so we should be fine.'

Wow, I thought, *she's a lot more casual about the deaths than I expected. Must be the cop in the family.*

'Fine with me.' I hopped up on my bike and let her lead the way, coasting out into the road. I pedalled a bit to catch up. 'I didn't know you were into riding.'

'I'm not a racer or anything,' she said, 'but I love to ride. And hike. Sometimes I can't believe how lucky we are to live here.'

I almost laughed. 'You're kidding. Clayton?'

'I love Clayton,' she said. 'We've got a lake, a forest, miles of trails and roads; if we could do something about the life expectancy we'd be in paradise.'

'I suppose you've got a point,' I said, following as she turned towards the lake road. We rode casually, barely pedalling, and I lifted up my head to look at the sun. It was bright and warm, and the air smelled like cut grass. I usually just used my bike to go places – to school, or to the library, or to the burned-out warehouse outside of town. I never just rode it for fun.

We reached the main lake road, leading out past a mechanic shop towards the wooded lake beyond. Marci pulled ahead, flipping into high gear and standing on the pedals to build up speed. I pushed hard to catch up, and the wind brushed past my face like a cool curtain. Marci was very fast, and watching her legs pump up and down I realised she was probably in much better shape than I was. It also convinced me that being a few bike-lengths behind wasn't really that bad of a place to be.

I used to have rules about watching girls: I simply never allowed myself to do it. I've lived half of my life in constant fear of my own thoughts – of my own darker nature that lurked inside, eager to snap up any lead I gave it and overpower me completely. I had dreams about killing my friends and family; I had fantasies, day and night, about catching and binding and torturing the people I met on the street. I'd even fantasised about embalming Marci. There was something inside of me that longed for blood and pain, not because it liked them but because it couldn't be satisfied by anything less. I didn't feel normal emotions in the same way as other people; things like love and kindness were foreign to me, while harsher feelings like hate and fear and envy were all too close to the surface. If I wanted to feel a powerful emotional experience, violence was pretty much the only way I could do it – so allowing myself to become attached to a girl was, rather obviously, a bad idea.

Brooke had gotten a glimpse of that side of me, locked away in Forman's house a few months ago. I didn't hurt her, but she knew. We hadn't spoken since.

But the thing was, now that I was a real demon hunter, everything was different. My dark side had a safe outlet, and my dreams at night were heroic tales of John the Conqueror, slaying all the dark things of the world – and if I enjoyed the slaying a little more than necessary, well, that was my right. It didn't hurt anyone but the demons, and hurting them was the whole point. Along with that change I'd let go of many of my rules, allowing myself for the first time to enjoy my life – to talk to people, to hunt demon, to look at girls. I was free.

Slowly, carefully, I let go of the handlebars and spread my arms wide. Marci glanced back, saw me, and did the same, whooping with exhilaration as we hurtled down the road. I closed my eyes and felt the wind on my face, sharp with danger and excitement. The town disappeared behind us, the wilderness rose up before us, and the road carried us headlong to nowhere.

Chapter 5

'How'd your date go?'

'Fine.'

It was the next morning, and I was trying to eat my breakfast in peace. Mom, on the other hand, was being a mom.

'What'd you guys do?'

'We just went out,' I said. 'It was nothing.' Which was true – it really was nothing. We'd ridden around on our bikes for a while, which was fun enough, I guess, but it's hard to carry on much of a conversation while you're twenty feet apart on a bike trail. That was fine with me, because I'm horrible at talking to people, but Marci had probably been bored out of her mind.

'Well, it's not *nothing*,' said Mom. She was standing in the hall, holding a curling iron to her hair while I ate a bowl of cereal in the kitchen. 'You've never gone out with her before, so that's got to be *something*.'

'I've barely ever gone out with anybody before,' I said.

'So it's even more of a something. You took your bike instead of the car: did you go bike riding somewhere?'

'I actually didn't ride it at all. I walked it all the way to her house, and then left it on her porch.'

42

'Don't be a smart aleck.'

'And then,' I continued, 'since I didn't have a car, I had to carry her everywhere we went.'

Mom smiled. 'Well, at least it wasn't a total loss.'

'What?'

'What do you mean, "what?" I know a hot babe when I see one.'

'I really don't need to hear that kind of comment from my mom.'

She ducked back around the corner to the bathroom, and I sighed in relief and ate some more cereal. A moment later she re-emerged, the curling iron wrapped up in a different lock of hair.

I rolled my eyes. 'Seriously, Mom, how long is that cord? I thought the kitchen would be a safe place to eat breakfast this morning.'

'I plugged it in here in the hall,' she said. 'It's just long enough to reach the kitchen and the bathroom if I walk back and forth.'

'Well, that's wonderful.'

'So you went bike riding, then,' she said. 'Just around town? Out in the forest trails somewhere?'

'Yes,' I said. 'We went out to Forman's place.'

Her face twisted: eyes widening, nostrils flaring. It was her 'shocked' face, with a dash of 'confused'. 'Really?'

'Of course not,' I said, 'but the face you just made almost makes this conversation worth it.'

'John . . .'

'It's still not worth it, but it almost was.'

'To the lake then,' she said, plunging onward. She was

tenacious this morning. 'It's wonderful weather for the lake. Did you go swimming?'

'We went skinny dipping.'

'Can you please just answer a simple question without the attitude?' She stepped back around the corner again. I thought I'd get a moment of respite, but she kept talking, shouting from the bathroom. 'It may surprise you to know this, but there are children – some of them teenage boys, just like you – who actually carry on open, honest conversations with their mothers.'

'I find it very hard to believe that there are other teenage boys just like me.' I finished my cereal and stood up. 'I also find it a little terrifying.'

She came back around the corner, having readjusted the curler again. Her face was no longer playful. 'I'm sorry; I didn't mean to talk about anything uncomfortable.'

I walked past her into the living room. 'Finally something we agree on. Let's stop talking right now.' I turned on the TV. I could probably still catch most of the morning news.

'Come on, John,' she said. 'I'm just asking how things went on your date. I want to be involved in your life.' I ignored her and flipped through the channels. 'The cord reaches in here even better than the kitchen,' she said. 'We can keep talking.'

'We can,' I said, 'but we can also stop. That's called "freedom of choice".'

'You know, I was really getting to like the fact that we didn't watch the news during every single meal any more—' She stopped abruptly, caught by the news footage. It had caught me at the same moment, and we stared at it. 'That's City Hall.'

'Yeah.'

There was a reporter at Clayton's City Hall, talking intently to the camera while several policemen milled around behind her, armed and edgy. In the background, parked right in front of the steps, was an ambulance with flashing lights, and near it a swarm of paramedics clustered around something on the ground. I caught a glimpse of Ron, the Coroner, standing with them. Someone was dead.

'Turn it up,' Mom said softly.

'We have Sheriff Meier with us,' the reporter said, and the camera zoomed out and panned over to reveal the Sheriff standing stiffly on the reporter's left. 'Sheriff Meier, what can you tell us about this attack on the Mayor?'

Mom gasped. 'The Mayor!'

'It appears to have happened late last night,' said the Sheriff. He looked tired, and I guessed that he'd been up for several hours already. 'The Mayor and one of his aides were the only ones in the building at the time, and both were attacked; the aide received a blow to the head but was otherwise unharmed, and he's on his way to the hospital now.'

'The Handyman typically attacks his victims in their homes,' said the reporter. 'Do you have any idea why he might have attacked the Mayor here, in his office?'

The Sheriff bristled at that, as he so often did with the press. 'This case bears remarkable similarity to the Handyman killings, yes, but we want to stress that the connection is still conjecture. We are investigating any and all evidence, and if it turns out that this is the real Handyman and not a copycat, we will proceed from there.'

'Besides,' I added, talking to the screen, 'the Handyman kills people at home *and* at work – he killed a police officer in his car once. This reporter doesn't know what she's talking about.'

Mom shook her head. 'I can't believe this is happening. The Mayor.'

I whistled. 'She's mad, all right.'

'The reporter?'

'No,' I said, 'the demon.'

'Then God help us all.' Mom stood up and walked back to the bathroom.

The reporter nodded solemnly. 'Thank you very much for your time.'

'You're welcome,' said the Sheriff, looking a bit impatient, and he left to walk back towards the crime scene. The reporter turned back to the camera, which zoomed in until she filled the screen.

'We also want to mention that City Hall and the adjoining courthouse will be closed throughout the day while police and other investigators look for evidence,' she said. 'Some county employees have been given the day off, others are being questioned, but there are still no solid leads as to the evidence of Clayton County's newest killer. This is Carrie Walsh, Five Live News.'

'City Hall is closed?' asked Mom. She was standing behind me, curling a new part of her hair. 'We have a meeting there today.'

'Not any more,' I said.

'Then why am I curling my hair?'

'Because if you stop halfway through you'll look like an idiot.'

'That was a rhetorical question, John.' She walked back to the bathroom and shouted: 'What is wrong with our town?'

'We're being hunted by—'

'I know,' she said, coming back into the room. 'I know it's a demon, okay? I know it, and I admit it, and it scares the living hell out of me. But what are we supposed to do? How can we just carry on? How can we stay here and do this job, for the love of . . . I feel like a war profiteer, getting rich while everyone dies.'

'We're not supposed to just carry on,' I said. 'We're supposed to stop it.'

'No, we're not!' she told me, her voice rising. 'The police are supposed to stop it, and you are not the police. You're not trained, you're not armed – you're not even old enough to vote!'

'Young or old, I am the only one who knows anything about this.'

'There has to be someone else,' she said, rushing forward to grab my arm. 'If they're really real, and really out there, there have to be other people that know about them. Maybe we can talk to them.'

'What, like some kind of conspiracy freaks off the Internet?'

'No,' she said, staring at the floor and rubbing her mouth with her hand. Her other hand kept a vice-like grip on my arm. 'Not other civilians, but trained people. Government people. They've got to know, right? There's probably a branch of the government designed just for this, some secret group that nobody knows about.'

'And if nobody knows about them,' I said, 'how are we ever possibly going to find them? What are we going to say? If we call the police right now and tell them we want to speak with the Special Demon Unit, no one would believe us.'

'We don't have to find them; we just make an official report and *they'll* find *us*.'

'We already reported it when Crowley died, remember?' I said. 'That put us in touch with the FBI, which put us in touch with Forman, who turned out to be another demon. Last time I trusted the FBI I ended up drinking my own urine in a hole under some guy's house. We're on our own for this.'

'You can't say that,' Mom objected. 'I will not let you do this.'

'So you're just going to ignore it while everybody dies around you?'

'What do you think you're going to do, John?' she demanded, putting her hands on her hips. 'What? Help me understand.'

'That's what *I* want,' I said. 'I want to understand.'

'You want to kill them.'

'If it comes to that, yes,' I said, 'but first we have to understand them. Doesn't it make you curious at all? Even a little bit? Don't you want to know who they are and why they're here and why they're killing everybody? Why does everyone insist on shutting their eyes to this?'

'Life is too short,' my mom said, folding her arms and leaning against the wall. 'It's too precious. We have to live in this world, but we don't have to wallow in it. We don't have to fill our lives with all of this darkness.'

'But somebody has to,' I said. 'Somebody has to take the hit and deal with the darkness, or it will never go away.'

A fierce look came into her eyes. 'But that somebody does not have to be my son.' She stared at me a moment, her eyes wet with tears. 'You're all I have left.'

She turned and went back into the bathroom, and for a moment I watched the empty space where she had been. I wasn't really all she had left. I was the only one left at home, sure, with Dad eight years gone and my sister Lauren barely on speaking terms with her, but she had Margaret, and she had . . . Well, she had to have somebody else – right? And things with Lauren were better than they'd been in years, so that was something.

Right?

I turned back to the TV. The news was cutting to a commercial, but the signout footage was a quick shot of the courthouse lawn, probably taken earlier that morning when the Mayor's body was first found. There was an indistinct shape on the grass, presumably the body, and rising up from its back were two long poles, just like with the pastor. Caught on the poles, or perhaps hung there, were two wide sheets of ripped plastic, flowing in the breeze and splashed with dirty red blood. They flapped in the wind like artificial wings, and then the screen fell to black.

Brooke's house was just two doors down from mine, a two-storey tract home that followed the same basic layout as every other house in the neighbourhood – except ours, of course, which was just an apartment over the mortuary. I sat in my car, parked innocuously on the kerb, and catalogued Brooke's house in my head: there was the front porch, with the door right in the centre; this led back into a long hallway that stretched to the rear of the house. On the left was the living room, small but cosy, with a large picture window, and on the right was a dining room that turned into a kitchen at the back; this had a large sliding glass door that led out to their backyard. The back corner on the left side was a bathroom and a large pantry.

The first floor I didn't know nearly as well, having never been up there, but I'd been in the Crowleys' house so I could guess where everything was. The staircase led up to a master bedroom – presumably her parents – at the top on the front right corner. I could see the windows from my seat in the car: white lace curtains and a couple of cutesy knick-knacks. Across the hall was a smaller bedroom which was probably her brother Ethan's. The back left corner was Brooke's room, with a wide view of the woods beyond. This I knew for certain, because I used to sit in the darkness of that wood and watch her through the uncurtained window. But I was better than that now.

Well, obviously not much better.

I don't know why I was watching her house. It's not like I needed the companionship – if I wanted to do something, I could just call my friend Max. I wasn't peeping into Brooke's windows, and I wasn't stalking her, I was just . . . thinking about her. I wondered if she ever thought about me.

It was late August, with just enough breeze to keep the heat from being oppressive. My windows were rolled down, and I hung my arm out the side, feeling it bake in the sun. Somewhere a lawnmower droned. I watched Brooke's house with a blank mind. The world was hollow, like a bell.

A few minutes later the lawnmower shut off, and a minute or two after that Brooke herself came into view, walking out from the backyard pushing a lawnmower. She lined it up on a corner of the front lawn and leaned down to grab the starter cord, ripping it up and back. The mower roared to life and she pushed it forward, carving a long, straight swathe into the grass. She was so different from Marci – taller, thinner, less curvy and more . . . willowy? That was a stupid word. Brooke was elegant, long and slender. Her hair was golden, and today she had pulled it back into a ponytail that hung past her shoulders. She moved simply and gracefully.

She reached the edge of the lawn and turned around, coming back towards me as she cut the second row. I slumped down in the car so she wouldn't see me, but her eyes were on the grass. When she turned again to go back the other way I got out of my car and walked slowly towards her, coming to a stop in her driveway. She reached the far edge and pulled the mower around again for another pass. She saw me now, and paused a moment. She turned off the mower and pulled a headphone out of her ear.

'Hey, John.'

'Hey.'

We stood there, silent. There was so much I wanted to say, but really nothing that I actually *could* say. Not because the words weren't there, they just weren't in any kind of order. Anything I said would be a string of random words: food shoes house, my not floor holding. Everywhere. Sky.

Language fell apart, not just for me but for the entire world, from now until the dawn of time.

How did anyone ever talk to anyone else?

She spoke. 'How you doing?'

'Fine.'

Silence again.

She bent back down to grab the starter cord, but I stopped her.

'Do you think . . . ?' I didn't even know what I wanted to ask her.

'John,' she said, 'I'm sorry for what I said. But it's still true. You're . . . I mean . . . I don't know what I mean.' She sighed. 'We talked about this already, right? I can't just forget everything. I can't just look at your eyes and see the person I used to see. I've seen . . .' She bit her lip. 'I don't know what I've seen. More than I wanted to.' She braced herself to pull, hand on the cord, but I stopped her again.

'Wait.'

She closed her eyes. 'Did Marci ask you out?' she asked.

I nodded. 'How'd you know?'

'She asked me if she could. Like I had any say in it. You're not my . . . anything. I mean, we only went on two dates, right?'

'You told her to ask me out?'

She let go of the cord and straightened up. 'I didn't tell her not to.'

'I thought you were scared of me. Seems like you would've warned her or something.'

She shook her head. 'Please don't think I hate you, John. You're a good friend. You saved my life, maybe more than once. But now every time I see you I see *him*, and I see the smoke, and then I see the way you . . .' Her voice cracked and I could tell she was trying not to cry. She kept her eyes down, avoiding mine. 'I see the way you looked at me. The way you looked when you asked him for the knife. I'm not scared any more, I just . . .' She looked up at the sky. 'I don't know. I think it's because I saw someone else, someone behind your face, like you'd taken off a mask. It was still you, but it wasn't. And I don't think that person is going to hurt me, or Marci, or anybody else, but . . . I guess the thing is that I don't know anything about that person. At all. And that's what scares me more than anything – that there could be two people, so different, and one of them so secret.'

I looked at her – bright blue eyes, clearer than the sky, wet with tears like drops of rain. I wanted to wipe away those tears, I wanted to run, I wanted to hold her and hit her and scream and disappear. I wanted to melt into a puddle of sludge, like Crowley and Forman before me – gone forever, like a drop of nothing. I wanted to deny it all, and tell her she was crazy, and act as normal as possible, and convince her I was just like everybody else. I should have stayed in my car. I should have stayed in my house.

She bent back to the starter cord, but I stepped forward, my hand held out desperately.

'Can we talk?'

'About what?'

'About . . .' *About what?* I had nothing to talk about. I had no hobbies, I had no interests, I had no life but the one I could never share with anyone. The only thing I ever thought about. 'I think Forman was a demon.'

'A what?'

'I know he was,' I said, taking another step forward. 'So was the Clayton Killer.' No one knew it was Mr Crowley. 'And I think the new one is too.'

'A demon?' said Brooke. 'Like, a literal demon, like with horns and a tail and all that?'

'I think that's a devil,' I said. 'I think demons just look like us.'

'What are you talking about?'

'That's not the point – I mean, it's not a real demon, not technically, but it's some kind of . . . like a monster, like a real monster. Like in a movie or something.'

She was staring at me, her jaw wide open and her brow furrowed in concern. 'John, are you okay?'

I shouldn't have said anything – I was usually so much smarter, so much more careful. Why did I think she would have any idea what I was talking about?

'Did you see anything when we were in the house with Forman?' I asked. 'Did you notice anything weird about him?' *Why did I keep talking?*

'Monsters aren't real, John,' she said. She looked worried. 'Do you need to sit down?'

'No, I'm fine. Listen, I'm fine, just forget it, okay?' I felt like I was drowning. 'That was just a crazy story, you know? Just a . . . just a joke.' I took a step back. 'I'll see you around.' I turned and walked quickly towards my house.

'John, wait.'

I ignored her, never turning or slowing or breathing until I made it home and got inside and locked the door behind me.

Chapter 6

The Mayor's body arrived in the mortuary on the first day of school, early in the morning as I was getting ready to leave. Dead bodies keep to their own schedule: a body decays at the same rate every time, no matter who it is, no matter how important it is, no matter how long the FBI studies it for evidence. The Mayor had been dead for a week now, and there wasn't much time left to embalm it if the family wanted a viewing. When the body showed up early in the morning like this it meant that the Coroners had stayed up all night finishing their autopsy – running final checks, performing a final cleaning, and dotting all the i's on their paperwork. The funeral was only one day away. We had very little time to work with.

I stayed in the kitchen, wolfing down my breakfast until finally the Coroner left, and then I ran downstairs like a shot. Mom was getting washed up, and I walked over casually to join her.

'What do you think you're doing?' she asked.

'Helping.'

'Not during school hours,' she said. 'You've got to leave in just a few minutes.'

'Then I have a few minutes,' I said. 'Let me help get you started.'

Mom paused, watching me, then sighed. 'Did you eat your cereal?'

'Yes.'

'And you washed your bowl?'

'Yes,' I lied. I hadn't really, but she wouldn't know that until it was too late.

'Wash your hands, then,' she said, turning back to the sink. 'The last thing Mayor Robinson needs is raisin bran in his chest cavity.'

I crowded up next to her and washed eagerly, then pulled on an apron, a mask and a pair of sterile rubber gloves. We unzipped the body bag and pulled it off, catching a powerful whiff of cleansers and disinfectants from the autopsied corpse.

'Let's hope the fan doesn't give out,' I said.

'Margaret's on her way,' said Mom.

'I can stay until she gets here,' I offered, but Mom shook her head and looked at the clock.

'You can stay for four more minutes, then it's off to school.'

'Smelling like a corpse.'

Mom sniffed the air and laughed. 'You'll smell like detergent, and most people don't connect that smell to corpses. Just tell everyone you cleaned the bathroom this morning.'

'That's sure to impress them.'

'Only the ones who appreciates a hardworking man,' said Mom. 'Girls will love it.'

I unwrapped the bandages on the wrists, then reached for

a bottle of Dis-Spray and froze, my hand stretched into the air. Something on the wrist had caught my eye.

I stepped back to the table and bent down to peer at the wrist more closely. On the first corpse, the wrists had been severed cleanly – no saw marks or serrations, no major tissue trauma – but the Mayor's left wrist was different. Instead of ending in a clean, indecipherable wall of meat and bone, this wrist was messy. There was a straight cut, yes, but behind it was a smaller cut, coming down through the flesh and glancing diagonally off the big knob of bone on the outside of the wrist. It looked like the demon had tried to sever the hand, missed, then hit home with a second swing.

What did it mean?

I had assumed that the demon used claws, like Mr Crowley's, and his claws had never been stopped by a bone – they'd been able to cut through anything. I'd seen him dig into the asphalt like it was clay. Did this demon have duller claws, or a weaker swing, or was she doing something else entirely? What if it wasn't a claw at all, but an axe? But that didn't make sense. An axe should have been able to slice through a wrist without any problem, and it couldn't possibly have made the stab wounds on the back.

'Time to go,' said Mom.

'Yeah,' I said absently, grabbing the body's shoulder to roll it over. 'I need to look at something.'

'You need to go to school,' she said, pushing the shoulder gently back down. 'That was the deal.'

'But look at this wrist,' I said, pointing at it.

'That was mentioned in Ron's report,' she said calmly, steering me away from the table.

'Does it say what made it?'

'Go to school,' she repeated.

'But I need to know!' I shouted, shrugging her violently off of my arm. I was breathing heavily, my teeth clenched. She stepped back, eyes wide, and I stepped back the other way, as if away from an electric shock. *Where had that come from?*

I took a deep breath. 'I'm sorry.' I hadn't had any kind of angry outbursts, physical or otherwise, in weeks. 'I'll go now.'

Mom regained her composure and nodded. 'What do we say?'

I paused. It had been a while since we'd bothered with this, but it was another little ritual we had – a mantra we used to say whenever I left the house, to help me remember my rules. I didn't want to start it again.

But it was better than the alternative.

'Today I will smile all day, and think good thoughts about everyone I meet.' Mom said it with me. It scared me, and I think it scared her, to know how quickly we both went back to the same preventative measure.

I took off my apron and mask, threw away my gloves and washed my hands in the restroom on the way out.

In hindsight, it was stupid of me to stop at Brooke's house on the way to school. Ever since I got my licence last year I'd driven her to and from school every day; I got to see her, talk to her, and smell the clean, soft scent that followed her everywhere. I cherished those car rides, and now, through force of habit and a powerful sense of delusion, I was right back at it on the first day of the new school year.

Of course she wasn't speaking to me, but she still needed to get to school, right? We'd never officially cut off the driving arrangement, so technically it was still on, and even if I drove her to school it didn't mean she had to talk to me. But over time we were sure to start talking again anyway – meaningless small talk at first, then more and more, until everything would be just like it had always been.

I waited by her kerb for three minutes, trying to get up the nerve to go knock on her door – she'd always come out on her own before – but it was stupid. I knew it was stupid even to come here, I knew it before I did it. It was just . . . well, it was worth a try, anyway. I put the car in gear and drove away.

I passed Brooke several blocks later, waiting at the bus stop. She didn't wave, and I drove by without slowing.

I'd never really liked school. I liked learning, but I liked a very specific learning environment. Noisy classrooms with yellowed floor tiles, fluorescent lights and a few hundred kids who thought I was a freak were, unsurprisingly, not a part of the environment I preferred. Give me a good library, an Internet connection and some educational TV, and I could sit and 'learn' for hours, as long as I enjoyed the subject; I'd venture to say that I knew more about serial killers and criminal profiling than almost anybody in town, up to and including the FBI team that had come to investigate the Handyman killings. But I was also a realist, and I recognised organised education as a necessary evil. I wanted to become a real mortician when I grew up, and that meant I needed college, and that meant I needed high school. If I could sit through just two more years of broken desks, social cliques and school spirit, I'd be in the clear.

I parked in the back lot. It was the end of August, and the weather was warm but cooling rapidly. Scattered groups of kids were shouting to each other cheerfully, leaning on their cars or strolling slowly towards the various buildings. Our school had three: the main building, the tech building (which was fairly low tech, despite its name), and the gym. I saw a couple of sophomores wandering about in a daze, still daunted by their first day in a real high school. They probably couldn't read their class schedules.

'Hey, John,' said Marci, leaning against one of the flowerboxes in the side lawn. Her best friend, Rachel, was with her. 'How's it going?'

I stopped. After our bike-riding date I hadn't heard from her, and I'd assumed she'd lost interest. Yet here she was, on the first day of school, ignoring everyone else on the lawn and talking to me.

'Not bad,' I said. 'Nothing like the first day of school to get you going in the morning.'

'Ug,' said Marci, 'it's like a Monday.'

'It is a Monday.'

'No, I mean like the Monday to end all Mondays,' she said. 'It's that same depressing "Oh no, the weekend is really over" feeling, magnified a thousand times.' She grinned mischievously. 'I'm taking bets on the first person to ditch class.'

'Counting the whole school?' I asked. 'I bet there's some people that don't even show up.'

'That's what I told her,' said Rachel.

'What's your first period?' asked Marci.

I looked at my schedule, though I had it memorised. 'Social Studies with Verner.'

Marci smiled. 'Sweet – us too. Then here's the rules: check out everyone in our first-period class, make your pick, and then we'll watch them for the rest of the day. First one to ditch is the winner.'

'You mean whoever bets on the first ditcher is the winner,' said Rachel.

'That's debatable,' Marci replied, standing up. 'Let's go grab some seats in the back, so we can get a good view of all our contestants.'

Rachel stood as well, and together they walked over to the nearest door for the main building. After a second of hesitation, I followed them. I'd never walked into school with anybody before, except Max, but that barely counted. He was only my friend because I didn't have anyone else, and I was only his friend for the same reason. Besides, I hadn't seen him in weeks, and I was with two very cute girls.

Marci and Rachel waved and smiled and chatted with a dozen or so people on our way through the halls, and I hung behind them like a shadow – not hiding, but not inserting myself into their conversations, either. It seemed like everyone knew them, and they knew just about everyone else. I suppose that's what 'popular' means, and it shouldn't have surprised me, but it did. I could go a whole week without talking to anyone at school, sometimes anyone at all. Marci was the exact opposite, to a degree that I hadn't even imagined was possible. It was a little annoying, but more than that it was exhausting. It was so much easier to be an outcast.

Mr Verner's room was the same as always; I don't think he'd put up any new posters since the 1990s, if that, which seemed weird for a Social Studies teacher. Shouldn't he have been more on top of current events? The door was in the rear of the room, and Marci went straight to the far wall to claim the back corner seat. Rachel sat in front of her, so I hesitantly took the seat next to Marci on the back row. It's hard to explain why I felt so strange. It wasn't because Marci was popular or pretty, though she certainly was; it was more because I'd just never really hung out with anybody before. I felt like I was forgetting something; like I was supposed to do or say something and didn't know what it was. I couldn't think of anything, so I just sat down.

'My next class is with Mr Coleman,' said Marci. 'Gag. Do you know how many times he's tried to look down my shirt?'

'So wear something else,' said Rachel. 'With a shirt like that on, I feel like I should be ogling you too.'

'He's a teacher,' said Marci. 'It's completely disgusting.'

'You should report him,' I said, glancing at her chest and then looking quickly away. I'd given up my rules against girl-watching, but they were still so ingrained that I hadn't even noticed her shirt yet – I'd been subconsciously avoiding it. It was a tight black tank top, the same colour as her hair, with a curly green leaf pattern that showed off her curves to perfection. She really was gorgeous . . .

And then I found myself thinking about Brooke. That's the weirdest thing.

'I almost did report him last year,' Marci went on, 'but when I got to the counsellor's office *he* checked me out, too, so I gave up. Obviously I enjoy a little attention, but it amazes me how brazen some people are about it.'

Two more girls wandered into the room, talking and ignoring us. I looked at Marci, keeping my eyes firmly on her face; her eyes were the same green as the vines.

'You shouldn't just give up,' I said. 'We have a . . .' I didn't know what to say, or how to say it: *we have a responsibility to stop people from doing bad things*. Why was that so hard to say? Everyone I talked to was so complacent. Had people always been like this, and I was just noticing it now?

'What do we have?' asked Marci.

'We have . . .' Did they really want to talk about this? Most people didn't care about any of the things I did, and I usually didn't realise it until I'd already said something insulting, boring, or controversial. I looked around at the classroom. *Think, John*, I told myself. *Find something to talk about. Talking is easy. People do it every day.* I saw the two people who'd come in earlier, Kristen and Ashley, and I pointed at them. 'We have our first two contestants,' I said. 'Do you think either of them will be the first ditcher of the day?'

Marci was looking at me out of the corner of her eyes, ignoring my question. What was she thinking?

Rachel laughed. 'There's no way Kristen goes first,' she said. 'Straight A students don't ditch.'

'They ditch all the time,' said Marci. 'I got straight As in ninth grade, if you'll remember, and I ditched my math class about once a week.' She grinned. 'That's a twenty per cent ditch rate.'

'Kristen is not just any straight A student,' argued Rachel.

'She's a straight A student taking every college credit class the school has, *and* she's the editor of the school paper. She's not going to ditch, the first day of term.'

'She will if we're counting school paper meetings,' I said.

'Leaving normal school to go to voluntary extra school does not count as ditching,' said Marci. 'It won't be Kristen, and I don't think Ashley will break first either. She's not a super-nerd or anything, but she's not all that rebellious. We're looking for a true wild woman.'

'How about a wild man?' I asked, watching as more people drifted into the room. Among them was Rob Anders, who I thought of as a bully though he wasn't really. He simply knew enough about me to be scared, without knowing enough to be smart about it. He hated me, but like most high-school kids he was completely powerless to hurt me; sticks and stones could break my bones, but Rob was too chicken to go that far. His suspicions about me were just enough to guarantee him a few seconds of 'I told you so' fame if anyone ever found out about the two people I'd killed, but between now and then he was just an angry kid. Even now, when he could have come over to taunt me or whatever, he didn't; he was probably scared off by Marci, actually. No guy in his right mind wanted to look like a jerk in front of her.

Through the door, in the crowded hallway, I caught a quick glimpse of Max walking past – still short, still chubby, still wearing his glasses, but different somehow. His head was down, and he was scowling. And then he was gone.

'You think Rob?' Marci asked, following my gaze to where he stood in the doorway. She pondered him a moment, then shook her head. 'I don't see it. Punching you at the Bonfire last year was the craziest thing he's ever done in his life, and I heard he spent the whole summer working it off for his slave-driver mom. He'll be on his best behaviour today, just to prove he's changed. We need somebody else.'

'Hey, guys.' Brad Nielsen flopped down into the desk in front of me, right next to Rachel. 'What's up?' He was a guy I'd known better as a kid, though we hadn't really hung out in years. He was nice enough, but I found myself suddenly hating him – hating him passionately, almost violently. Who did he think he was, invading my group and talking to my girls?

This was exactly why I'd stopped hanging around people – I didn't want to think like this. How quickly had I gone from nervousness to jealousy? He'd done something so little – he had sat down in a chair – and I'd felt myself burning with rage. Why couldn't I just have a normal relationship, without seeing everyone I met as a possession or a competitor? I breathed deep, counting slowly to ten while he talked, willing myself to calm down.

'Did you guys hear about Allison?' His face was grave, and the girls leaned in, frowning.

'Allison Hill?' asked Marci.

'Yeah,' said Brad. He looked at me. 'You didn't hear?'

'Nothing,' I said. 'What happened?'

'Killed herself,' said Brad. He swallowed. 'They found her this morning – wrists slit, just like Jenny Zeller.'

Rachel covered her mouth, her eyes wide, and Marci's jaw dropped.

'You're kidding,' she said. 'What the hell?'

'It came on the radio right as I got to school,' said Brad.

'She just called me last night,' said Rachel, tears welling up in her eyes. 'She called me five times – I thought she was just being annoying. I had no idea!'

Another suicide. I looked around the room and saw for the first time the worried looks of the other students: the furrowed brows, the pursed lips, the teary eyes. Everyone was talking about it.

Allison Hill had been a pretty normal girl, as far as I could tell: she didn't have a ton of friends, but she had more than Jenny Zeller. She was in the choir and the dance team; she had two good parents; she had a job at the bookstore. I'd bought a book on Herb Mullin from her just a few weeks ago.

Why did normal people kill themselves?

'I don't understand,' I said.

'I know,' said Brad. 'It's nuts.'

'Suicides always go up during periods of trauma,' I said, 'and we've had plenty of trauma over the past year, but why teenage girls? They're not in the target demographic of any of the three killers, so it's not personal fear, and I don't think either of them have had connections to the other victims. Did the two girls know each other?'

No one answered, and I mentally kicked myself. There I went again, spouting off about the technical details of a crime and making everyone think I was a freak. I looked up quickly and sighed with relief, seeing that Rachel was ignoring me altogether, too lost in her tears to listen, and Brad was only half-listening, probably out of politeness, while he tried to comfort Rachel. When I stopped talking he turned away altogether to focus on her.

But there was Marci again, looking at me with that same look as before; not judging, and not really studying, just . . . looking. Thinking.

Brad and Rachel were whispering now, locked in some tearful private conversation. All around us the class was involved in a dozen similar hushed conversations, as the other kids struggled to come to terms with their emotions. I watched them blankly, unsure how to react. I wasn't sad about Allison, I was . . . confused. Angry. *Why was I even bothering with these idiots if this was how they valued their lives?* I told myself I shouldn't think like that, but it was hard to think of anything else.

Marci pulled out a notebook, turned to a clean sheet and started writing. When she finished she sat up straight and smiled at me – a fake smile, trying to be playful but leaving her eyes dull and sad.

'I've made my prediction,' she said, tearing out the page and folding it carefully in fourths. 'Are you ready?'

'I haven't thought much about it.'

'That's okay,' she said, handing me the note. 'We can work together on this one.'

I took the note and unfolded it.

John Cleaver

I looked back at Marci and raised my eyebrows.

'You think?' I asked.

'I do,' she said. 'And as for your guess, I have it on very good authority that a girl named Marci Jensen absolutely cannot handle any more school today.' Her eyes misted up, just the tiniest fraction of a tear, and she blinked it away. 'Pick her, and who knows? Maybe we'll get lucky, and we'll both win.' She smiled again, more real this time, but still a mask of sadness. 'It could happen.'

I looked at the classroom – a mess of crying, confused students, and still no teacher. It was already five minutes after class was supposed to start. School wasn't likely to be much of anything today anyway, after the news about Allison. I looked back at her.

'Where do you want to go?'

'Out,' she said, closing her eyes. 'Out and away.'

The windows in the classroom were dark and blurry, made of some ancient plastic that had yellowed over the years. The sky beyond looked old and sour, like a jaundiced eye.

We didn't need demons. It almost didn't matter how many they killed, because we just rolled over and killed ourselves. Would it ever stop? Would there be anyone left when it did?

And I was the one who'd called them here.

I grabbed my backpack and stood up. 'Let's get out of here.'

Chapter 7

Marci had a much newer car than I did, though, that's not saying much, and she drove me to her house to pick something up on our way to Friendly Burger. The front door was open, as before, and the twin four year olds were still there – and still, as nearly as I could tell, wearing the same clothes as before. Marci smiled at them as we walked inside, and ruffled the boy's hair.

'Hey dude,' she said. 'Mom in the garden?'

'Is school over already?' the little girl asked.

'Yes, it is,' said Marci, holding out her hands. 'Isn't that awesome?'

'Momma's in the garden,' said the boy.

'Why is school so short?' asked the girl.

'Because we already know everything,' Marci answered, leading us into the kitchen. It was old, like the rest of the house, and the kitchen table was sticky with jam that I assumed had come from the twins' breakfast.

'Momma's in the garden,' the boy repeated.

'Thanks, Jaden, I heard you the first time.'

'Do you really know everything?' the girl asked. 'Do you know how many stars there are?'

Marci turned to face the twins, squatting down to meet their eyes. 'Four billion, five zillion, six hundred and twenty-three. Do you guys want to watch cartoons?'

'Yes!' they shouted. Marci herded them back down the hall, and I heard a TV come on. A moment later she returned to the kitchen, smiling, and walked to the sink.

'I remember being that happy.' She picked up a wet rag, went over to the table and started scrubbing away the jam.

I turned to look at the fridge. It was covered with calendars, flyers, crayon drawings, magnetic letters and more. One of the magnets was a splash of rubber water, with a rubber fish dangling in front of it on a stiff spring. I turned back to Marci and saw her leaning forwards, her hands braced against the table, watching me. I looked away again, at the window this time, and felt suddenly stupid. *Why did I keep looking away?* She probably thought I was a jerk. But just as suddenly, an answer popped into my head: it was my rules again, cutting in to stop me from looking at Marci's chest. It was a force of habit so embedded that I hadn't even noticed I was doing it. I needed to pay attention to her, not my rules. I forced myself to look back and saw her standing upright, leaning lightly against the counter with her arms folded.

'You're different,' she said. 'You know that?'

'I'm sorry.'

She raised her eyebrows. 'Don't be sorry, whatever you do.' She grabbed a purse off the counter and held it up. 'You hungry?'

'Not really.'

'Me neither.' She pulled out a kitchen chair and sat down, then shook her head. 'Can you believe this?'

'You mean the Handyman, or the suicides?'

'Any of it,' she said. 'All of it. What's happening to us?' She caught me with her gaze, staring intently. 'Did you know the Clarks left town?'

The Clarks lived next door to Max, in the neighbourhood called The Gardens. Max's dad had been killed in front of their house just nine months ago, when Mr Crowley had ripped him in half. I'd been there, hiding, and I'd hesitated just a second too long to save him. I pushed the thought away and looked back innocently.

'They moved?'

'They haven't sold their house yet,' said Marci, 'but they left. Three days ago. Said they wanted to get out before school started, so their kids could start the new year somewhere safe.' She closed her eyes. 'Fifteen people dead in a year, seventeen if you count the suicides.' She opened her eyes and looked up at me. 'Is that totally freaky, that I know that? Of all the sick things to keep track of.'

It was actually nineteen dead, because Mr Crowley had killed two drifters nobody knew about, and hidden the bodies so well no one had ever found them. One, I knew, was in the lake, and the other was probably there as well. There might be even more; it had taken me almost two months to trace the killings to Crowley, and who knew what he'd done before I found him.

Marci was staring at the wall now, her elbow planted on the table and her fist in front of her mouth. She was blowing into it, her face slack and her eyes moist.

I pulled out a chair and sat across from her. 'Knowing how many people have died isn't freaky at all,' I said. 'I know them all too. I could probably name them.'

Marci laughed – short and humourless. 'Sometimes I wonder what it's like to grow up where people have other things to talk about. Weather, or football games, or movies. You know?'

'We have all that stuff,' I said. 'It's just too boring to bother with.'

'I guess that's true enough. But we used to live like that, you know, boring or not.'

It was time for me to do something – to say something, to involve myself in this conversation. On our first date I'd barely said a word, and even when I was dating Brooke I hadn't been especially active. She'd planned everything, she'd done everything, she'd said almost everything. I was just along for the ride back then, and now I was doing it again. I needed to act; I needed to *be*. I needed to step up and be a real person. But . . .

What could I possibly say? Her little brother had said she had lots of boys over all the time – what kinds of things did they say? Did they talk about sports? Did they tell her she was pretty? I couldn't hold her hand or gaze into her eyes or anything like that. If I wanted to act, I needed to stop acting like I thought other people were supposed to act, and start acting like myself. I was the one she'd invited into her kitchen: John Cleaver. But how much did she really know about John Cleaver?

And how interested could she possibly be in the things that interested John Cleaver?

I spread my hands on the table, flat against the wood. I had no one else to talk to: Mom wouldn't talk about the killings, and Brooke wouldn't talk at all. I was desperate to talk to somebody, and if I told everything to Marci I'd either gain a confidante or destroy a budding friendship. But what good was a friend I couldn't talk to? I wanted to be the real me. I decided to test the waters.

'Your dad told you about me, right?'

She looked up. 'What?'

'No one knows what I did in that house. Most people don't even know I was there – but your dad does, and he told you, right?'

She nodded. 'You saved all those people. And you attacked Agent Forman.'

'And you asked me out anyway?'

'That's *why* I asked you out.'

I paused just a moment before continuing, 'What else did he tell you?'

'About you?'

'About anything. About Forman, or the Handyman, or the Clayton Killer. Does he tell you other things?'

'He . . .' She paused. 'I ask him about his job a lot, actually – I think it's fascinating – but he hasn't said much about the killers. But he told me about Forman's house, and what Forman was doing in there – what he did to you, and to those women. He wanted me to know what was happening, so I'd be prepared if anything happened to me.'

'So are you?'

She paused again, longer this time.

'I think so,' she said. 'I know some self-defence moves, I

carry Mace. I know what parts of town to stay away from, and what parts are safe, but the Mayor was just killed inside of City Hall, so I don't know if anything's safe any more.'

'Forman kidnapped me inside the police station,' I said. 'He pulled a gun, he beat up Stephanie, and he abducted us both right there. No witnesses, no chance for help, nothing.'

'That's horrible,' she said. She looked at me, and her eyes softened.

'It was horrible,' I agreed, 'but it wasn't the end. We hung on for two more days, and we won. And it wasn't because I had Mace, or because I stayed away from danger zones, it was because I knew what was going on, and I knew how he thought and what he did. I knew what he wanted, and I turned it against him.'

She was watching me, resting her chin in the palm of her hand. 'You know, you really are different.'

I had her interest now; she was really thinking about what I was saying. 'Do you remember what you said this morning about Mr Coleman?' I asked.

'Jeez, what a dirtbag.'

'You said you gave up. He did something wrong, you were going to stop him, and then you just gave up.'

'Well, come on now, it's not like I can have every guy who looks at me arrested—'

'I'm not accusing you of anything,' I said, holding out my hand to calm her down. 'I tell you right now, if I looked like you I think the attention would drive me insane; I don't know how you do it.' She smiled a little at that, and I went on, 'What I'm saying is that the killers in town are just like that – it's on a bigger scale, but it's the same thing. Something

74

bad happens, and you can try to do something about it or you can sit back, and when you *do* try to do something it usually gets worse before it gets better. That's what happened to you, and that's what happened to me with Forman.'

It was time to show her who I really was. 'Do you know why I was in the police station that night?'

'No.'

'I was helping Forman track the killer, though it turned out to be him all along. He was . . . I know this sounds weird, because I'm only sixteen, but he was running the case past me, bouncing ideas around to see if I had any insights.'

She raised her eyebrows again. 'You're kidding.'

'I was there when the Clayton Killer attacked my neighbours,' I said. 'I mean, everyone knows I was there, but I was *really* there, right in the middle of it, and not just because I lived across the street and heard a noise. I'd been studying the Clayton Killer for months, trying to figure out who he was, and who he was attacking, and why, and once I figured all of that out I thought I could figure out how to stop him. I *did* figure out how to stop him. I saved Kay Crowley, and I almost saved Dr Neblin.'

'And Mr Crowley, too,' she said.

She didn't know Mr Crowley was the killer – nobody did. I nodded, and went on; it wouldn't hurt to bend the truth a little bit.

'I almost saved him too,' I agreed. 'And Forman knew that – he knew everything I'd done to track the Clayton Killer – so when the second killer started dumping bodies all over town, Forman asked for my help tracking him, too. And then it turned out that he was the killer, and he was really just trying to find out how much of a threat I was. Once he realised that I was almost there – that I'd almost traced the whole thing back to him – he locked me up so I couldn't stop him.' It wasn't the full truth, but it was all I dared to trust her with at the time. The demons would stay secret.

'You're kidding,' she said again, laughing, then stopped and frowned. 'You're serious?'

'Yeah.'

'I had no idea.' She sat back in her chair, staring at the table, then looked up at me. 'What are you, some kind of genius detective?'

'That's just the thing,' I said. 'Anyone can do this, but nobody ever does. They leave it all to the police or the FBI, but if you pay attention and follow the case, you can find all the clues.' I couldn't tell her that I planned to go after the killer myself, so I took the safe route. 'We can tell the police everything we find, and help them stop this killer.'

That was it – I'd said it all. I'd told her who I was: John the Dragonslayer. I'd either piqued her interest or driven her off completely. I watched her, waiting to see what she said.

She watched me back, her eyes moving over me, searching.

'You really are serious,' she said.

I didn't even nod, I just stared back, waiting. After a long moment she shrugged.

'So what do we do?'

'Are you sure you want to do this?'

She nodded. 'My dad's a cop, John. You're going to have to try pretty hard to freak me out.'

'That's a challenge I'll accept,' I said, and she smiled warily.

'So let's get right into it. The central question of criminal profiling is this: what did the killer do that she didn't have to do?'

'She?'

'I think the Handyman might be a woman,' I said.

'Why?'

'Just a hunch.'

She smirked. 'I'm beginning to think this isn't nearly as scientific as you led me to believe.'

'There's very little science in criminal profiling,' I admitted. 'It's all educated guesses and shots in the dark.'

'Does it ever work?'

'It works all the time,' I said. 'How about . . . okay, here's an example: the Trailside Killer, from San Francisco. He killed a bunch of people, both women and men, in the middle of the woods, and he kept at it for a year before they finally caught him. The forensic evidence showed that the attacks were all fast, like really fast, which usually means that the killer doesn't want to be seen, but this was in the middle of nowhere – there was no one else around for miles. The profiler on the case decided that the only reason to go that fast when there was no danger of getting caught was that the killer was ashamed of something, and he didn't want the victims to notice it.'

'So the profiler predicted that the killer had a big ugly scar or something,' said Marci, 'and the police started looking for people with scars. Does that really help?'

I smiled. 'It's even better than that. You see, even though there were no witnesses in the woods, there were plenty at the trailheads and the parking lots, and nobody they interviewed had ever mentioned somebody with a physical deformity. So the profiler guessed that the killer had a deformity nobody could see, but that still made him feel awkward and outcast. He told the police to look for a guy with a stutter.'

'He got all that just from the speed of the attacks?'

'Well, there was obviously more to it than that – I'm just paraphrasing – but your reaction is pretty typical. Even the police laughed at the profiler. And then they caught the guy, and he had a really debilitating stutter.'

Marci shook her head, her mouth open. 'That's freaky.

'Freaky and crazy and incredibly accurate,' I said. '*If* you know what you're doing.'

'So the Trailside Killer did something he didn't have to do,' said Marci, nodding, 'and figuring out the reason for that told them something valuable about him.'

'Exactly,' I said. She'd picked this up a lot quicker than Max had.

'All right,' said Marci, 'I think I get it. But how does the Handyman thing make you think she's a woman?'

'Just forget the gender thing for now,' I said. 'Let's go back to my question: what did the killer do that "it" didn't have to do?'

'He cut off their hands.'

'Correct.'

'And that tells us what – that he hates hands?' She laughed. 'You realise this is impossible.'

It gets even harder when you factor in the knowledge that the killer's a demon, I thought. I still don't know what the demon is doing with the hands and tongues she steals.

'I don't really have any good ideas about the hands,' I admitted. 'It could be anything. So we start with something else.'

'Like what?'

'Like, well . . . the wounds are all very clean; the hands and tongue were removed very carefully. What could that tell us?'

'That the killer is very clean,' she said. 'That's what all the plastic drop cloths are for, too, right?' She grinned wickedly. 'So maybe it is a woman, after all.'

'Very funny,' I said, 'but certainly possible. Strong attention to cleanliness also suggests age: younger killers are sloppier, more impulsive, and old killers tend to be more meticulous.'

'So this is an older killer, possibly a woman,' said Marci, 'who plans ahead and is very careful about everything. That fits perfectly, because she attacked the Mayor in City Hall instead of at home, where the security system was so much better.'

'How do you know that?'

'Dad said something about it.' She whistled. 'Wow, this profiling stuff actually works.'

'Told you so.'

'Then it also stands to reason,' she said, 'that the killer carries around a pretty big bag of stuff.'

'Why?' Nowhere in my analysis had I ever considered a bag.

'Because she has so much stuff she needs,' said Marci. 'A woman is never without her purse, especially not an organised woman like this, so she has to have a big bag full of plastic sheets, and a gun, and a hacksaw, and whatever else she uses. That's a lot of stuff.'

'That . . .' I paused. 'You're right, that is a lot of stuff. I hadn't thought of that.' *Because I was so sure the demon used her own claws for the killing, and that was colouring the rest of my theories. It's entirely possible that she just uses a normal weapon, like Forman did, and that means she'd have to carry it with her – but then, what kind of weapon could have made the wrist wounds?*

'You're good at this,' I said.

Marci rolled her eyes. 'This is the last thing I ever wanted to be good at.'

'But the thing about the hands,' I said, 'is that they weren't removed with a hacksaw – there was none of the tissue damage that you'd expect with a saw.'

'Now it's my turn to ask how you know something.'

I stopped short. The lack of tissue damage was something they'd never mentioned on the news. I'd learned it in the mortuary, and my involvement in the mortuary was supposed to be a secret. How much should I tell her?

Marci was looking right at me, not accusing but simply curious. She was being completely honest and open. I needed to learn how to be the same.

'I help my mom in the mortuary,' I said. 'I helped embalm Pastor Olsen.'

'Holy crap.' She shifted in her chair. 'Isn't that completely . . . icky?'

' "Icky?" '

'That's the technical term for "ohmygoshgross",' she said. 'I never knew that about you.'

'Believe me,' I said, 'there are a lot of things you never knew about me. But let's think about the wrist wounds: do you have any idea what could have made them?'

'No saw-marks?' she asked.

'Nope.'

'A knife?'

'It's a single cut,' I said. 'There's no way you could get that kind of force behind a knife. Maybe a machete.'

'Or an axe,' she said, tapping her chin. 'Or a shovel.'

'An axe and a machete are probably too big to conceal,' I said, 'let alone a shovel. Even if we think big and give our killer a duffel bag for her stuff, she's going to have trouble carrying anything big enough to make that kind of cut.' I kept going back to the claw; it had to be a claw – nothing else fit. But telling Marci about the demons would be another giant step, and I still wasn't comfortable with it.

'What about a hatchet?' she asked. I looked up, struck by the idea, and she went on: 'A hatchet handle's not as long as an axe, so you can't get quite as much power behind it, but it might be able to cut through a wrist bone like that.' I stared at her, and she smiled nervously. 'I guess? I don't know how to cut through a wrist bone.' I kept staring. 'Look,' she said, 'you started this, don't look at me like that.'

'No,' I said quickly, 'no, I'm not looking at you weird at all. I think that's brilliant.'

'Thank you.'

'I mean, it's not brilliant—'

'What?'

'I mean, it's something I never thought of, and I should have. A hatchet. I can't believe I didn't think of a hatchet.'

'I liked this conversation better when I was brilliant.'

'What?' I asked, smiling. 'Now *you're* some kind of genius detective?'

'Hey,' she drawled, 'this stuff's easy.' She narrowed her eyes and winked. 'Stick with me, kid; we'll catch this psycho.'

'Wow,' I said, cocking my head to the side. 'Was that a cowboy or a film noir mobster?'

She threw the wet rag in my face. 'That was a *brilliant* criminal investigator. Who is also hungry.'

'I know how she feels,' I said. 'Does she want to go get something?'

'Yeah,' said Marci, smiling. 'I think she does.'

Chapter 8

The next night was the Mayor's funeral, starting with a viewing at 5 p.m., and the place was packed. Mom and Margaret and Lauren had spent the entire day finishing the embalming, coordinating with the cemetery and running all over town between flower shops, city organisers, and even printers for the programmes. When I came home from school at three o'clock they threw me into it as well, to vacuum the chapel and roll out the good entry rugs and make sure that everything was perfect. The police were there too, securing the area tighter than I'd ever seen. We'd had plenty of murdered nobodies in our chapel, but this was our first murdered government official. Officer Jensen waved at me, and I waved back. I wondered if he knew that Marci and I had skipped the entire first day of school.

At four thirty, with the chapel prepared and the corpse ready for display, Mom and Margaret and I went upstairs to change. I had a white, collared shirt I used for funerals, with a thin black tie and a black suit-coat to wear over them. I kept the tie knotted on a hanger in my closet, because I could never remember how to do it; I pulled it on now and tightened the loop.

There were still a few minutes left before I needed to be downstairs, and I walked to the window. On the other side of the road, maybe 100 feet away, was the Crowleys' house. There was the white Buick where I'd found Dr Neblin dead; there was the old shed where I'd dragged his body. There was the mark in the road where Mr Crowley's claws had torn up the asphalt. I'd stopped him, but it had taken too long. Too many people had died. Now we had another demon, killing more people, and I still didn't know anything about it.

A cloud passed overhead, darkening the air just enough that I could see my reflection in the window, faint and ghostly. I straightened my tie and went downstairs.

A viewing is an odd thing: families like to see their dearly departed one last time, so we morticians spend hours with make-up, putty and string trying to make a sack of dead meat look as much like a person as possible. Corpses, especially when they've been dead a week like this one, simply don't look like they used to – not because their flesh is rotting off or anything, but for smaller, subtler reasons. The muscles are slack, without even blood pressure to form them, so the face is shaped differently: it is more gaunt, with none of the expression it had in life. The jaw hangs open, so we pin it shut with hooks and wire. The eyes shrivel, so we fill the cavity with cotton to give the eyelids their proper curve. With no blood to give it colour the skin grows pale, so we mix the formaldehyde with dyes, and paint the face with foundation and blush. We work from photos, doing our best to approximate not just any dead guy but *your* dead guy; not just any father but your father, your mother, your sister, your aunt. Then we dress it up in your dead father's suit, like a giant stuffed animal, and lay it in a coffin for you to wander past, awkward and uneasy.

People grow uncomfortable at viewings because, for most, it is their only contact with death. They don't know how to deal with it. They stand there, silent, maybe piping up with a comment about how peaceful he looks, or how much he looks like himself. It's never true – he never looks like himself. Whatever 'himself' used to mean, it's gone now, and the thing left behind in the suit and the coffin could just as easily be anything: it could be a stranger; it could be a tree. Eventually, it will be. The friends and family stare blankly, wondering why this lifeless thing holds no comfort, and then they wander away and talk about how long it's been, and how are the kids, and don't you love my new shoes?

My job was to stand in the doorway with funeral programmes, handing them out and occasionally answering a question about the restrooms. I was an informative table: deferential, glad to be of use. Eventually I left the programmes on a chair and retreated to the office, watching the sombre crowd through the crack of the open door. Someone still managed to find me and ask about the restroom. I gave him directions and closed the door completely.

At six o'clock the viewing ended, and I stepped out to help usher everyone into the chapel for the funeral itself. Usually I pushed the coffin as well, from its home in the antechamber to its place of honour in front of the podium, but tonight the police were performing that function. Sheriff Meier and Officer Jensen, their dress uniforms cleaned and pressed, led a long procession of family with the dead Mayor at the head. I watched from the back. Marci was on the other side, sitting alone. She watched the procession through dark eyes.

Mom stood next to me. 'Where have you been?' she whispered.

'Upstairs,' I lied.

'I looked upstairs.'

'Outside.'

'I need your help, John,' she said. 'This is a job, you know. This is how we pay our bills. We need to do it right.'

'Does everyone have a programme?' I asked.

'That's not the point—'

'Everyone has a programme,' 'I said, 'so I did my job fine.'

Mom glared at me, but the family was almost seated, and she needed to start the ceremony. She left me and walked to the front, and I knew she was putting on her polite, practised mortician face: understanding and professional; serious yet calm. I turned to leave again, but another soft whisper pulled me back.

'You got somewhere we can hide from this?'

I turned and saw Marci, standing quietly behind me. She was wearing a slim dress, and heels that made her nearly as tall as I was.

'I hate funerals,' she said. 'I only came to be with Dad, but he's sitting in the front with Meier.'

'Come on,' I breathed, and led her into the hall and back to the office. If Mom hadn't found me there before, it was probably still the best place. 'In here,' I said. I held the door for her, followed her in and offered her the nice chair behind the desk. I then closed the door behind us and sat across from her.

'So,' she said, looking around. 'This is where you work.'

'Yep. I don't do a lot here in the office, I'm mostly in the back. Clean a lot of restrooms, vacuum a lot of floors. Embalm a lot of Mayors.'

'Ug,' she said. 'It's one thing to see them on the news, but getting right up and touching them is so not for me.'

'We have a week,' I said.

'You have the bodies for a week?'

'No, I'm saying we have one week before the next death. The other attacks were two weeks apart, one on Sunday, the next on a Monday, so number three will be one week from tonight if the pattern holds. We have one week to figure it out.'

Marci grimaced. 'What, you and I? We don't know anything. Not anything important.'

'What about the bag and the hatchet? We figured those out.'

'The police already knew about them,' said Marci. 'I asked my dad. I might be able to get more out of him, if I know what to ask.'

'Ha,' I laughed, smiling thinly. 'The daughter of a cop and the son of a mortician: teen crime-fighters. We're like a bad TV show.'

'I know.' She stretched her arms, pushing her chest forward, and I looked away instinctively. My gaze fell on the filing cabinet, and I stood up quickly.

'Hang on,' I said, walking to the files and opening the top drawer. 'I think the son of the mortician may have another trick up his sleeve.'

'What do you mean?'

'I didn't get to help embalm the Mayor,' I said, flipping through the files, 'but his paperwork's in here somewhere. If we still have the body, we still have the state files on it.'

'What's on the papers?'

'A complete listing of all wounds,' I said, closing the drawer and moving to the next one down. 'Man, I have no idea how Lauren's files are set up.' I found the Mayor's name on a folder and pulled it out. 'Here we go. You might want to look away.'

'Why would I— *holy sheez.*'

I flopped open the folder on the desk, exposing a sheaf of autopsy photos clipped to the stack of papers. Marci looked away, gagging and muttering, while I flipped through the files.

'There were wounds on the first body that the police didn't tell the media about,' I said. 'Wounds on the back – dozens of them, hidden by the victim's shirt so nobody could see them.'

'I cannot believe that you work here,' she said, staring at the wall. She was gripping a chair for support.

'You get used to it,' I said, then tapped my finger on a pink sheet of carbon paper. 'Here it is. *Bullet wound in the head . . . both hands severed . . . tongue removed . . . two pole wounds in the back . . . thirty-seven stab wounds in the back.* Wow.' I sucked in a slow breath. 'Thirty-seven.'

'I'm going to be sick.'

'It's okay,' I said, closing up the folder. 'I'm putting it away.'

'That's not going to help.'

'Sure it is,' I said, sliding the folder back into the drawer and rolling it closed. 'There – photos are gone, everything's gone. You can turn around.'

Marci turned reluctantly. 'You know, I could have gone my whole life without seeing those photos.'

'If we don't figure this out in time, there'll be plenty more where those came from.'

'Don't remind me.' She leaned back, looking at the ceiling. 'Thirty-seven times. Who stabs a guy thirty-seven times?'

'That's exactly the question,' I said. 'She didn't have to do it, which means it's important. So: who *would* stab a guy thirty-seven times?'

'Someone really . . .' Marci closed her eyes '. . . angry. So angry she couldn't stop stabbing, even when the victim was dead.'

'The victim was dead when she started,' I said. 'He was shot in the back of the head.'

'So she's really, really angry,' said Marci. 'Angry enough to stab a dead body. I've been that angry a couple of times.'

'Really?'

She opened her eyes and glowered at me. 'No, not really, but sometimes you just wanna . . . vent your frustration, you know? You just want to pound something.'

'I'll be sure not to make you angry, then.'

'We have a punching bag in the basement,' she said. 'Many a bad date has been erased from my memory thanks to that thing, I assure you.'

'So we have a killer who's venting his anger,' I said. 'But that would suggest an angry attack – something violent and impulsive. This woman attacks very calmly, with everything carefully planned in advance. She gets in, she shoots, she lays down plastic, and only then does she start stabbing. Plus, the hands and tongue are removed very precisely. That doesn't suggest anger at all.'

Marci looked back up at the ceiling, sitting silently. She didn't look like she was getting into it – she hadn't come here for this, and she probably had plenty of subjects she'd rather talk about. I was trying to think of something I could say to bring back the same excitement she'd shown the day before, when suddenly she spoke again. 'Do you think her victims see her before she attacks?'

'I don't know,' I said. 'I guess it's possible.' *It's also possible that she can turn invisible, or change her shape, or some other crazy supernatural thing that would help her hide from her prey,* I thought. Trying to profile a demon was getting harder and harder.

'I was just thinking,' said Marci. 'This guy showed up at my house one time just incensed about something – another bad dating story, sorry. But this guy was so mad, I didn't even go out with him. He terrified me. I called off the date right there on the porch.'

'Which probably only made him madder,' I said.

'Obviously,' said Marci, 'but he couldn't freak out on me with my dad's squad car parked twenty feet away, so he just left. But the point is, if someone came up to these victims looking mad enough to stab them thirty-seven times, they would have run away screaming. But none of them did.'

'You're right,' I said, going back over the news stories in my head. 'Nobody heard screaming, nobody found any sign of a fight, and there were no defensive wounds on either of the bodies. So whatever the killer looks like, she doesn't look scary.'

'Or angry,' said Marci.

'Or,' I said, 'she might not even be angry at all. We might be misinterpreting the stab wounds completely.'

'Can you think of anything else it could be?'

'Well, what if it's a message?' I asked. 'She leaves these bodies outside where everyone can see them, so she's obviously trying to say something. Maybe the stab wounds are part of it.'

'But they were covered up,' said Marci; she was getting excited again. 'You said the stab wounds were hidden by the shirt. As a proud graduate of Home Ec I can assure you that thirty-seven cuts in the back of a shirt would completely destroy it – you wouldn't be hiding anything under there. This woman had to take their shirts off, stab the living crap out of them, and then put their shirts back on.'

'So if anything,' I said, 'she's trying to hide the stabs, not display them.'

'All right,' said Marci. 'We have a killer who starts out calm and then gets angry. All we have to do is figure out what the victims did to make her angry – probably something pretty simple, since both of them did it.'

With that comment, another piece of the puzzle snapped into place for me, as clear as a bell. I looked up at Marci. 'The only common factor between the two situations is her. The killer is making herself angry.' *Forman said that demons are defined by what they lack,* I thought. *She kills because she's trying to fill a hole, in her mind or her heart, and somehow that hole is filling her with rage.*

'Why would she make herself angry?'

'It's not on purpose,' I said. 'It's just the side-effect of something else. She's calm, and then she kills, and then she flips out.'

'And then she tries to cover it up with a shirt,' said Marci, nodding slowly. 'It fits. But what does it mean?'

'It means she doesn't want to kill,' I said. 'She probably hates it, but she can't stop it, and she promises herself she'll never do it again and then she does it again anyway. And she goes nuts.'

'This is . . .' Marci grimaced again. 'This is really vile.'

'But really cool,' I said. 'This is a piece I'm sure the police don't have yet.'

'I'll tell my dad as soon as the funeral's out.'

'No,' I said, 'not yet. This is a good piece, but it doesn't lead to anyone.' She looked troubled, and I held out my hands to soothe her. 'Let's wait until we have more to give him; there's no sense jumping the gun when we're this close.'

Marci looked uneasy. 'How close do you think we are?'

'Very close,' I said. 'Maybe close enough to predict the next victim.'

'And if we can predict him,' said Marci, smiling for the first time that night, 'we can warn him.'

Chapter 9

I went to Marci's house every day that week, trading theories and combing through every piece of evidence we could remember. At first we sat in the kitchen, but Marci got nervous with the little kids so close by, and we took our talk of serial killers and dismembered corpses outside.

'What about the poles?' Marci asked. 'That's got to mean something, right?' It was Saturday, and we were still no closer to an answer.

'It's a message,' I said, 'but that doesn't tell us much. Most of the time when a serial killer leaves a message like that, it's just the standard "here I am, you can't catch me".'

'Even if it's just to get attention,' said Marci, 'the fact that the killer needs attention is still a pretty good clue, right?'

'Absolutely,' I agreed. I don't know if Marci was a natural psychologist, or if it was just the fact that she wasn't sociopathic like me, but she was really getting good at this. Sociopathy is defined as the lack of empathy: sociopaths like me can't identify with other people, which means we can't really understand them either. Marci didn't have that handicap, so she was finding connections I'd never thought of.

'The poles are like flags,' she said, thinking out loud, 'to make sure people see the body. One of the poles in the Mayor was an actual flagpole.'

'But with the flag ripped off,' I said. 'If they were supposed to be flags, why would she strip it down?'

'It was an American flag, so maybe she hates America. Or maybe she loves America and didn't want the flag associated with the murder.'

'Serial killing isn't murder,' I said, the words slipping out before I could stop them. It was a pet peeve of mine, but from the shocked look on Marci's face I knew she'd misinterpreted it. 'I mean, it is murder, but it's not *just* murder. It's like saying computer hacking is theft. It is, but it's got its own set of reasons and methods that make it so different from any other theft that you have to look at it differently.'

'That seems like a weird distinction,' said Marci. 'Killing someone is murder. That's that.'

'It is,' I said again, 'but it's a very specific kind of murder that needs to be looked at very differently.' She was still staring at me strangely, so I tried to change the subject. 'Look, it doesn't matter – let's get back to the flag. You think the killer loves America and doesn't want it associated with killing.'

Marci watched me silently for a moment longer before speaking. 'Could be a war protest.'

'Clayton County is a weird place for a war protest.'

'I know, I'm just thinking. The poles really do act like flags, though, and I'm trying to think of why she rips the actual flags off. Maybe it's just the pole. She doesn't want something up there to distract from the poles themselves.'

'I don't think so,' I said, remembering back to the shot I'd seen on the news. 'When the Mayor died, she hung plastic sheeting on the poles. It was like she was making her own flags.'

'Did they look like anything?'

'Kind of like wings, actually. But it was a flagpole, and she hung her own flag on it.'

'So she's replacing America.'

'Or removing it,' I said.

'Removing it?'

'Maybe not completely,' I said, 'but from the crime scene, at least. How about this: the Handyman always puts poles in the victims' backs, because that's how she sends her message. This time, because she was in City Hall, the only pole she could find was a flagpole, but she didn't want the flag to interfere with her message: it's not about America, it's about something else, so she had to take the flag off so people wouldn't get the wrong idea.'

'That works,' said Marci, 'but it means there's probably more to her message than just "here I am".'

'There you are,' said Marci's mom, opening the screen door. Marci and I were sitting on the porch, our feet on the steps, and her mom set down a plate of buttered bread on the floor between us. 'This isn't fresh out of the oven or anything, but I thought you might like a snack.'

Marci's mom was large – not fat, just big – and her hands were weathered and callused from constant work in the yard and garden. She was nice enough, but it was obvious Marci had gotten her good looks from somewhere else.

'Thanks,' said Marci, smiling widely. She seemed grateful

for the interruption, though I wasn't sure. She picked up a piece of bread. 'Mom's bread is great, John, you'll love it. This is, what, like five wholegrains?'

'Six,' said her mom. 'I added another one.'

I took a piece and held it up to inspect it. It looked like a slab of birdseed.

'Wow,' I said. 'I didn't know you could get that many wholegrains into one piece of bread.'

'I don't want to interrupt,' said her mom, opening the door and stepping back in. 'Just bringing a snack. Have fun!'

' "Have fun",' said Marci, laughing. 'She thinks we're out here talking about our favourite bands or something.'

I held out my bread. 'Do you seriously eat this?'

She laughed some more. 'Of course we eat it. What else would you do with it?'

'You could hang it from a tree and feed every bird in the neighbourhood.'

'It's *good for you*,' she said, in a voice that meant she knew exactly how stupid that sounded, but then she took another big bite. She obviously enjoyed it.

I took a bite; it was rough and chewy. I tried to say something, but it took so long to chew I couldn't form any words.

'Mom's been perfecting this recipe for years,' said Marci. 'You should have tried it when she first started – it was pretty heavy-duty.'

I finally managed to swallow, and shook my head in disbelief. 'Holy crap, that's like a buttered granola bar.'

'We eat it all the time,' said Marci. 'It's totally normal to us now. Anything else feels too flimsy. Wonder Bread's practically tissue-paper compared to this.'

'Wonder Bread's like tissue paper compared to anything,' I said, 'but if I can reverse the metaphor, this is like titanium compared to Wonder Bread.'

'That's actually a simile, not a metaphor. You can tell because it has "like" in it.'

'And this is actually a construction material, not a food,' I said. 'You can tell because it has wood pulp in it.'

'Poor baby,' said Marci, making an exaggerated frown. 'Wood pulp is good for you – it'll put hair on your chest.'

'And you've been eating this for how long?' I asked. 'That's horrifying.'

Marci laughed again. 'Shut up!'

I heard a car engine rumbling closer, and looked out to the street just in time to see Marci's dad pull up to the kerb in his squad car. I set the bread back down on the plate and tried to look innocent. I wasn't afraid of cops, I actually quite liked them, but I'd never met one at his own house before. The last thing I needed was for Officer Jensen to freak out and tell me to stop corrupting his daughter.

'Hey, Dad,' said Marci, swallowing another bite of bread.

'Hey, babe,' said Officer Jensen, stepping out and closing the car door behind him. 'And the venerable John Cleaver – it's an honour.'

'Hi,' I said. I gave a small wave, uncertain what else to do.

'What brings you here?' he asked, stopping a few feet away with his hands on his hips. He seemed cheerful enough.

Would he stay cheerful if he knew we were talking about the Handyman?

'We're talking about the Handyman,' said Marci.

'Cool,' he said.

Well, I guess that answers that question.

'We're doing our own investigation,' said Marci. She sighed, long and fake. 'Just a little criminal profiling; you know, nothing big.'

Her dad laughed. 'Well, John's the one to do it with. A little too much personal experience with psychos – huh, kid?'

I'm sure he didn't mean anything rude by it – he didn't know I was a psycho too.

He folded his arms. 'So, what do you have so far?'

Marci glanced at me quickly, then turned back to her dad. 'How much do you work with the profilers assigned to the case?'

'Not at all,' he said. 'I'm only marginally involved with the Handyman case.'

'Well,' she said, 'we've got some stuff you might want to pass along.' She glanced at me again. *Why did she keep doing that?* 'For example, we know that killing makes her angry.'

So that's why she keeps looking at me: she told him the thing I wanted to keep secret. I kept my face impassive. Did she tell because she didn't trust me, or just because she didn't understand my reasons for secrecy? It's not like I could tell her my plan: that we could find the killer on our own, and then I could go after her myself. Having the police and the FBI running around following the same leads would make my plan a lot more difficult.

' "Her"?' asked Officer Jensen. 'You think the killer is female?'

Oh come on, she was giving away everything.

'That's another thing,' said Marci, nodding. 'We're pretty sure she is.'

'A woman who gets angry when she kills, but does it anyway,' he said. 'Interesting.' He smiled, just barely in the corners of his mouth, and spoke again. 'So what have you deduced about the hands?'

That smile meant something – it meant he knew something. They had evidence about the hands they hadn't shared yet, or more likely new evidence that had just come in; if it was a secret, he wouldn't have mentioned it. But would he share the whole thing? I had to frame my answer carefully.

But what could I possibly say, when the only real answer was, 'The killer's a demon who uses the stolen hands and tongue for an as-yet unknown supernatural purpose'?

I spoke slowly, cautiously. 'The killer removes the hands and tongue very carefully, almost surgically. This is probably after the bout of rage that comes from the initial kill, because she's obviously very calm when she does it. She takes off the hands with a hatchet, a single blow for each one, and the tongue with some kind of scalpel, I think.'

'And what does he – or she, if you prefer – do with them?'

'Most serial killers keep souvenirs of their kills,' I said, trying to spin a plausible lie, 'because they like to remember them. They can pull out a piece of jewelry or a driver's licence even months later and relive the crime. Body parts don't last that long, especially soft tissue like the tongue, so it's more likely, statistically speaking, that the Handyman is eating them.'

'Gross,' said Marci.

I was positive that wasn't the case here: if the demon was just looking for food, she wouldn't need to be nearly this careful about it. There had to be some other purpose. But if I gave Officer Jensen a false answer, I gave him an opportunity to prove me wrong, and the natural human response to that opportunity would be to take it: to show what he knew. I had to hope it worked.

'It's the only explanation that has any real precedent,' I said. 'Jeffrey Dahmer, Ed Gein, Albert Fish; the ones who take body parts are usually cannibals. Usually. There are some we don't know much about, like Charles Albright. No one ever found out what he did with the body parts he stole.'

'What did he steal?' asked Marci.

'Eyeballs.'

'I knew I shouldn't have asked.'

Officer Jensen wasn't smiling any more, but he wasn't frowning either. His face was flat, his mouth turned down; he wasn't mad, he was . . . professional. I'd slipped him into lecture mode. He was going to take the bait.

'So you think he eats the hands and tongue?' he asked.

'It seems likely,' I said. I watched him carefully.

'And what if I told you that he didn't?'

Perfect! It was exactly like I'd hoped – they'd found some new evidence. Having a friend with ties to the police was awesome.

'What have you found?' I asked.

He lowered his voice. 'We got a call this morning: two

hikers out by the lake came across a firepit, with the fire still burning; they got there just in time to hear someone running through the trees towards the road. A few seconds after that, a car started and drove away. They didn't think anything of it until they smelled meat in the firepit, and poked it with a stick.' He looked down at the sidewalk. 'It was the Mayor's hand.'

No, I thought, *that doesn't make any sense. She had to be saving the hands for some kind of special purpose. What purpose did it serve to save them, and then turn around and destroy them?*

'So she was cooking them, to eat,' said Marci. 'Just like John said.'

'Only if she likes her meat really, really well done,' said her father. 'These weren't on a grill or a spit – they were down inside, under the logs.'

Years of pyromania leaped into my mind, and I knew that the area in the centre, under the logs, was the hottest part of a campfire. That's where the fire pulled in new oxygen, and it burned like a furnace. Anything in there would be incinerated.

But why? What could the demon possibly gain from burning them? Was she destroying evidence? Was someone too close? But if she could absorb them or disintegrate them the way Crowley had, she wouldn't need to burn them. I couldn't believe it. It had to be something else – they must be unrelated hands from an unrelated attack.

'You can't possibly have ID'd the hands already,' I said. 'The fingerprints would be unreadable, and you haven't had time for a DNA test.'

Officer Jensen smiled grimly and held up his wrist, tapping

the knob of bone. 'This is called the pisiform bone. The blow that took the Mayor's left wrist – probably done with a hatchet, like you said – bounced off of this bone the first time, and then cut slightly through it on the second stroke. It left a very distinctive cut, and the bones we recovered from the fire match perfectly.'

'Did the hikers see the killer?' asked Marci.

'Not a thing,' he said, shaking his head. 'Not even a silhouette, or a flash of colour through the trees. Certainly not a confirmation of gender. I'm afraid your female theory is still just a theory.'

'What about the car?' she asked.

'Our hikers didn't see anything,' he said, 'but we're still questioning everyone we can find who was out by the lake today. Someone may have seen the killer, so we might be able to get a description.'

No. This was wrong. It didn't jive with anything I thought I knew about the killer: why would a demon need to burn evidence? Why would the killer save the hands so carefully just to destroy them later? Did the destruction imply more rage, or more control? More planning, or less? It didn't make sense.

'What about the tongue?' I asked. 'Did they find the tongue?'

He nodded. 'There was some kind of charred lump in addition to the hands, which was probably meat and might be the tongue, but there's no way to confirm that yet. The Feds have it; we'll see what they come up with.'

The tongue too. *So it was the same killer.* I wracked my brain, searching for an explanation, but nothing came. What was I missing? We needed another victim, and we needed it soon, so we could find the next piece of the puzzle.

'Are you okay, John?'

I looked up and saw Marci looking at me, her face marred by a frown. She was concerned. How bad did I look?

'He's probably just squeamish,' said her dad, but Marci snorted.

'John's the most unsqueamish person in the world,' she said. 'I'm the one who gets grossed out; he's only bothered by . . . by letting the bad guys get away, I guess.' She looked into my eyes. 'We're not going to make it, are we?'

'Make what?' asked her father.

'We wanted to predict the next victim,' she said, 'so you could try to warn him, but there's only a few days left, and your new evidence changes everything. It sets us back.'

Here I was, upset about being wrong, and she thought I was worrying about the victim we wouldn't be able to save. I was desperate for another killing, and she only thought the best of me.

Just like Brooke had, before she'd learned the truth.

I was a killer. I had known when I first called Nobody that she would kill people here, and I'd been willing to accept it as the only way of tracking her. I followed corpses like bloody footprints, and when I reached the end I made another corpse of my own. I'd killed two men – two demons – but how many more bodies had I left in my wake? How many people had died so that I could pretend to be a saviour?

Was I really a saviour at all? Or just another killer?

'You gonna be all right?' asked Officer Jensen.

I looked up, shrugged, and nodded. 'Yeah, I'll be fine.'

'It's probably just Mom's bread,' said Marci, laughing half-heartedly. 'Six whole grains today.'

'Six,' her dad said, and whistled. 'No wonder you look like that. I can barely handle four – but don't you dare tell her I said that.'

He stepped up to the porch, passing between us and reaching for the door. He was already pulling it open when Marci stopped him.

'Hey, Dad.'

'Yeah, babe?'

Marci shot me another quick glance, but different than before. That had been a guilty look, when she had known she was about to tell our secret. This was more searching, more . . . nervous. She looked back to her father.

'Did you have a chance to follow up on that teacher I told you about?'

'Mr Coleman?'

'Yeah, the one who leers at me all the time.'

So, she'd told someone after all. Good for her.

'Of course I did, honey. I thought you'd heard.'

'Heard what?'

He looked at her, then at me, as if surprised we didn't know something. Officer Jensen's eyes went grim as he spoke.

'The Vice Principal checked his classroom after I mentioned your concern,' he said, 'and it turns out Mr Coleman's computer was filled with pornography, most of it depicting underage teens. Girls and boys. He was fired this morning.'

Chapter 10

Mr Coleman was found dead four days later, on Wednesday morning, his hands severed and his tongue removed. It was unexpected. Nothing in the previous crimes, or in any of our profiling, had led me to think that the next victim would be someone like Mr Coleman. The first two victims were older men, late fifties to early sixties, with families and jobs and good reputations in the community. Coleman was in his thirties, single, and the community pariah. Everyone hated him.

I expect widely-hated people to be murdered now and then, but serial killers choose their victims through entirely different methods. What was it about this guy that put him into the Handyman's sights?

'Are you going to Marci's house again?'

It was Wednesday night, and Mom and I were eating dinner. I kept my eyes on my food and answered blandly.

'Yeah.'

'Doing anything fun?'

'Just hanging around.'

'You know,' said Mom, poking at her food with her fork, 'you could hang around here sometimes. I wouldn't mind.'

'Yeah,' I said. I had no intention of ever bringing Marci here, but it was easier to just agree and then not do it.

'I'm serious,' said Mom. 'You don't have to just go to her house all the time. We have some board games, and movies, and I could make popcorn or something—'

'No thanks,' I said, still looking down. 'Her house is fine.' I took another bite of food; as soon as I finished I could leave.

'Oh, I know,' said Mom. 'I'm sure her house is great, and I've met her mother – she's a lovely woman. And obviously her father is very nice.'

I shrugged noncommittally. 'Yeah.'

We sat in silence for a minute, and I started to think I was free. Then I glanced up at Mom, and she still wasn't eating. That wasn't good – it meant she was thinking, and that meant she was going to talk again.

After another long pause she whispered softly, 'I'm sorry there's no father here.'

Oh, please no . . .

'Mom,' I said, 'can we please not start this?'

'I wish you had a good father, John, I wish it every day, and I try to be the best mother I can—'

'My father is fine,' I said, 'especially because he's not here.'

'Do you know how painful it is to hear you say that?'

'Why? Come on, Mom, you hate him more than I do.'

'That doesn't mean I'm happy about it,' she said. 'It doesn't mean I'm happy about the way things turned out. Yes, he was a bad father, and a bad husband, and a bad everything, but that doesn't make it any easier for you to grow up fatherless. You have no male role models, you have no positive male influence—'

'Wait, are you saying I'm going to Marci's house because I'm looking for a male role model?'

'Officer Jensen is a good man, and you don't have one at home.'

'And Marci is practically a model, and we don't have any of those at home either. Maybe as long as you're out shopping for new dads you can pick up some hot teenage girls in the next aisle over. We can place them around like lamps, liven the place up a little.'

'That is not what I'm suggesting at all.'

'I have a friend, Mom,' I said. 'That's it. You are always begging me to go out and make new friends, but then as soon as I do you start psycho-analysing me.'

'I am not—'

'And then you wonder why I don't bring Marci over here,' I continued. 'Halfway through the popcorn and the dusty kid games from the laundry closet you'd tell her I'm only dating her because I don't have a dad. That would be fabulous.'

Mom stopped, eyes wide. 'You're dating her?'

'What?'

'Like, officially dating?'

'No, I'm not dating her. We're just . . . friends.'

'Well, how am I supposed to know these things when you refuse to talk to me?'

'We're talking right now, aren't we?'

'*I'm* certainly trying to talk,' she said. '*You're* just yelling.'

'I am not yelling.'

'Tell me about Marci.'

'I actually don't even knock,' I said, sitting back and folding my arms. 'I sit outside and peep through the windows while cutting myself with a razor.'

'And there you go again,' she said, shaking her head. 'As soon as I ask you to open up about your life you start spinning some ridiculous lie you know I won't believe. I'd expect someone with as much therapy experience as you to have a little more subtlety with his deflection tactics.'

'Ouch, Mom, bring up the therapy. Go ahead and mention how much it cost you, too, if that's where this is going.'

'This is not about money, it's about your life.'

'No, it's about you getting into my life. It's about your money and your expectations and your meddling and your everything else. It is always about you.'

She slapped me, hard, right across the face. I stared at her in shock.

'Don't you ever say that again.'

My face stung, hot and red. She'd never struck me before. Dad had, of course, but he'd struck everybody. That's why they got divorced. But Mom was different – hard as iron inside, but never physical. Never violent. I stared at her, expressionless, and she stared back with her eyes wide and her mouth pinched tight. She was determined; resolute. She was as surprised as I was.

My cheek throbbed in pain, but I didn't raise my hand to touch it. I simply stared back. We sat that way for an eternity before she spoke again, softly.

'When you were younger I used to have nightmares every night about my little boy, all alone and small and away from his mommy. I used to check on you three times a night, sometimes four, seeing you huddled up in your blanket, a spark of heat in a cold, empty room. Some nights you came into our bed, and then one day you stopped, and you just called for me from your own room, and then one day you stopped that too, and you . . . didn't do anything. You didn't need me any more, and you didn't talk to me any more, and then one day I realised I wasn't Mommy any more.' Her eyes moved, almost imperceptibly; she was no longer focusing on my face but on some phantom point beyond it. 'I used to be "April"; I used to be "dear". Now I don't know what I am.'

I stood up calmly, carried my dishes to the counter, and dumped the uneaten food in the garbage. I stood there for a moment, staring at the wall.

'I'm sorry I slapped you,' she whispered.

I reached out to the counter, to the knife-block by the sink, and pulled out a long kitchen knife. Mom gasped behind me. It was the same knife I'd threatened her with nearly a year ago. I turned, walked to the table and set it gently in front of her.

'Remember this the next time you doubt me,' I said. 'Of the two of us, I'm the one who held back when an argument turned violent.'

I walked out of the door and drove away.

'Hi, John,' said Marci's mom, opening their front door. 'Are you okay?'

'I'm fine,' I said. 'Why?'

'Your teacher died,' she said, pulling me inside. 'I'm sure you're just sick over it.'

'He was a pedophile,' I said. 'He was leering at your daughter; I say he got what he deserved.'

'He deserved to be fired, and worse.' Her voice was hard. 'But he didn't deserve to die.'

Didn't he? Pornography leads to violence – that's exactly how Ted Bundy got started – and a pedophile in a position of control over minors, like Mr Coleman, was a crime just waiting to happen. He'd worked at the school for years, so there were bound to be students and former students coming out now with tales of illicit offers, molestation, perhaps even rape. If he hadn't done it yet, he would have. What was so bad about stopping it for good?

Logical or not, it wasn't an argument I wanted to get into at that moment. I needed to analyse the new evidence, and for that I needed Marci.

'You're right,' I lied, 'nobody deserves that. Is Marci here?'

'She's upstairs in her room,' said Mrs Jensen, 'and I'm so glad you're here. Perhaps you can cheer her up.'

Cheer her up? I thought, following Mrs Jensen up the stairs. *Even if her mom's upset over the death, why would Marci be? She hated Mr Coleman.*

We stopped outside a door, and Mrs Jensen knocked softly. 'Marci, honey?'

'I want to be alone for a while,' said Marci, her voice soft and cracked. She'd been crying.

So she was upset. People with empathy are so weird.

'John's here,' Mrs Jensen said. 'Do you want to talk to him?'

There was a pause, then a shuffle of stuff being moved around behind the door.

'Sure,' said Marci at last. She opened the door, rubbing her eye with the palm of her hand. Her clothes were rumpled, and her eyes were red and raw. She saw me and laughed awkwardly. 'I'm sorry, I look hideous.'

'You look fine,' I said.

'Come on in,' she said, standing to the side and gesturing into her room. 'Sorry it's a mess.'

'Keep the door open,' said Mrs Jensen sternly, then turned to go back downstairs.

I walked into Marci's bedroom, which was indeed a mess, and sat on the desk chair. Marci sat on her hastily-made bed, cross-legged, and combed her fingers through her hair.

'Seriously,' I said, 'you look fine.'

'Good, then screw this.' She stopped fiddling with her hair and fell backward, lying down on the bed with her legs still crossed. 'This is the worst thing ever.'

'Yeah,' I said, looking around the room. It was covered with posters and photos and knick-knacks, some of them new but some of them obviously several years old. The room wasn't so much decorated as attacked. 'Your mom said the same thing,' I continued, 'but I didn't expect you to take it this hard.'

She laughed hollowly. 'You didn't expect me to take it this hard? I'm the one who got him killed!'

'What?'

'This never would have happened without me. I'm the one who reported him, I'm the one who got him into the public view, I'm the one who made him a target. I may just as well have pulled the trigger myself.'

'That's ridiculous,' I said.

She started crying again. 'You don't know what it feels like to be responsible for this.'

Oh, I knew what it felt like – I just didn't know what it felt like to feel bad about it.

'Listen,' I said, 'if you were responsible, you'd have done the world a favour. But you're not responsible because this is not a punishment killing, so exposing him didn't lead straight to his death. There's nothing about the Handyman that suggests she's punishing people; the first two victims were completely innocent of anything.'

'How could this not be a punishment?' she asked. 'Didn't you hear about the eyes?'

'The eyes?' This was new.

'Oh damn, that's not even public yet.'

'Your dad told you something?' I asked. 'What was it?' Something about the word 'eyes' was bothering me – niggling at my memory – but I couldn't put my finger on it.

'Not tonight, John; I can't do this any more.'

'But this is important! If the manner of the killing has changed then it's a new clue, or it's an escalation from the killer. If you've got something new you've got to tell me.'

'Don't you even care?' asked Marci, sitting up. Her face was wet. 'Somebody died last night, and it was my fault!'

'Of course I care,' I said. 'If I didn't care I wouldn't be trying to stop her.'

'I'm not talking about her,' she said, her eyes pleading. 'I'm talking about me.'

She started sobbing again, and flopped back down on the bed, curling up on her side.

I knew I had to say something, but what? I'd felt awkward

enough talking to Marci when she was happy, and now that she was sad I had no idea what to do.

Eyes . . . eyeballs . . . It was right on the tip of my brain.

Charles Albright, the Eyeball Killer. I stopped abruptly, shocked by the sudden recollection. I'd mentioned Albright to Marci and her dad just a few days ago. I'd mentioned stealing eyeballs to a man who already had a strong reason to hate Mr Coleman, and a few days later Mr Coleman was killed, and his eyes were either damaged or stolen. Was it just a coincidence?

Or was Officer Jensen the Handyman?

Obviously it wasn't the Eyeball Killer himself – Charles Albright was in jail, happily drawing pictures of eyes on the walls of his cell – but it might be a hint or a clue. Maybe it was a message to me: 'I killed the man you were talking about, in the manner you were talking about. You have to know that it's me now.' Was he getting tired of waiting for me to figure it out? Was this little piece of escalation designed to spur me into action?

But it didn't fit: if Officer Jensen was a demon, and wanted me dead, why not just kill me? And how had he become a demon? Even if Nobody was a genderless shapeshifter, able to assume a man's identity as easily as a woman's, why choose Mr Jensen? Marci and I hadn't even talked yet when the first victim died . . . I paused, feeling sick. We didn't talk before the first killing but we talked right afterwards, specifically because Marci's dad had told her about me. Had he been orchestrating this entire thing, bringing us together and planting these careful crime scenes, all for some purpose of his or her own? What could Nobody possibly be planning?

There were so many holes in the idea: yes, if Officer Jensen was human he'd have great reason to hate Mr Coleman, because he was harassing his daughter, but a demon masquerading as Officer Jensen wouldn't hate him at all. There would be no reason to break his pattern and kill Coleman, when the eyes of any other victim would serve just as well. There were too many pieces that didn't fit at all . . .

. . . and yet there were other pieces that fit almost too perfectly. Marci's dad had pushed us together. Marci's dad had told her the secret of Coleman's eyeballs, knowing she would tell me. Marci's dad.

Marci.

I looked at Marci again, curled up on her bed, sobbing. Was it her? If Nobody was a shapeshifter then she could be anybody – Marci, Marci's dad, even my own mother. If Marci was a demon, that could explain why she'd been so friendly to me: she was a smart, popular, beautiful girl who'd never given me the time of day until three weeks ago. What was her plan? What did she want? If she wanted to kill me, why not do it now when she had the chance? Why lie there and pretend to cry?

The skin of her waist was exposed where her T-shirt had rumpled up away from her waistline; I could see her smooth, pink skin, the soft ridge of her hip, the intoxicating outline of her breasts and backside pressing against her clothes.

I could kill her now – strike first, before she knew I'd learned her secret. And then with time and the proper tools I could learn all her secrets; I could pry her open and find the demon inside. I could finally understand.

My hands were shaking, trembling in time to Marci's sobbing body.

Get up and leave.

I shifted in my chair, moving just slightly to see more of her exposed back, but without any conscious decision found myself moving further, turning away from her completely. My rules against looking at girls. I faced the wall, breathing heavily, focusing on the tacks and creases in the corner of an ancient poster.

I shouldn't be here. I was acting paranoid, seeing demons everywhere I looked. I was a threat to Marci, and a threat to myself. I had to leave.

I stood up. 'I have to go.'

Marci rolled over. 'Please don't go, John. I'm sorry, I'm just a wreck . . .'

'No, I have to go.' I took a step towards the door as Marci stood up. Her T-shirt cascaded back down around her body, and the desire to stay welled up even stronger, a bursting, violent geyser in the pit of my stomach. I forced myself to look away again; everything I'd thought tonight was stupid and paranoid. I was losing control. 'I have to go.'

'Why?'

There was something in her voice, but my mind was too muddled to read it. Was she sad? Confused? Sorry? Happy? Angry? I was destroying our friendship; I was abandoning her in her hour of need.

I was saving her life.

'I'm sorry,' I said, but my voice sounded stiff and robotic. I tried to think of an excuse, anything to make me look less cruel, less suspicious, less hollow. Nothing came. I put a hand on the doorframe and ground out a final goodbye: 'Don't hate me.' It was the best I could do.

I walked down the hall, down the stairs, and out the front door, ignoring Mrs Jensen's confused farewell. I had to think, and I couldn't do it here. I couldn't risk any more than I had. But I couldn't just stop, either. Something had happened to Mr Coleman's eyes, and I needed to know what it meant. I needed to solve this puzzle and stop this demon – but how? I couldn't talk to Mom, I couldn't talk to Brooke, and now I couldn't talk to Marci, maybe ever again.

I supposed there was always Max, but that's not what I needed – another dumb kid with tunnel vision. This was a real demon, not a regular killer, and trying to treat it like a regular killer had gotten me nowhere. Either Mr Coleman's death literally made no sense, or it made perfect sense within a set of factors I hadn't considered. I'd missed those factors thus far because I was brainstorming with people who didn't acknowledge the supernatural, but that had to change. It was time to visit the only person left who I could talk to about demons.

It was time to visit Father Erikson again.

Chapter 11

Father Erikson lived in a ranch-style brick house on the east side of town. He answered the door in a thick cotton bathrobe draped over his regular clothes; it was dark blue, with a Disney logo in the corner.

'Hello?' he said.

'Hi. Can we talk?'

'And you are . . . ?' He studied me for a second. 'Wait, I know you. You're the kid who was asking about demons.'

'Yeah,' I said. 'Can we talk?'

'How did you find my home address?'

'It's called the Internet,' I said. 'Now listen. I need to talk, and I need to talk right now. Can I come in?'

'Um, sure, come on in. Do your parents know you're here?'

'Of course,' I lied, 'I never go anywhere without telling Dad all about it.'

'Well, that's good.' I wasn't sure he believed me. He closed the door behind me and pointed to the couch. The TV was showing some kind of soap opera, but I couldn't understand the words. 'I'm trying to learn Spanish,' he said, grabbing a remote and turning it off. I sat on the couch, and he eased himself into a well-worn recliner. 'Last time we talked, I asked the newspaper about their high-school intern,' he said. 'Apparently your name is Kristen.'

'I'm not really an intern at the paper.'

'So I gathered. What's your name?'

I paused. 'John.'

'Do you want to tell me what you're doing?'

'Mr Coleman was killed,' I said. 'He was a teacher at school.'

'And a member of my congregation,' said the pastor. 'It was a terrible tragedy.'

'Why does everyone think it's such a horrible thing for this guy to be dead?' I asked. 'He was a pedophile. He was a horrible person. After he got fired, all anyone could talk about was how terrible he was, and how lucky we were to get him out of the school, and now someone's taken him out of our lives altogether and that's a bad thing?'

'I wasn't talking about his death,' said the priest, 'though that was a tragedy too. I was talking about his life.'

'I think you're overusing the word "tragedy".'

'Maybe,' he said, shrugging. 'But I think you're overestimating David Coleman's evil. Yes, he sinned, and yes, that deserves punishment, but he also did a lot of good things that deserve praise. He was a very good teacher, and he was a very good friend. No one is all or nothing.'

'Fine,' I said, 'he was a great man. Whatever. That's not why I'm here. I'm trying to find out who killed him.'

'And, as before, you think a demon did it.'

I nodded. The priest was taking this all remarkably calmly. He must have dealt with a lot of weirdos at church.

'Why are you bringing all this to me?' he asked.

118

'Because I'm trying to find this demon and stop her, and I need help, and you're the only person I know who admits to a belief in paranormal creatures. And also because you're a priest, so if I ask you to, you have to keep this conversation confidential.'

He raised an eyebrow. 'What makes you say that?'

'Again, it's called the Internet. Seriously. As Catholic clergy, you are bound by your Church to treat a private conversation as confidentially as possible. It's not as legally binding as a psychologist, but a good clergyman, as I assume you are, will honour the request anyway in good faith.'

He sat quietly, watching me, as if sizing me up in his head. 'You're a stranger off the street, under-age, obsessed with a killer, and convinced of the reality of mythological monsters. If I'm as good a clergyman as you say, I should probably take you to a counsellor.'

'So you be my counsellor.'

'I'm not equipped to act as a—'

'Listen,' I said, standing up, 'swear to secrecy right now or I walk out. You want to help me? This is how you do it.'

He looked at me, waiting, and finally nodded. 'To the extent that I do not see you as an immediate threat to anyone's life, and provided that you let me introduce you to a therapist I know, I won't tell anyone about this conversation.'

I stared at him. He stood and offered his hand. 'You have my solemn promise.'

I looked at his face: mouth set in a thin line, eyes open, jaw slightly clenched. He was telling the truth. I shook his hand. 'Thank you.'

'Thank you,' he said.

We sat down. 'All right,' I said. 'This demon has thus far followed very strict criteria when choosing her victims. If you look at the first two in Clayton and the seven or eight before that in Georgia, the pattern is remarkably consistent. They're all men, they're all older, they're all married, and they're all respected members of the community. Pastor Olsen; Mayor Robinson; Steve Diamond, who was a policeman in Athens; Jack Humphrey, who was some kind of religious leader in Macon; and on and on. Everyone fits this pattern but Coleman: he was younger, he was single, he was hated by the community, and he wasn't even employed at the time. All the other victims had strong, stable jobs.'

'He may have been targeted before he lost his job,' said Erikson. 'It's only been a few days.'

'That's possible,' I said, nodding, 'because she definitely puts a lot of thought into these attacks, and she might not have had time to find a new victim. But there are even more differences. It turns out that this time the demon did something to his eyes – she's never messed with anybody's eyes before. There's no precedent for it, by which I mean there probably is a precedent and we just don't know enough to see it.'

The priest frowned. 'Why do you say that the killer – the demon – is a woman?'

'Force of habit,' I said. 'I honestly have no idea what gender this thing is any more. It's very possible that this demon can change shape and look like anyone, so honestly the person we're looking for could be male or female, and it could even be someone we know.'

'Demonic possession.'

'In a sense, yeah.'

The priest scooted forward in his chair, looking me in the eye. 'This is the part where I start to get nervous, because you're not just talking about hunting a demon any more – you're talking about hunting a member of this community.'

'Someone who looks like a member of this community—'

'No,' said the priest. 'You can't think that way. You came to me because you think I'm some kind of demon expert, so listen to me: if a person is possessed by a demon then the original person is still inside. That's how they work. Demons are supposed to be cast out, not killed, and that's a very long, very careful process designed to protect the human host.'

'You want to do an exorcism?'

'No, I don't,' he said. 'I'm not trained, and I'm not convinced it's even necessary. But the point I'm trying to make is that in all likelihood the thing you think is a demon is just another guy, just like you and me, and that there is nothing paranormal going on at all.'

I laughed drily, remembering Forman melt away into ash. 'You've got to trust me on this one.'

'But I can't trust you,' he said. 'I've known you for maybe half an hour total. You haven't given me a last name, and for all I know, the first name you gave me is a fake. You come in here, you talk about hunting demons, and I have no way of knowing if you're serious or joking or completely deranged.'

'I need your help.'

'I agree,' he said, 'but I'm pretty sure we're talking about different kinds of help.'

We stared at each other, silent and intent, my mind seething with rage. *Why wouldn't he just answer my questions?* His hands were pressed tightly around the armrests of his chair; his knuckles were white and his arms were trembling – just barely – and I knew that he was scared. He really thought I was dangerous. But he'd confronted me anyway, alone in his home, with no way of defending himself. If I were really as dangerous as he thought I was, I could kill him right here.

Maybe I should. Maybe he's the demon.

Even as I thought it, I knew it was stupid. There was no way he was the demon, just like there was no way Marci was the demon. I was desperate for anything, desperate to stop hunting and just kill something, and I was seeing demons in every shadow, behind every face, looking out from every pair of eyes.

Eyes. The eyes had to mean something. When a killer changed her methods, it always meant something. But Father Erikson wasn't going to help me figure it out. No one wanted to help me stop the demons, they just wanted to save me from myself. *I am not the biggest threat here!*

But the priest thought I was. And he didn't know my name.

I could use that.

The same thing had happened with my old therapist, Dr Neblin. We had started talking about the bad guy, and we just ended up talking about me. People like Max and Marci were legitimately interested in this kind of stuff, but adults always assumed I was talking about myself – that the scenarios I posed were some kind of convoluted metaphors about my inner feelings. Neblin, the priest, my mom ... it was the only kind of help they ever wanted to give. So why not let him help me?

'Let's say I'm as dangerous as you think I am,' I said. *Stay imposing – even if he's only talking to stall, at least he's talking.* 'Let's say, for the sake of argument, that I am the Handyman.'

'I don't think you're the Handyman.'

'Pretend,' I said. 'Now: what do you want to say to me?'

His eyes widened. 'What?'

'I've just killed three people. Why?'

'I ... don't know why.'

'I just cut out a man's eyes, which I have never done before. Why did I do it?'

'Why are you asking me these questions?'

'You said you wanted to help me, so help me. Psycho-analyse me. Offer me sage counsel from the Bible.' I clenched my fists, trying to stay calm. 'A serial killer is asking you for help, dammit, so help him!'

'I ...' He paused. 'You'll have to tell me more.'

'About what?'

'If you're a killer, why are you here?'

'In your house?'

'In Clayton.'

I nodded. *That's a good question; this might actually work.* 'I'm looking for someone.'

He swallowed. 'Someone specific?'

'Yes,' I said, 'but I don't know who it is. Someone in this town has done something to make me very angry, and I'm here to find him.'

'What did this . . . mystery person do to make you angry?'

Who does he think I'm talking about? 'That doesn't concern you,' I said carefully. 'I know he exists, but nothing else.'

'So why are you killing?' he asked.

'You tell me.'

'You're . . .' He paused. 'You're sending a message. The people you kill, and the way you kill them, are messages to the man you're looking for, somehow representative of whatever made you mad enough to come and look for him in the first place.'

'That's good,' I said, 'but remember that I killed eight people in Georgia before coming here, and all by the same method.'

'So if the deaths are messages,' said the priest, 'then the killer – you – is sending the same message here that you sent before.'

Interesting, I thought. *And if the current messages are directed to a demon hunter – me – does that mean the older messages were directed at another demon hunter in Georgia? The demons have been around for ages – I can't possibly be the first human to learn about them.*

'Are you saying the missing hands and tongues are threats?' I asked, continuing my line of thought.

'Are they?'

'It makes sense,' I said. 'Kind of a "This is what I'll do to you when I find you", sort of thing.'

'Are we still talking about you?'

'Are you more comfortable that way?'

'I'm not really comfortable either way.'

'Then it doesn't matter,' I said. 'Just keep talking. If the mutilated bodies are threats, why change a pattern ten bodies long and start mutilating eyes?'

'What exactly happened to his eyes?' the pastor asked. 'That wasn't on the news.' He stopped suddenly, his voice quiet. 'How do you know about the eyes?'

'I'm the Handyman.'

'You're not the Handyman, but you're . . . something. What are you not telling me?'

'Do you think I'm dangerous?'

'You're definitely dangerous.'

'To you?'

He paused, watching me through narrowed eyes. After a moment he replied, 'Only if you think I'm the person you're looking for.'

'It's the demon who's looking for someone, not me.'

'And you're looking for the demon, or whatever it is, and when you find the person you think it's in, heaven help them. You're focused, I'll give you that. You're like a loaded gun, cocked and aimed, and as soon as your target walks into your sights, you'll destroy it.' He sighed. 'I beg you: be careful of your aim. If you choose the wrong target, you'll destroy yourself as well.'

I thought of Marci lying defenceless on her bed, of Brooke chained to Forman's table. I thought of my own mother, cowering under the tip of my knife, of a hundred mothers throwing their phones at the wall, screaming for me to stop calling, huddling terrified with their children in the dark.

'Then help me,' I whispered. 'I can't do this alone.'

'Then stop.'

'I can't stop.' I closed my eyes, growling through clenched

teeth, 'If I stop, she keeps going. She dies or we all die. Why won't anyone see that?'

'If thy eye offend thee . . .' he murmured.

Thy eye. I looked up quickly. 'What?'

'It's a scripture,' he said. ' "And if thy right eye offend thee, pluck it out, and cast it from thee". Matthew, chapter five, verse twenty-nine.'

I felt a tingle of anticipation. *This is important.* 'Keep going.'

'It's a metaphor,' he said. ' "For it is profitable for thee that one of thy members should perish, and not that thy whole body should be cast into hell".'

I paused to deconstruct it. 'It's saying that one part can spoil the whole, so it's better to get rid of that part than to let the whole thing get corrupted.'

'Exactly,' he said. 'Taken out of context, that scripture could be seen as a justification for murder.'

'Is there any more?' I asked. 'To the scripture, I mean. Does it say anything else?'

'It does,' said the priest, looking startled. 'It does. The very next verse says the same thing about hands.'

'Hot damn.'

He stood up, eyes wide and unfocused. 'It's real.'

'So we were right about the message,' I said, 'but we got the nature of the message all wrong. We thought it was an announcement, "Here I am, I'm coming for you", but it was a lesson. Coleman died because Coleman was a sinner; he looked at something he shouldn't have looked at, so he lost his eyes. He was destroyed for the greater good.'

'But the others weren't sinners at all,' said the pastor. 'Why would anyone kill them?'

126

'You said it yourself: no one's all or nothing. They were killed because of things they said, I guess, because their tongues were cut out. And the hands were cut off because of things they'd touched, or things they'd done.'

Pastor Erikson stared at me, his eyes wary. 'You really believe this, don't you? That these people need to die so the rest of us can be saved.'

I shook my head. 'No, not me, it's the Handyman.'

'But you said the same thing.'

'That was an exercise to get you thinking,' I said. 'Of course I'm not saying we should kill people.'

'But you said we should kill the Handyman,' he said, stepping slowly towards me. 'And you said the same thing before that, when you first got here: that we shouldn't feel bad about David Coleman's death. You said we were better off without him, and we should be glad he was killed.'

I stopped, bewildered. 'Look – I'm the good guy here,' I said. 'I'm trying to stop a killer.'

'By killing,' he said. 'Whether you succeed or fail, our community will still have a killer.'

No! 'I am not a killer!' I shouted. 'I am not a threat to anyone in this community. I am trying to help people!'

'You think the Handyman doesn't tell himself the same thing?'

I lunged toward him with a roar. 'Stop saying that!'

He held his ground, and I stopped just inches from his face. I forced myself to breathe evenly; I fought back the feral growl I could feel growing in my throat. I held his stare a moment longer, then turned and stalked to the door.

He called out grimly: 'What are you going to do?'

I stopped, my hand on the doorknob. 'What are *you* going to do?'

'We made a promise,' he said. 'You keep your end and I'll keep mine.'

I turned round, trying to read his face. *He can't possibly be ready to let me go.* I watched his eyes. *He knows I'm a danger to everyone around me. Is he really going to just let me go?*

He didn't move. Neither did I.

'You said your name was John?'

I nodded.

'I want to help you, John. I want you to talk to my friend.'

'The therapist.'

'Yes.'

I glanced at the door, then back at him. 'If I walk out right now, all you have is my word.'

'Is your word good?'

I paused. 'No.'

'Then tell me your name.'

'So you can turn me in?'

'So I can contact you and introduce you.'

The thought of it made me nervous. *I have to stay anonymous.* My stomach soured, and I balanced lightly on the balls of my feet, ready to run. The pastor didn't move.

Can I trust him?

I stared into his eyes. 'What if I threaten you?'

'I'm not the demon,' he said, 'and you know it. You won't hurt me.'

'And if I run?'

'Then I do my civic duty and tell the police about the

young man who told me he wanted to kill a woman in town.'

I breathed deeply. *Just kill him. Just take him now, while he's not expecting it – knock him back against the wall, crack his neck against the chair. Hide him in the basement. No one will ever know a thing.*

'Give me a week,' I told him. 'Just one week.'

'You said I can't trust you.'

I met his gaze. 'You can trust me for a week.'

He paused a moment, eyes flicking as he thought. Finally he nodded. 'One week, and you come back here. But if you hurt anyone, I swear to God your torment will not end in this life.'

I took a breath. 'One week.' I opened the door and disappeared into the darkness.

Chapter 12

I drove home via a long, convoluted route, looking over my shoulder for anyone following me. Everywhere I looked I saw movement in the corners of my eyes, shapes and shadows that I knew were watching me, hunting me, and then I turned to see them and they disappeared. *I told him too much*. I felt sick and nervous, and I couldn't stop shaking.

Parking several blocks from my house, I walked into a stranger's backyard and climbed over the fence into the forest beyond. It was a haze of dark on dark, shadows and shapes barely distinguishable from the smothering blackness of night. I waited, watching and listening with every ounce of concentration, but no one followed. I was alone.

I felt my way through the trees, passing darkened houses on one side and the endless forest on the other, until I reached the parking lot of the mortuary. No one was waiting; there were no police cars, no slavering monsters. It was nearly two in the morning. I went inside, locked the door tightly, and collapsed on my bed.

The religious theory made sense: all three killings could be the work of a self-styled holy avenger. But why would Nobody, a demon, want to punish sinners? She wasn't here on her own agenda. I had called her, and she had come to hunt me. Everything she did had to make sense through that lens.

Did she see me as a sinner, too? I'd killed her friends.

There were two main possibilities: either this was part of a complex plan to figure out who I was and take her vengeance, or she was merely passing time while she searched for me in other ways. Each demon I'd met thus far was missing something – they had no identity, or no body, or no emotions. They killed because it helped them to fill that hole, even if only for a little while. This demon wasn't killing people because they were sinners, but because believing they were sinners gave the killing some kind of vital meaning in her mind. It was the only way she knew to try to fix the holes in her soul.

I needed to know what the victims' guilt meant to her, which meant I needed to know exactly what she thought they were guilty of. Mr Coleman was guilty of looking at underage porn, so he was killed and his eyes – the offending organs – were removed. It was relatively clear and simple. But what had the other two victims done?

Neither Pastor Olsen nor Mayor Robinson had lost any extra body parts – just the hands and tongue. It seemed to serve as a baseline. It might be that the hands and tongue were taken from every sinner, regardless of their specific crime, and an extra part was taken from those who were especially evil.

The tongue was easy enough to guess at: it represented what people said. But what had the pastor said to invoke the Handyman's wrath? What had the Mayor said? None of the three victims had very much in common when it came to speaking: one spoke about religion, another about politics, and the last taught math in school. The Mayor and the teacher maybe overlapped on the subject of economics, but the pastor certainly didn't – not unless he'd preached a sermon on supply and demand or something.

Preaching. Preaching and teaching . . .

Maybe the common overlap had nothing to do with what they said, but to whom they said it. All three of them were in positions of authority. All three had made a living talking to others. They made plans for others; they guided others' lives. The Mayor was not an actual teacher, like the pastor and Mr Coleman, but he held a huge influence over the entire town. When you boiled it down, all three men were leaders.

That made Father Erikson an obvious target – him and every other pastor and schoolteacher in town – but so far they'd been safe. The demon wasn't killing indiscriminately; the mere fact that she posed the bodies so carefully meant that she was trying to teach us something. She had a message, and she wanted it to be heard and understood. We'd missed her point on the first few killings, so now she was taking more care; that's why she'd 'signed' the Mayor's corpse with bloody plastic wings, marking herself as an Angel of Death, and it was why she'd made the lesson even more obvious by taking Coleman's eyes. That meant the next victim would be similar to Mr Coleman: a community leader with a sordid past, so no one would miss the point. All I had to do was find the most likely candidate and then lie in wait, ready to catch Nobody on her way to the kill. It was perfect.

But it wasn't.

Father Erikson had cut me right to the core, obliterating all the careful lies I'd built up to protect myself from the truth: that I too was a killer, no different from any other. But I couldn't just stop: there was simply no way, no physical way, that I could turn myself around and walk away from this. If I didn't stop Nobody, she'd keep killing – and that would make me responsible; and I refused to be responsible for any innocent deaths.

If I could figure out who the next target was, and stop Nobody before she got there, I'd be saving lives – *if* everything went perfect. Of course, nothing ever went perfect. But if I could think of a way to involve the police, they could move in first and protect the target. I wouldn't have to kill.

But I want to kill.

No. One thing at a time. I identify the target, I tell the police, and then I can find out if I'm right or not without putting anyone at risk. Then the next time, I can do it myself. I can be ready. I can kill the demon.

If the demon kept to her pattern, the next death would be in two weeks: late at night on Wednesday the twenty-second, or early the next morning on Thursday the twenty-third. It seemed like a lot of time to find one sinner, but it wasn't.

There were an awful lot of sinners in Clayton County.

The next afternoon I parked in front of the Jensens' house and turned off the engine, too nervous to go inside. Marci's dad was the only policeman I knew personally, so if I was going to present my plan to the police it had to be through him. We'd talked before – he knew that I knew what I was talking about, and he trusted my opinion. But if Marci hated me as much as I thought she did – or even if she simply didn't like me any more – my chances of talking to him were slim to none.

Not to mention the possibility, still lurking in the back of my mind, that he was the demon. Just because I'd figured out why the demon was killing didn't mean I knew who the demon was – and if Nobody could steal bodies and identities like Crowley had, she could be anybody. Still, even if Officer Jensen was a demon, he hadn't killed me yet, and now that I knew to be suspicious I could keep my eyes open and try to stay one step ahead. The only way to figure out his plan, if he had one, was to observe him as much as I could. I took a deep breath and got out of the car.

It was a cooler day than usual, and I shivered as I walked up the steps and knocked on their door. It was open, as usual, warm air spilling out through the screen. I heard the common noises of Marci's family – a loud TV, children shouting, footsteps pounding up and down the stairs and running through the halls. I waited only a moment before Marci appeared and stood behind the screen. Her face was blank.

'Hey,' she said.

'Hey.' Despite all the time I'd spent preparing for this visit – planning my pitch to Officer Jensen, and my escape strategy if he turned out to be a demon after all – I had no idea what to say to Marci. I stood still, feeling robotic again, watching her face for some sign that I could grab on to and know what to do. She was looking off to the side, avoiding my face.

I remembered her crying, remembered how sad she was, and tried to force myself to empathise through pure force of will. Nothing came. Instead I fell back on my old standby: faking it. What would a normal person say to a sad friend?

'Are you okay?' I asked. It sounded clumsy, too loud and direct. I watched her carefully for a response, and she nodded.

'Yeah. You?' She looked up, catching my eyes with hers. They were red from crying. She hadn't been in school all day, and I wondered if she'd been crying straight through since last night.

'I'm fine,' I said. *What would a normal person say next?* I was no good at this. Just like before, the first time I'd sat down and talked in her kitchen, I knew I couldn't pretend with her. I couldn't be somebody else. I took a deep breath.

'Look,' I said, 'I'm not very good with people. I don't know how to talk, and I don't know how to react, and I definitely don't know how to comfort anyone. I know you were really sad last night, and I wish I'd been able to do something about it, but I couldn't. Sorry.'

She started crying again. 'No, no,' she said, and I braced myself for the worst. 'I was such a mess last night, I was hysterical, it's not your fault at all.' She paused. 'After the way I treated you, I didn't think you'd ever come back.'

That was not what I had expected.

She put a hand on the screen. 'You want to come in?'

I hesitated just a fraction of a second. 'Sure.'

She pushed open the screen and I started to step in, but she caught me mid-step and drew me into a tight hug, wrapping her arms around me, burying her face in my neck. Her tears were wet against my skin, and I could feel her chest against mine, her heart pumping steadily.

'I don't hate you at all,' she whispered. 'I'm so sorry you would ever think that.'

Slowly I put my arms up around her, touching her uncertainly. I could count on one hand the number of times I'd hugged someone in the last eight years – I had no idea what to do. I patted her a couple of times before letting my arms fall still and simply hold her.

'I'm sorry,' she said, sniffing and pulling away. 'I'm gonna get snot all over you. Come on in.'

The phone rang twice before Father Erikson picked up.

'Hello?'

'Don't call the police.' I was on the payphone by the truck stop; I hadn't bothered to disguise my voice.

'Is this John?'

'Yes.'

'We made a deal, John. You talk to my friend, or I call the police. I can't just let this slide.'

I'd worked this out beforehand, planning my moves carefully to throw him off my trail. 'Do you think I'm crazy?'

He paused. 'It's just a therapist, John, not a psychiatrist. She'll just help you work some things out.'

She. I'd looked up every therapist and psychological counsellor in town, and of the three I found, two were female: Mary Adams, a recovery counsellor at the hospital, and Pat Richardson, the high-school counsellor. Which one was his friend?

'I'm not trying to back out of the deal,' I said. 'I'm just
... I don't want anyone to think I'm crazy. You know?' I
tried to sound embarrassed and sincere, but I was never good
at faking emotion. Was he buying it? 'I've never had therapy
before. I'm scared.'

'It's nothing to be afraid of,' he said, and I tried to read
his voice. Reassuring? Impatient? I really hated talking on
the phone, but sometimes it was the only safe way. He couldn't
see me or touch me, and had no idea where I was. 'She's
completely discreet; no one you know will even see you
talking to her.'

I smiled. *That means it's not the school counsellor.* Dr Adams
at the hospital was an odd choice, given her specialty, but
I could make this work.

'Please,' I said. 'I know it's not our deal, but I already took
your advice, and I got an appointment with a counsellor at
the hospital. It's the only place I could think of to go. Please,
just let me talk to her – don't call the police.'

He said nothing, and I knew he was thinking it over.
He knew I was potentially volatile, and now he thought I
was already seeing the counsellor he wanted to introduce
me to, so why force the issue any further? It wouldn't hold
him off forever, but it would give me more time. A week,
at least.

If he bought it.

'Are you there?'

'Yes, John, yes, I think that will be fine.'

I closed my eyes and breathed deeply. 'Thank you.'

'If you need anything else,' he said, 'if you ever want to
talk again, I'm always available.'

'Thank you. That's very kind.'

I hung up.

Sociopath or not, I knew it was stupid to bring up the Handyman in my first few days back with Marci. Instead we sat on the couch and watched TV silently together, while I bit my tongue and tried not to talk about killers and corpses and holy avengers. Finally, playing poker in her room on a rainy Saturday, I couldn't take it any longer. I set down my hand of cards.

'We haven't talked about the Handyman all week.'

'Thank goodness,' she said, and pointed at my cards. 'Call or fold?'

'I'm serious,' I said. 'I think I've cracked it.'

She frowned. 'You know who it is?'

'No, but I think I know why she's killing. And I think we can figure out who's next.'

She stared at her cards, silent for a long time. Finally she shook her head. 'No, I don't want to.'

'What?'

'I don't want to get back into it. It's too much – it's too close. I don't want to be responsible for another death.'

'That's exactly why we need to do this,' I said, 'so there won't *be* any more deaths.'

'But there will be,' she said. 'We're just two kids – we're sixteen. We can't stop a killer. We *shouldn't* stop a killer. We should let the police do their job, and we should do ours. This isn't a game.'

'Do you want to know why Mr Coleman was our fault?'

'For the love of all that's holy, no.'

'Because the Handyman is punishing sinners,' I said, 'and we exposed one, which made him a target. It's not just any sinners, but sinners in positions of authority. Leaders in the community, like pastors and teachers and government officials.'

'John . . .'

'Every attack is getting worse,' I said. 'Remember how Mayor Robinson had thirty-seven stab wounds in his back? Well, Coleman had sixty-four.'

'Please stop.'

'Sixty-four,' I repeated. 'And in a week and a half our time will be up, and she'll purge another sinner – someone important, and someone in the public eye to make sure that everyone gets the message. But now we've figured it out, and we can find the next victim before she kills him.' I stared ay Marci, holding her gaze intensely. She stared back. 'Please, Marci – you've got to help me.'

She stared back, her eyes hard. I tried to guess what she was thinking. Would she go along, or refuse?

'It's impossible,' she said. 'There's no way we can guess one specific person this creep thinks is a sinner.'

That means she's considering it, I thought. *She's thinking about it. I have to feed the fire.*

'It could be another pastor, or a teacher,' I said. 'Maybe the Principal at school.'

Her face went white. 'It could be a cop.'

I nodded. 'Anyone who's in a position of authority is game, but only if they have some kind of shady background – not a secret, but something everyone knows about. Your dad should be totally safe.'

She continued staring, her mouth a thin pink line. Her eyes were shadowed by her brow, and she looked out darkly. 'Sheriff Meier should be safe,' she said. 'Mick Herrman, Craig Moore; they should all be fine.' I stayed silent, and she squinted her eyes. 'This is why I didn't want to do this. I don't want to think about all the bad things people have done, and I don't want to feel guilty when I forget about some terrible thing that gets somebody killed.'

'What about—'

'Ellingford,' she said suddenly, opening her eyes. 'Larry Ellingford. He was an officer that got called under review two years ago for abuse of power. He was writing fraudulent speeding tickets to people he didn't like. I don't even know if he's still in town; I haven't heard anything about him in ages.'

'That's good,' I said. 'Can you think of anyone else?'

'Why am I doing all the work?'

'Okay,' I said, nodding. 'How about Ms Troyer, the Vice Principal? There was that whole thing last year about her fudging the results of the student body election.'

'You think that's enough?' she asked. 'If the Handyman'll kill someone for that, none of us are safe.'

'I'm just brainstorming,' I said. 'I'm trying to think of anyone I can.'

She paused, then said slowly, 'How about Curt Halsey?'

A host of thoughts rushed to my mind, crowding each other out. *If ever anyone deserved to be killed by a demon . . .* 'You mean the guy that burned down Forman's house?'

'Why not?' she asked. 'He's currently under suspicion of homicide – that's a pretty big sin.'

'He's also in police custody,' I said. 'She couldn't get to him. Besides, it's stretching the requirements quite a bit to call him a community leader.'

'People think he killed Forman,' she said. 'He's getting all the hero credit that you'd be getting if the truth came out.'

'True,' I said. 'That gives us three leads: one who might have moved, one who's only a sinner by the widest definition, and one who's in jail. Not a very good list.'

'But good enough for tonight,' she said, pointedly picking up her cards and fanning them out. 'I'm not thinking about this any more for now. Call or fold.'

I looked at her and she looked back, cocking her head with an expression that said, 'Just try to disagree with me.' I picked up my cards and fanned them out. 'Give me all your fours.'

'Wrong game,' she said sternly, then slowly broke into a smile and laughed. 'I count that as a fold, though. I win.' She scraped the pile of M&Ms across the carpet and into the much bigger pile by her legs. 'You still have a few left. Shuffle up and I'll take them off your hands.'

'You'll just share them with me anyway.'

'Try me, punk.'

I gathered the cards and shuffled, all the while running through lists of possible victims in my head.

Chapter 13

On Monday night the phone rang during dinner. The caller ID said Jensen.

'Hello?'

'John,' said Marci quickly, 'are you watching the news?'

'Not at the moment.'

'That's fine, I don't even know if it's on yet.'

'What?'

'Can you get over here?'

'Slow down, you're talking in circles.'

'William Astrup was arrested,' she said. 'My dad's radio just went off, and I heard it from the hall. He was arrested in Springdale for soliciting prostitution.'

I frowned. Springdale, despite its fancy name, was the poorest neighbourhood of Clayton County – a massive string of apartments that sprawled through the heart of town. It was exactly the kind of place someone would go to solicit a prostitute, but not the kind of place anyone would expect to find a community leader.

'Who's William Astrup?' I asked. 'Is that another cop?'

'You're kidding me,' she said. 'He's the owner of the wood plant – he's the richest man in the county, and the biggest employer. No one else even comes close. How can you not know that?'

'I'm kind of amazed that you *do* know it,' I said. 'How do you know the guy who owns the wood plant?'

'Just get over here,' she said. 'This is our next victim – it's got to be – and I'm not telling Dad about this without you.'

She was right. This sounded like the ideal victim for the Handyman, and there were only a few days left. But as ridiculous as it sounded, I still couldn't shake the idea that Officer Jensen might be the demon. Did I dare go and spill my whole plan to him? I paused, trying to study the situation: if he was the demon, then he had a much bigger plan I hadn't begun to grasp yet; embedding myself in his life was the best way to discover it. And if he wasn't the demon, then he could save the victim while I slipped by in the dark and took the demon out.

For just a moment I considered not telling him at all, to make absolutely sure that no one interfered with my trap for Nobody. This William Astrup would be perfect bait if he suspected nothing, and if the police stayed far away. But it was too late now. By bringing Marci into this, I'd brought in her ethics as well. She wanted the victim protected, and she would make sure it happened whether I was the one to say it or not.

'I'll be there in a minute,' I said.

'See ya.' We hung up, and I turned to leave.

'Something happened to William Astrup?' Mom asked.

'How does everybody know this guy but me?'

'What's going on?'

'Nothing,' I said. 'I just need to run over to Marci's.'

'Can't you finish your dinner first?'

'No.' I ran down the stairs and out the side door, then drove quickly to Marci's house. Her father was walking out to his squad car right as I pulled up, with Marci close on his heels.

'Here he is,' she was saying as I stepped out of the car. 'Just listen to him.'

'Make it quick,' he said, turning to look at me. 'Apparently you've got something to tell me about the Handyman?'

'Yes,' I said, stumbling over my own thoughts as I tried to get them in order. 'You need to . . . I mean . . .' I wasn't ready to explain all of this yet. I liked to take my time and plan things, not rush into them blindly. 'She's going to try to kill William Astrup.'

Officer Jensen narrowed his eyes. 'What makes you say that?'

'Because she's targeting community leaders she thinks have done wrong,' I told him. 'The Handyman is a holy avenger – it's not a very common serial-killer profile but I promise you it's true in this case. She's trying to save us, or teach us, or cleanse us, or whatever, and a rich, powerful guy like Astrup getting arrested is exactly what she's looking for.'

'Wait – how did you know about . . .' He studied me for a second, then growled under his breath and turned to Marci. 'Marci Elizabeth Jensen. Have you been eavesdropping again?'

'I didn't try to hear it, it's just loud.'

'I have told you a hundred times that you are not allowed to interfere with my job. This is very serious. If word of this arrest gets out—'

'Word *is* going to get out, no matter what you do,' I interrupted. 'Astrup is too important, and people will find out, and then the Handyman will try to kill him. Late Wednesday night, if he sticks to his pattern – and that's only two days away. You have to trust me. He fits the profile exactly.'

'If he fits a profile,' Officer Jensen said, 'the FBI will already know about it.'

'Then no one will think you're weird when you suggest protecting him,' I said. 'Listen, the Handyman probably lies awake at night praying for someone as important as William Astrup to make a mistake this big. Killing him is exactly the message she is trying to send, and if she cut out Coleman's eyes for porn I don't have to tell you what she'll cut off of Astrup for solicitation.'

'Ew,' said Marci.

'You know about the eyes too?' said Jensen sternly, whirling on Marci again.

'You told me that one yourself!' she snapped.

'Look,' I said, 'I know you have no reason to trust us, but—' I stopped suddenly, unsure of what to say next. *If he leaves Astrup defenceless I'll be able to see exactly what the demon does to him, and how. If I'm lucky I'll spot a weakness and find a way to kill Nobody right there, on the spot, with no more waiting and no more speculation.* But I didn't want Marci to think I was backing down.

'You know he's probably going to post bail right away, so you won't be able to hold him anyway,' I went on, 'but you could send him some guards or something. Maybe – I don't know.' *What am I really doing here? I have to learn more about*

Nobody, and yet I'm sabotaging my best chance, just to save one criminal's life. Or am I doing it because I'm afraid of what Marci will think of me?

What's really important here?

Officer Jensen looked at me again, eyes intense. I could tell he was thinking about it.

'What about the prostitute?' he asked. 'Aren't you worried about her?'

'The Handyman doesn't care about her,' I said. 'Only the authority figure.'

He paused again. 'I can't just walk in there and tell them my daughter and her boyfriend cracked the Handyman case.'

'Then tell them you did it,' said Marci, 'but just tell them.'

No! He almost said no and you ruined it!

He looked back and forth between Marci and me, then sighed. 'Fine, I'll tell them, but I won't guarantee anything. And in return,' he pointed at us sternly, 'you two will keep absolutely quiet about this, and you will stop "accidentally overhearing" my radio, and you will keep out of this permanently. Am I clear?'

'Loud and clear,' said Marci, nodding. We stepped up onto the kerb, and Officer Jensen got into his car. He gave us one last look before driving away, and Marci waved as he left.

'Thanks for coming,' she said, patting me twice on the chest before turning towards the house. I turned with her, silently cursing that we'd managed to convince him, and we walked slowly to the front steps. 'I'm so glad to be rid of this.'

'Yeah,' I said, already trying to think of my next move. I needed to find a way to watch Astrup, to see who contacted him and how they reacted to the police. But how could I get close enough?

'Marci,' her mom called from the doorway, 'phone's for you.'

'Who is it?'

'Rachel again.'

'Oh my gosh,' Marci muttered, then shouted back, 'just tell her I'm busy, and I'll call her later.'

Mrs Jensen faded back into the house, and Marci shook her head. 'That girl will not leave me alone! "What are you wearing to the dance?" "Who are you going with?" "Can we go in a group?" "What diet should I use so I can fit my dress?" She's driving me crazy.'

I wasn't paying much attention, too preoccupied with my plans, but I nodded and tried to look as if I was listening. 'She's going to a dance? Cool.' *The victims are all killed without a fight, usually inside their own homes, which means they let the killer in of their own free will. That usually means the killer is someone they know, but with this many victims it has to be something else. Whatever disguise or cover Nobody is using is apparently non-threatening, and somehow familiar to everyone she killed.*

'Yes, there's a dance,' said Marci, enunciating each syllable. 'The Homecoming Dance – you may have heard of it? A little social gathering this Friday?'

'Oh yeah, the Homecoming thing. There's the posters at school and stuff.' *I've been assuming that Nobody can change her face and body, like Crowley did, but Crowley could only do it by killing someone – by literally stealing their bodies. The Handyman doesn't steal bodies, and the few parts she does steal she just destroys later on. How is she disguising herself?*

147

'Rachel's going with Brad,' said Marci, 'and we're kind of hoping to go in a group, though I don't have a date yet.'

This pulled me out of my thoughts. 'You don't? But you're, like . . . It seems like someone would have asked you weeks ago.'

Marci was staring at me, her mouth wide open, as if she didn't know what to say. I realised I'd said something stupid, and tried to cover it up.

'I mean, you're amazing,' I said. 'Everyone loves you – you have more friends than anyone I think I've ever met. How could no one have asked you yet?'

'As a matter of fact,' she said, fumbling slightly with her words, 'five people have asked me. Five. And I've said no to all of them.'

'You don't want to go?'

'No, I'd kind of like to go, actually.'

I looked at her, awaiting an explanation. *Girls are so weird.* She gazed back for a moment, then rolled her eyes and looked up at the twilit sky. 'Do I have to do everything myself?'

And that's when it finally hit me: she wanted me to ask her.

'I . . .'

'Yes?' she said, turning back to face me. 'Something you want to say?'

'Are you . . . ?'

'Something finally clicking in that remarkably thick head of yours?'

'Wait.'

'Oh, I've been waiting.'

'Do you actually want to . . .' I trailed off.

' "Go . . ." ' she prompted.

'Go . . . to the Homecoming dance . . .'

' "With . . ." '

'Me?' I finished.

'I am astonished at the level of meddling it took to make that happen.'

'I'm confused,' I said.

'Obviously. Let me explain: first, yes, I would love to go to Homecoming with you, thank you so much for asking. Second, what in the hell is your problem?'

'What?'

'You're over here for hours every day, you obviously like me, I obviously like you, and frankly we don't spend enough time apart for you to even have time to ask anyone else to the dance, let alone flirt enough to make asking a possibility. How long would you have waited if I hadn't forced the issue?'

'I . . . I'm not really a dance kind of guy.'

'You mean never?' she asked. 'Here I was, waiting all this time, and you weren't even thinking about it?'

'I'm sorry?'

'You are without a doubt the weirdest guy I have ever met.'

I took a breath. 'But that's just the thing,' I said. 'I *am* the weirdest guy you've ever met. I'm like the opposite of you. You have lots of friends, I have no friends; you're beautiful, I'm weird-looking; you're popular and interesting and fun, and I work in a mortuary. I'm obsessed with death and I study serial killers for fun. Guys like me don't go to dances, and when we do, we don't go with girls like you.' I

149

didn't think I had to actually explain how messed-up I was – couldn't people just tell by looking at me?

Marci looked astonished. 'Is that seriously how you think of yourself? Is that seriously how you think of *me*?'

'As beautiful?'

'As above you. As . . . too good for you. Listen, John, how should I put this?' She licked her lips. 'Girls aren't stupid, okay? We know when guys like us, and we usually know why: yes, we know we're attractive, and yes, we notice when guys check us out. I can't tell you how many conversations I've had in just the last month where I have to look at a guy's forehead the whole time because he's staring at my boobs. And yes, I admit that sometimes I use them on purpose to get attention. I've done it with you. But you're the first straight boy since sixth grade that it hasn't worked on. The first one who doesn't just stare.' She shrugged, and looked out at the street. 'You're the first boy in years who's more interested in talking to me than checking out my rack.'

'But I'm just . . .' How could I explain this? 'I'm just following my rules. I'm trying to treat you like a person. With respect.' *The alternative is to treat you like the bodies in the mortuary, like a doll to play with, and I don't dare allow myself to think like that.*

' "With respect",' she repeated. 'One of the best things about you, John, is that you have no idea how rare that is.'

I didn't know what to say, so I said nothing. We sat for a moment while the sky turned bright orange with sunset above us. After a moment I spoke up, hesitantly.

'So . . . does this mean we're dating?'

Marci laughed out loud. 'Holy crap, you are such a geek!'

150

'Well, how am I supposed to know these things if you don't tell me?'

'Even my dad called you my boyfriend, just now when he drove away. *Everyone* thinks we're dating; I have no idea how you missed it.'

'Well,' I said. 'Boyfriend, huh?'

She pulled up her knees and rested her head on them, looking at me sideways. 'Yup.'

'And that would make you my girlfriend.'

'It would.'

I paused a moment. 'Then I should give you a mushy nickname, like "Sweetums" or "Cupcake".'

'I don't think we have to go that far.'

'How about "Sugar Booger"?'

'Call me that again,' she said, laughing, 'and I'll find another date for Homecoming so fast your head will spin. Five guys I turned down – remember that. Five.'

'Five,' I repeated. *Why did you choose the only one who's dreamed about killing you?*

I let Marci make our Homecoming plans, and busied myself with plans for trapping Nobody. I drove to William Astrup's house and scoped it out. He hadn't been released by the police yet, and the news hadn't broken, so his house was empty and I could wander through his yard at will.

There was a large hedge by the front door, and the back door that faced the forest was surrounded by plenty of good hiding-places. Which one would be best? Assuming that Nobody wasn't completely invisible – which, given her name, she might well be – she was liable to show up under some kind of harmless pretence. Delivering a pizza? A package? 'Hi, my car broke down and my phone won't work – can I use yours?' Whatever it was, it would almost certainly happen at the front door. That's where I needed to watch.

I checked out the front hedge: I could hide behind it for hours if I had to, completely obscured. If I had a gun, I could just sit there and shoot the first person to show up with a big duffel bag – assuming that a gun would even work on Nobody. They hadn't worked on Crowley, but Crowley had been much more physical, more brutal; Nobody was a finesse killer who used tools and took her time. She might not be able to shapeshift or regenerate at all; obviously Forman couldn't.

A gun might actually work, especially if it had a silencer. I could shoot her before she even rang the bell, and be gone just as quickly, and the evidence would melt away to almost nothing: an ashy smear on the front porch. I could do this, as long as the police didn't get in the way. Had Officer Jensen really believed us? Had he really taken us seriously?

The whole point was moot if the Handyman didn't hear about Astrup's arrest and didn't choose him as her next victim.

That same night I used the pay phone to call in an anonymous tip to the newspaper. It was on the news Monday night, and by Tuesday everyone in town had heard about it; the bait was set. All I needed was the gun. I thought about stealing one from Marci's house, because I knew Officer Jensen had some, but I discarded the idea immediately. I'm not dumb enough to steal a gun from a cop. Max, on the other hand, was another story. His dad had a huge gun collection, and now that he was dead nobody ever used them. They'd never even know it was missing.

I woke up Wednesday morning ready to visit Max and steal a gun, and turned on the morning news while I ate breakfast. The story hit me like a kick to the stomach. The killer had struck early. William Astrup was fine. Instead, Sheriff Meier was dead, his hands and tongue removed, his body pinned to the grass with two long poles rising up like wings.

Chapter 14

'Hold still,' said Mom, fussing with my bow-tie. 'This would be a lot easier if you didn't fight me the whole time.'

'Imagine how easy it would be if you just left me alone,' I said, pulling away for the fifth time. 'It looks fine.'

'It's crooked,' she said. 'For goodness' sake, let me fix it for just twenty seconds so I can take a picture, and then you can mess it up as much as you want.'

I stalked down the hall to the fridge, where Mom had stashed the corsage she bought me. 'I don't want a picture.'

'But you have to get a picture!' she said, following me through the house. 'This is my baby's first dance!' I glared at her. 'I mean my handsome young man's first dance! Of course I need a picture.'

'So you can never look at it and accidentally delete the memory card?'

'That only happened once,' she said sternly. 'And no, it's so I can show everyone.'

' "Everyone"? Who's "everyone"? All the friends we don't have, or all the family that aren't here? Lauren left work an hour ago without even coming upstairs, and Margaret didn't come in at all, so I can't imagine they care about seeing a picture of it. And if Dad wanted to see my first dance he gave up his shot a few years ago.' There was a knock on the door, which gave me the perfect opportunity to look away from my mother's stunned face. 'That's probably my ride.'

I opened the door and saw Brad Nielsen, Rachel's date, standing out on the landing. 'Oh, good,' he said, 'I wasn't sure if I had the right door. I was half-afraid I'd open this up and find a bunch of dead bodies or something.'

'The mortuary's downstairs,' I said. 'And nobody's dead right now.'

'Well, that's good to know,' he said, and waved politely at my mom. 'Hello, Mrs Cleaver, how are you?'

How could anyone not know if someone in town is recently dead or not? I thought. It's the only interesting thing that ever happens around here.

'Hello, Bradley,' said Mom. She'd regained her composure after my outburst, and now raised her camera. 'Stand close.'

'No, Mom,' I said. 'No pictures.'

'But your friend's here now,' she said, waving us together. 'Smile!'

'I don't need a picture with—' the flash snapped '—another guy. That's great, Mom, thank you. Send that one to Dad and tell him we're going steady.'

'Sweet!' said Brad. 'Don't worry, man, they take photos at the dance; we'll get some of those. How is your dad, anyway?'

'He's awesome,' I said. 'He's currently my favourite parent.' I pushed Brad back onto the landing and shut the door behind me, then led him down the stairs to the side door and out into the night air. It was the last week of September, and already the evenings were darker and cooler. We got into Brad's car – he had the best car out of the four of us – and drove off to pick up the girls.

'It's been a long time, hasn't it?' said Brad. I looked over at him.

'A long time since what?'

'Since we did anything,' he said. 'We used to hang out all the time in elementary school; what happened to all that?'

'I don't know.'

'What was that game we used to play, on that thing in the playground? The big wooden thing?'

'I don't remember.'

'No, it was a game you made up, with that ramp thing made out of tyres, and we had to call the pockets, like in pool, and then try to jump into the right one.' He laughed, and the memory came back – fuzzy and immaterial, like a memory of someone else's life. Kids at recess, laughing and shouting and jumping and falling, playing all day without a care in the world.

'That barely seems like us any more,' I said, watching the cars and houses and people roll by outside. *It's a different world, now, and darker. It's full of demons – real live demons that want to kill us all. It's hard to imagine that anyone could ever be that carefree again.*

'I know what you mean,' said Brad. 'It's like, we used to pretend to do things, but now we're actually doing them – we have jobs, we play sports, we go to school. I mean, of course we did those things before, but now they mean something; now it's not just football in the street, it's football on the big field with lights and announcers and the whole town watching.'

I stared blankly out the window – different houses than I'd seen a minute ago, and different cars, and different people, but still somehow the same. Blocks and blocks and miles and miles, all the same. *Lights and announcers. Is that really as far as your ambitions reach?*

'And the girls!' said Brad, slapping the steering wheel. 'You think *we've* changed, holy cow. I remember when Rachel had pigtails and skinned knees and screamed at the PE teacher every time we played soccer. And Marci was like a total hippie or something, like a feral child, until one day bam! The girls disappeared and these gorgeous women appeared out of nowhere.'

Everyone grows up. I thought about Marci's little sister, Kendra, fours years old with frizzy hair, growing up to be a young woman; filling out, becoming beautiful. Somebody's girlfriend; somebody's obsession; somebody's victim. All grown-up and sexy and dead.

'Yeah,' I said. 'That's just the way things go sometimes.'

'Rachel's right up here,' he said, turning down a street and pointing ahead. He parked and ran to her front door while I shuffled into the back seat. A few minutes later Brad led Rachel to the car, opened her door, helped her in, and closed it after her. I watched carefully, preparing to do the same thing.

'Hi John,' she said, turning slightly to wave from the front seat. 'Lookin' good!'

157

'Hi,' I said. I was starting to remember how much I hated spending time with people; the bigger the group, the worse it got. This dance was going to kill me.

We drove to Marci's house, and I walked up to the door with my plastic corsage box. The front was open, as always, and I knocked on the screen. There was an instant crash and rumble as her siblings jumped off the couch and ran to see me. The house filled with shouts of, 'Marci! John's here!' and the hallway filled with kids.

'My sister looks beautiful,' said Kendra. 'You're going to love her, but Mom says she's immodest.'

'Back! Back inside!' said Marci, coming down the hall. She was wearing a long, dark green dress, lifting the hem carefully off the floor as the kids charged past her and back into the TV room. The bottom of the dress shimmered softly in the faint light of the hallway, while the top was an elegant, embroidered corset. Her shoulders and collarbone were bare, with more cleavage than I'd expected after her speech to me the other night.

She opened the door and beckoned me in. 'You'd better come inside. Mom wants pictures.'

'Everyone's going to want pictures,' I said. 'You look incredible.'

'Thank you.'

'I thought you were going with me because you didn't have to show off the . . .' I gestured vaguely. 'You know.'

'I'd already bought the dress over the summer. How was I to know I'd end up dating an actual gentleman? Plus there was a really good sale online.'

I held up the corsage. 'That's great for you, but there's

158

literally nowhere for me to pin this. Plus I think your dad would shoot me if he saw me trying.'

'I'll do it,' she said, taking the box as we walked into the kitchen. 'But this means you have to do your own boutonnière.' She pulled a little flower box of her own from the fridge, handed it to me, and we pinned on our flowers while her mom laughed and took pictures. We posed, we held hands, I did my best to smile, and finally we escaped back out to the car. Brad threw it into gear, and we were off.

We ate dinner at the nicest restaurant in town – a steak place that, precisely because it was the nicest restaurant in town, was crammed full of high-school kids in rented tuxedos and an explosion of multicolored satin. Marci had planned ahead and made reservations early, probably the same time she'd bought the dress.

I'd spent several months as a vegetarian, trying to keep myself from thinking about dead meat in general, and dead humans in particular. Once I'd found my purpose and focused on killing demons, I'd been able to let some of those rules slip, and I figured it was okay to have a little meat for a special occasion. I looked over the menu and ordered a porterhouse steak – my favourite cut. Brad got the same, and Marci and Rachel ordered salads.

'I absolutely love your dress,' said Rachel, reaching over to Marci. She stopped just shy of touching her. 'So much better than this boring thing I've got on.'

'I love your dress!' said Brad. 'You look great.'

'Thanks,' said Rachel, flashing him a smile. 'You're so

sweet.' Her smile was quick, and her face turned towards him, but I caught a glimpse of something . . . off. There and gone in a flash. *Did Brad say something wrong?* I wondered. *Even compliments are hard to give right in a situation like this. I hate social politics.*

'Did you guys hear about the Sheriff?' asked Brad.

'Marci and I looked at each other silently; we hadn't had much chance to talk about it yet, though I'd been working on my own theories all week. The demon had broken her pattern again, in ways we hadn't anticipated, and that scared me. It meant I didn't know as much as I thought I did, and that was a very dangerous situation to be in. I was desperate to learn more, and elated that Brad had brought it up.

'Let's not talk about that,' said Marci, and shot me a warning look. I leaned back and sighed, listening as the conversation turned into gossip about the other kids in the restaurant.

Brooke was there, on the far side of the room, in a light blue dress and a matching satin jacket. Her hair was up in a pile of curls on top of her head, and she looked radiant. She was sitting next to Mike Larsen, it looked like, and I found myself hating him passionately.

A troupe of waiters brought out our plates, and my three companions dug in to their food. I stared at mine, suddenly queasy. The meat was red and juicy – medium rare, just like I'd asked – and staring out starkly from the centre was a sawed-off cross-section of bone. It was a piece of the vertebra, perfectly trimmed and perfectly normal, but all I could see – all I could think of – was the parade of severed wrists that had come and gone through the mortuary. Red, juicy meat around a neat central column of bone.

It's okay, I told myself, *just eat*. I pressed my fork into it, watching the juices run out from the holes, and I raised up my knife, and suddenly it was Mike Larsen on the plate, dead and bleeding: meaningless food to be chewed up and swallowed. I felt no wave of nausea; no rise of bile in the back of my throat. I knew that those thoughts were wrong, but they didn't *feel* wrong. It was just another thing. It was the way I'd used to think, in the times before I'd gained control.

My old thoughts and habits were all creeping back, one by one; my dark side, the part of me I called Mr Monster, was stirring. My angry fight with my mother; my paranoid suspicions of Marci – my urge to kill her that night in her room. It was all coming back. Why? Wasn't it enough that I was hunting a demon? Wasn't it enough that I was planning to kill?

Of course not, I whispered, deep in the caverns of my mind. *I don't want to think about killing, I want to really kill. I'm a creature of action. Thinking about it will never be enough.*

The room grew dark, and I felt my skin grow hot. *I shouldn't be here. I have a demon to catch, and here I am wasting my time – and everyone else's lives – at a stupid dinner before some stupid dance. I'm an idiot. I'm a fool. I'm sitting idly by while Nobody teaches her vicious lesson with a trail of death. I have to act. I have to find her, and I have to kill her. It's the only way to stop her.*

But what then? Who'll be next after Nobody, and how many people will die before I find that demon?

I pushed my plate away.

'Something wrong?' asked Marci.

'I don't think I can eat it,' I said. *I don't think I can even have it on the table.* I flagged down a waiter and said, 'Can you take this back?'

'Is there a problem with it, sir?'

If I blame them, I can dodge the embarrassing questions. 'Yes,' I said. 'I ordered it medium rare, and this is barely medium.'

'Of course, sir, I'll have the chef prepare a new one immediately.'

'Actually,' I said, looking over at Marci, 'that salad looks really good. Could I just get one of those instead?'

'Of course, sir. Would you like it with grilled chicken?'

'No, thanks,' I said. 'No meat at all.'

Chapter 15

The Homecoming Dance was held in City Hall, in a large open room with a marble floor circled by rows of ornate wooden pillars. It was probably too small for a crowd this size, but it was really the only choice. Whenever the city needed a bigger venue than City Hall they used the gym at Clayton High, and nobody wanted to hold the dance there. Instead, the students crammed into this small space, jumping and pulsing in time to the music, and retreating to the cool shadows outside whenever it grew too loud, too noisy, or too hot.

Marci grabbed my hand and ploughed her way through the crowd, becoming almost instantly separated from Brad and Rachel. I followed her, holding tightly to her wrist and apologising mutely to everyone we bumped into on the way. Nearly everyone smiled and waved at Marci, followed by a polite wave to me; people were accustomed to seeing us together, but that didn't mean they knew how to react to us. To them I was still just the weird kid who lived over the mortuary.

When we reached the centre of the room Marci turned around, cheered loudly, and started dancing. I did my best to follow along, which mostly just meant shifting my weight back and forth from one foot to the other. I decided in that moment that I was never meant to be a dancer. I also decided that of all the torture I'd experienced in Agent Forman's house of death, nothing could compare to the torture of a high-school dance.

Marci laughed, tried to show me what to do, then laughed again as I continued to suck. A more empathetic person would have said, 'At least she's enjoying herself,' but I was ready to turn around and run. Thankfully, blissfully, the song ended and the dancing stopped. There was a chorus of cheers from the eager crowd, and then another song started – slow and bluesy. Marci stepped in close, wrapped her arms around my shoulders, and began to sway softly.

'You know,' she said, 'this works a lot better if you touch me back.' I glanced at the other couples around us, saw how they did it, and tentatively put my hands on Marci's waist. It was soft, and perfectly curved, and I touched her lightly, like a balloon I was afraid of popping. She chuckled and sighed.

'How are you liking your first dance?'

'A few seconds ago it was also my last dance,' I said. 'But I have to admit that this part is pretty nice.'

'It is,' she said, stepping in closer. We moved back and forth, hesitantly awkward and blissfully comfortable at the same time.

We were close to each other, yet still worlds apart. I have rarely felt truly connected to anyone, but those few connections were all powerful memories: brandishing a knife at my mom; staring hungrily at Brooke in Forman's house.

Each event was a scar in my mind, violent and intense, like a white-knuckle ride in a speeding car. I lived my whole life behind a hazy, emotionless curtain, cutting me off from the rest of the world, but for just a few seconds here and there I'd been able to break through it; I had been connected, sharing my emotions with another person just like a real, empathetic human being. Even then it was limited – not in the depth of emotion, but in the variety. It only ever worked with fear and control.

Then Marci shifted slightly, beginning to rotate, and without thinking I went along with her: step forward with one foot, step back with the other. Forward with one foot, back with the other. Words were unnecessary; we were perfectly coordinated. Perhaps it was a coincidence. Perhaps we were thinking the same thoughts. Perhaps . . .

Perhaps it was best to think no thoughts at all.

We danced that way for an ageless eternity, locked in perfect sync, moving and turning and shifting in a harmony I'd never known. *This is real.* The song faded and still I clung to her, desperate to keep going, to hold onto that connection like a lifeline to humanity.

Another grinding dance song exploded over the speakers, and the crowd cheered loudly. They shook the floor, stomping and waving, and I cocked my head towards the refreshment table on the side.

'Can we sit this one out?'

'What?'

I leaned in close, whispering in her ear, feeling her hair on my face. 'Can we get a drink?'

'Sure!'

We made our way back to the side, ducking into an alcove that made the sound less oppressive, and reached the drinks table just as Rachel found us in tears and grabbed hold of Marci's arms.

'Rach, what's wrong?'

Rachel was too much of a mess to speak, and I turned to the punch bowl while she composed herself. I reached for the ladle just as another hand got there first – slender and pale, flanked by a flash of blue in the corner of my eye. Brooke. I looked up just as she did; we stared at each other a moment, faces blank. She poured her drink, offered me the ladle, and slipped into the crowd.

'This whole night is a disaster!' cried Rachel, while Marci clucked and cooed to try to soothe her. 'This dress looks horrible, I spilled some salad dressing on it, and Brad was just looking at you the whole time anyway.'

'Oh, come on,' said Marci, pulling her into a hug. 'You're gorgeous, and he can't take his eyes off you.'

'Are you sure?'

'Of course I'm sure,' said Marci. 'You look great, and he looks great, and he's had a thing for you since last year. You need to get out there and enjoy yourself!'

'Thank you,' said Rachel, crying. 'I wish I was as happy as you, or as pretty.'

'Seriously, Rachel, you're gorgeous.'

'You're the best friend ever. I wish I could be . . .' And then she left, melting back into the crowd, and Marci stepped next to me.

'Sometimes I don't know what to do with that girl,' she sighed. 'She is an emotional issue with legs.'

'She's right, though, you know.' I turned to face her. 'You're always happy, you're always . . . there. I can read people really well, most of the time. I can look at a face and figure out almost exactly what that person is thinking. But that's as far as I can go – I know what people are feeling, but I don't know what I should be feeling about it. You can do the same thing, and then you actually use that knowledge productively.'

Marci smiled and leaned in closer, grabbing my hands. 'John Wayne Cleaver, you give the weirdest compliments in the entire world.'

'You have empathy like I've never seen,' I went on. 'You know exactly how to talk to people, exactly how to connect. You think it's weird because it's easy for you, but for people like me, it's . . .' *How could I explain what she had done?*

'People like you, huh?'

'Yeah.'

'And what kind of people are you, precisely?'

In her heels she was nearly the same height as I was, and standing this close our eyes were perfectly level; our lips were level; our noses were almost touching. I stared deeply into her eyes. *Does she really want to know what I am? Do I even dare to tell her?*

No, I don't. I can't. But if she could figure it out on her own . . .

'You're the social genius here,' I said, pasting on a smile. 'Why don't you tell me what kind of person I am?'

'Well,' she said, grinning, 'you're smart, but very eclectic about it; you focus on the things that interest you and ignore everything else.' While she was speaking, a movement caught my eye – not an individual motion but a wave of activity rippling across the crowd, accompanied by a rustle of voices audible above the music. I stood on my toes to get a better look, and Marci turned, crinkling her brow. 'What's that?'

Someone shouted, though I couldn't hear the words. The music stopped abruptly and in the sudden silence a girl screamed, harsh and terrified.

'Get away from me!'

The shout was like a signal for the dance to collapse into chaos, and the whole crowd started screaming and backing into the wall. Marci and I were pressed back; the drink table tipped and crashed to the floor, and a swarm of terrified dancers surged into it, scrambling on the wet floor, trapping people behind the overturned table, desperate to get away from . . . what? There was an old radiator behind us, and I stepped up on it to get a better view.

'That scream sounded like Ashley,' said Marci.

'It is,' I said, looking over the heads of the maddened crowd. Ashley Ohrn, a girl from school, was walking through the centre of the hall, eyes squeezed shut and sobbing loudly. There was a black harness draped over her satin dress, a web of straps holding six brown blocks to her chest. It was an image I'd seen in a hundred movies, now horribly real and barely fifty feet away – bricks of C4 explosive, strung together with brightly coloured wires. 'She's wearing a bomb.'

'Ashley,' called someone. 'What are you—'

'Don't talk to me!' she shrieked. The crowd by the doors was fleeing in two trickling lines, but the rest of us were being trampled back into the walls, leaving a wide circle of terror with Ashley at the centre. 'Everybody just get away!'

'What's going on?' asked Marci.

'She's here for me,' I whispered. *Nobody's here, but she doesn't know who I am. She narrowed it down and discovered I was a teenager, but not which one specifically. She stole Ashley's body and made a bomb big enough to kill every teenager in town.*

Ashley reached the centre of the room, crying hysterically. Marci grabbed hold of my arm and stood up on the radiator with me, balancing precariously against the wall.

'She's really going to do it,' I said.

'She's terrified,' said Marci. 'If that's a bomb, she didn't put it on herself.'

I glanced back at the door, and the black night beyond. *Marci's right: Ashley's not the killer, she's the pawn. Nobody's out there somewhere, watching where it's safe.* I flexed my fingers in frustration, curling them around imaginary weapons. I had nothing – there was no way I could confront her. I didn't even know if I could reach the door, and the window behind me was too high to climb to. I thought about calling her, begging her to cancel the attack, but Forman's phone was still at home, hidden away. *There's nothing I can do.*

The press of people surged against us, squishing screaming students into the wall and almost jostling us down from our perch on the radiator. Someone else was scrambling up now, pulling heavily on Marci, and I shoved him back.

'I can't just stand here,' I said, staring out at Ashley. She had something in her hands; her knuckles were white around it. 'I've got to do something.'

'Are you crazy?' asked Marci.

'Technically, yes.' *But what could I do?* I caught a glimpse of Brooke on the far side of the ring, eyes wide with terror, and I made my decision. 'Do you have your phone?'

'What are you doing?'

'I'm going to stop this,' I said. 'Do you have your cellphone?'

'Where would I hide a cellphone in this dress?'

'Then find someone who does,' I said, 'and call the police. And stay here.'

She called after me again but I ignored her, diving down into the crowd and shoving my way through a sea of stomping feet and frightened faces. Ashley's voice rang out, wet and hoarse with tears. 'I'm sorry! I'm so sorry!'

'Let me through!' I shouted, but the only people lucid enough to pay attention merely shouted back insults as they pushed past me in a futile rush towards safety. I struggled against the current and finally got through, stumbling into the wide circle that had formed around her. Students and teachers and chaperones were pressed tight against all four walls, rigid with terror.

'John, move back!' bellowed a teacher. 'You'll get us all killed!'

'She doesn't want to kill everyone,' I said. The next words stuck in my throat, but I forced them out. 'This doesn't have to happen.'

'It's not me,' Ashley said, her voice cracking. 'I swear it's not me.'

'I know,' I said, walking slowly towards her. 'I know it's not you – it's the woman who put the bomb on you.'

'What woman?'

I stopped. 'The woman who's making you do this.'

'It was a man,' she cried, 'only a man. I didn't see a woman.'

170

So I was right; she's taken a new body somehow.

'That's fine,' I said, and took a step closer. 'It was a man. What did he tell you?'

'Stay back!' the Principal warned me. 'It's not safe.'

'It's fine,' I told him. 'Ashley is not going to hurt anybody, and nobody is going to hurt Ashley. Isn't that right?'

She nodded, and I took another step closer. 'What did he tell you?'

'He said,' she choked on her tears, swallowed, and continued, 'he said he'd push the button and kill us all.'

There has to be some way out of this. 'He'll kill us no matter what?' I asked. 'Is that all he said?'

'He said I had to read this letter.' She held up her hands. She'd been clutching a sheet of paper.

'That's good,' I said, nodding and grasping at the sliver of hope. 'If he wants us to hear something then he's not gonna kill us – there's no point. He needs us alive so the message can get out.' I looked at her. 'Just do what he said. Just read it.'

She trembled, and I could hear the paper rattling in her hands. ' "Why won't anybody listen",' she began.

That's right, I thought, *we're listening now. Just don't kill us.*

' "I have tried to be reasonable. I have tried to be—" ' she swallowed ' "—polite. Your city is plagued by evil, and I am trying to destroy it, but all you do is fight against me".'

Am I the evil she's fighting against? But these four killings seem designed to lead me towards her, not drive me away. It doesn't make sense.

' "When I . . ." ' Ashley sobbed, squinting through her

171

tears, ' "killed the . . . the great liar, I sent a letter to the newspaper, which they refused to print. When I killed the pedophile I talked to them directly, but they still refused to share my teachings".'

Slowly it dawned on me: *This isn't about me at all. It's not a plan or a trick or anything else. The Handyman really cares about his message, more than anything else.*

' "Now this is the final straw",' Ashley continued, fighting back sobs, ' "You have understood my teachings, but you have turned against them. You have tried to protect the adulterer. But still I am merciful, and I have slain the one who led you astray".' At this point Ashley dissolved into tears, too terrified to continue.

'Is that all?' I asked. 'Ashley, look at me. Come on – look at me.' She did so, and I held her gaze. 'He said you'd be safe if you read it,' I told her. 'You have to read it all.'

She nodded and looked back at the paper. ' "I didn't want to put these innocent children in danger, but it was the only way to make you listen. This is your final warning. Walk in the ways of the Lord, and make His paths straight. Thus you shall be purified . . ." ' She trailed off, then finished: ' "By fire".'

The hall was silent, no one daring to move or breathe, everyone waiting. A single second ticked by, as long as an hour. Nothing exploded.

'Is that all?' I asked.

'Yes.'

'Are you sure? There's nothing else at all?'

'That's every word, I promise.'

'Then I want you to drop the paper, and turn around,' I

told her. I was only ten steps away now, and I walked slowly forward. 'Just turn around, so I can undo that harness.'

She turned slowly, gingerly, as if expecting to blow up at any second. I was three steps away, two steps, one. The harness was a simple web of straps and plastic buckles, hanging loosely over her shoulders and around her chest; he hadn't even tightened it. I inspected the first buckle carefully for wires or metal contacts, saw nothing, and slowly squeezed the plastic nubs until the buckle popped loose. Nothing happened. I undid the next one, then the next, then reached around to grab the pack of explosives before opening the last clasp.

Something's not right.

I didn't know anything about explosives, but I'd seen enough movies to know that a block of C4 was supposed to be like a heavy brick of clay that you pressed the detonators into. This wasn't anything like I had expected. I moved around to face Ashley directly, getting a better look at the blocks.

'What are you doing?' she asked.

'Quiet.'

I'd assumed that the subtle differences between the Hollywood image and the bomb on Ashley's chest were because the ones on TV were inaccurate, but I could see now that it was more. Seen up close, these bombs were completely different – almost handmade. *Almost fake.* I reached out and grabbed the edge of the paper wrapping, digging my finger into a crease, and tore it away.

'No!' screamed Ashley, but nothing happened. The torn paper revealed woodgrain and saw-marks; the bright red stamp of a lumberyard.

'They're made of wood.' I pulled the paper away on the others and found the same: long wooden blocks, cut into pieces and wrapped with paper. The wires that ran into them were held by hidden nails. There was no explosive, no power source, and no detonators, just a carefully crafted prop designed to remind us of the movies. 'The whole thing's a fake.'

Ashley pulled away from me, reaching behind her back in a frenzy and pulling apart the last buckle. She tore the fake bomb off and held it up, grimacing, then threw it down and backed up a step. The crowd gasped. The wooden blocks knocked against the marble floor, echoing in the high room. Nothing happened.

I jumped forward and grabbed Ashley's arm, whispering urgently, 'What did you see out there? What happened?'

'It was a man,' she said, trying to pull away. I held her like a vise. 'He had a gun. He told me to put the vest on or he'd shoot, and then he said to come in here and read the letter or he'd blow me up.'

'Did you see him? Can you describe him?'

'No, no!' she cried. 'It was dark and I couldn't see a thing – just his outline. He was short, maybe five feet tall, I don't know!'

'And his voice,' I demanded. 'Describe his voice.'

'He didn't say anything,' she said. 'It was all written on a note. Let me go!'

The crowd was parting and police were coming in. I let go of her just as the police caught up to us, shouting for paramedics, and they pulled Ashley and me outside. More cops were directing traffic through the double doors, trying to get everyone out of the building. A bomb squad rushed past us going in, but I shook my head.

'It's fake,' I called after them. 'He was never going to blow up anything.'

I felt a hand on my shoulder, and turned to see Officer Jensen; Marci was right behind him, and raced to my side. I reared back, suddenly afraid that he'd come to kill me, but he held up a clear plastic bag containing a small, discarded pistol. 'He was never going to shoot anybody, either. This was out in the shadows, just over there, clean as a whistle – no clip, and nothing in the chamber.'

'He left his gun?' I asked.

'He probably wanted us to find it,' said Officer Jensen. 'It looks like he scrubbed it clean of evidence and then left it where he knew we'd see it.'

I leaned against Marci, suddenly tired. 'He wanted us to know it was really him. I'll bet you anything the ballistics of that gun match all four killings, but you won't find any evidence to tell you who he is.'

Officer Jensen nodded. 'That's exactly what I thought, too.' He cocked his head to the side. 'You're very good at this, you know?'

I studied him closely, sizing him up, trying to match him against Ashley's description of her attacker, but he was far taller than she'd described. It couldn't have been him.

But it was a man, that much she was sure of. Which meant either Nobody really was a shapeshifter, or . . .

. . . it wasn't Nobody.

I stumbled, feeling drained, and Marci caught me and led me out onto the park lawn.

'You need to sit,' she said. 'You're going to come down off a killer adrenaline buzz any second now, and you don't want to be on your feet for it.'

'I'm fine,' I said, but allowed her to lead me to a bench. It was dark, lit by the flashing lights of a dozen cop cars and fire trucks, and the sidewalks were filled with lines of terrified students. My hands were shaking, and Marci pulled them into her lap and held them tightly.

'He didn't say anything,' I said, 'he just gave her a note. That either means he couldn't talk, or he wouldn't.'

'You're an absolute idiot,' she said. 'You could have been killed – do you realise that?'

'This is important,' I told her. 'None of the victims have ever fought the Handyman, which probably means he gains their trust, which almost definitely means he can talk. So why would he talk to them, and not to Ashley?'

'Just let it go,' said Marci, 'just for one night.'

'No,' I said, fixing her with my eyes. 'He just told us he's going to keep killing, and he just showed us that most of our profile is garbage. We can't just let it go, we've got to figure him out. Or her – we don't even know that for sure any more.'

Marci reached up and touched my cheek, running her hand up the side of my face and straightening my hair. I found myself suddenly unable to think about anything else.

'You're a hero,' she said, 'but even heroes need a rest sometimes.'

'He might have a speech impediment. Like the Trailside Killer. But it's probably not something, um, debilitating.' She was stroking my head, and I could barely concentrate. 'It's probably just an identifier, like an accent. He didn't want Ashley to hear his voice because he knew he was going to leave her alive. The Handyman has an accent, I'll bet you anything.'

'That's your whole thing, isn't it?' said Marci, leaning close to my face. I could see the blue and red lights from the police cars reflecting on her skin and flashing in her eyes. 'You see something wrong and you have to fix it, and damn the consequences.'

'But it's important,' I said again. 'She, or he, or whatever it is, will just keep killing and killing until I stop it.' I looked up at the stars. 'Now I've wasted two whole months building a profile that can't predict anything, and we're not any closer now than when we started.'

'You don't have to solve everything by yourself,' Marci said softly. 'I know you're trying to do your best to make things right, and I love that about you, but you can't let it eat you alive. The Handyman left evidence, and the police can use it to track her down, or him, or whatever, and you don't have to do everything.' She smiled weakly. 'You don't have to march into hell every single time they open the gate.'

I studied her face, cataloguing every familiar line and curve. I let out a long breath, pushing out the air like a poison. *Calm down*, I told myself. I turned and looked at the street. Cars crept past slowly, trying to get a good look at the chaos. 'You know, I am suddenly struck with the horrifying realisation that you and my mom might really get along.'

'Then you're lucky to be surrounded by smart women,' she said. 'I can see we have our hands full.'

She said 'we'. She'd seen me be stupid, she'd seen me be obsessed, she'd seen me put my life at risk . . . and she said 'we'.

'You're not leaving,' I said.

She smiled, curling her mouth into a mischievous grin. 'Are you kidding? My boyfriend just saved the whole school – he's a hero! He's a stupid, reckless, idiot of a hero, but hey. He's mine.'

'I'm yours, huh?'

We watched the chaos swirl around us, curiously separated by darkness and grass: there were police on the front steps, interviewing witnesses; there were long lines of students trying to get to their cars, and long lines of cars trying to get out onto the street. I tilted my head back and looked up at the stars again.

'You know,' said Marci, 'it's getting kind of chilly out here.'

I smiled up at the sky. 'Now you're regretting that immodest dress.'

She punched me lightly, laughing. 'I'm not complaining, you dork, I'm asking you to put your arm around me. I swear, it's like dropping hints off a cliff.'

I lifted my arm and curled it around her shoulders; she laid her head on my shoulder, warm and soft and perfect.

'So,' she said. 'How'd your first dance go?'

'Not bad, overall.'

'I take it this is also your first bomb threat?'

I smiled. 'Yep.'

'How about your first kiss?'

I paused, lost for words, my brain a hollow, buzzing sphere. 'Nothing's happened yet, but it is a night for firsts.'

She lifted her head, bringing it level with mine. 'Well, if it's your first, I'd better make sure it's memorable.'

And she did.

Chapter 16

I slept in the next morning, dreaming of Marci, and finally crawled out of bed at ten o'clock. Mom was gone, and I flipped on the TV; there was nothing on, and I turned it back off. I poured a bowl of cereal and was just sitting down to eat it when the doorbell rang. I ignored it, but it rang again, then a third time, so I dragged myself out of my chair, went down stairs to the outside door and opened it up. Brooke was outside, walking away.

'Hey,' I said, suddenly conscious of my wrinkled pyjamas and mussed-up hair.

She turned around. 'Hey.' She was dressed simply, in jeans and a long-sleeved shirt. She stood silent a moment, shuffling her feet. 'I just heard about Rachel, and I wanted to say I was sorry.'

'Rachel?'

Her face, already pale, went white. 'You haven't heard.' It wasn't a question, but a sudden shock of realisation, and in that instant, reading her eyes and her face and her stance, I received the same shock. I knew exactly what she was going to say.

'She killed herself,' I stated.

Brooke nodded.

'Dammit.' I stepped back, feeling the blood drain from my head, leaving it light and useless; an empty, worthless thing that buzzed with static and noise. The walls were dark and oppressive; the sun was too bright, and too cold. 'She was a mess all night – crying and depressed and everything – but I didn't think she'd take it that far. I had no idea.'

I turned away from the door, saw the wall too close, and punched it in rage. 'Why!' My scream devolved into a roar, loud and harsh until it scratched my throat and raked it raw.

'I'm so sorry to be the one to tell you,' said Brooke, standing in the doorway. 'I knew you were spending a lot of time with her lately, and I thought I'd better come see if there was anything I could . . . I'm so sorry, John.'

'Why do they keep killing themselves?' I demanded. 'Everything we do, everything we risk, is just . . . meaningless! It's like we never even stopped the killers; it's like they're all still out there, killing anyone they want, and we can't do anything about it. I don't know why we even try!' I threw myself down on the stairs, hurting myself as I sat, and I relished the bright focus on pain. I gritted my teeth and punched the wall again, hammering it over and over until my hand throbbed red. Brooke put her hands in her pockets, then took them out again.

'You want to talk?' she asked.

'Doesn't matter if I do, since nobody ever listens.'

'I'll listen.'

I looked up, watching her framed in the doorway. 'You think I'm a freak.'

She shrugged awkwardly. 'Even freaks need to talk

sometimes. I wouldn't mind talking about it myself, to be honest.'

I stood up slowly, rubbing my hand, waving weakly at the wall as if to say *that was nothing; just forget it ever happened.* 'Come on up, then,' I said. 'My cereal's getting soggy.' I walked back up the stairs and she followed. I sat down to eat, and pointed in the general direction of the cupboard.

'Bowls are in there if you want some.'

'Thanks.' She poured a bowl of cereal and sat down across from me, pressing the flakes down into the milk with her spoon. 'Did you know Rachel well?'

'I don't think I know anyone well.' I took a mouthful, chewed and swallowed. 'She's Marci's best friend, I guess, but we never really did much with her.'

Brooke said, 'I kind of think you're Marci's best friend now.' She smiled, then winced. 'I mean, even before her other best friend died. I'm sorry, that sounded totally bad.'

I shrugged. 'It's hard to make a suicide sound worse than it is. Say whatever you want.'

'I don't know if I have a best friend,' said Brooke, staring at her cereal. She hadn't eaten any yet. 'I knew Rachel pretty well, though; we always got along.' She looked up. 'I remember this one time when we had a slumber party at her house, in seventh grade, and we dared each other to call the boys we liked. She called Brad.' She looked down again. 'I'm glad they got to go to the dance, even just once, before she died.'

I scowled. 'She didn't just die – it's not like she was hit by a meteor or something. This wasn't an act of nature, or an attack, or an accident: she killed herself. She was sitting there, perfectly alive, and said, "You know what? I'm going to end my own life", and now she's gone. What makes a person do that?'

Brooke shook her head. 'I don't know.'

'Mom talked about leaving,' I said. 'We can't, obviously, because scary, dangerous times are the only times we make any money in this pit. We have to take care of the dead; we'll have to take care of Rachel, now. But sometimes I just want to get out. I just want to get out on the highway and drive and drive until I can't even remember this place. Until I get somewhere good.' I laughed without humour. 'I guess everywhere sucks, though.'

Brooke stared at nothing, her eyes wet.

I played with my cereal, tapping the spoon against the bowl, then set it down. 'I thought I could stop it.'

Brooke looked up.

'I thought I could wave a magic wand,' I continued, 'or a knife, or whatever, and make all the killing stop; make all the sadness stop; and no one would ever have to die again. No one would ever go away. But that doesn't happen. People always go away, and it doesn't matter if they're shot or stabbed or hit by a truck or killed by cancer or worn out by old age; it'll never stop.'

'Everybody dies,' said Brooke. 'It's just that not everybody dies when they're supposed to.'

'How do you know when they're supposed to?'

She shrugged. 'You don't. I think you just try to help everyone as much as you can, and even if you only give them one more day, then that's one more day they didn't have before.'

'And you think one more day is going to change anything?'

'I don't know. You can do a lot in one day, I guess, but I think the real people it changes are the ones who do the helping. You know? When you help somebody, even if it's only for one day, then that means you're the kind of person who helps people.' She looked back up. 'I think the world needs more people like that.'

The outside door banged loudly, muffled by the intervening walls, followed by footsteps on the stairs and then another bang as the inner door opened and Mom came in, arms full of groceries.

'John, can you help me with— Oh, Brooke.' She froze in place, mouth open, 'I didn't know you were here. What's up?'

Brooke wiped her eyes with the tips of her sleeves. 'Hi, Mrs Cleaver, we were just talking. Do you need help with the groceries?'

Mom pushed past us to the counter, looking back and forth between us, still surprised. 'No, that's fine, I can manage.' She set her bags on the counter. 'Is everything okay? You've been crying.' She stepped forward. 'You've both been crying.'

'Rachel Farnsworth killed herself,' I said.

Mom's eyes went wide. 'No.'

'It was last night,' I said, 'after the dance, I guess. Brooke just came over to tell me.'

'I'm sorry,' said Brooke.

'Wasn't Rachel in your group for the dance?' asked Mom, sitting down. Her hands were on the table, hovering just above the surface as if she wanted to reach out and hold onto mine; she didn't. 'Did she seem okay?'

'She was kind of depressed all night, actually,' I said. 'I didn't really see her after the police showed up. Brad took her home, and then Marci and I got a ride with her dad.'

'Have you talked to Marci?'

I looked over at Brooke, who grimaced and sucked air through her teeth. I knew that face; it meant she felt guilty.

I shook my head. 'Not yet.'

'I should go,' said Brooke, standing up. 'I didn't mean to take all your time. I'll go so you can call her.'

'Goodbye, Brooke,' said Mom. 'Thanks for coming.'

'Yeah,' said Brooke, and looked at me. I said nothing, and she left.

'Are you sure you're okay?' asked Mom. 'You seem upset, and you don't usually get upset when people die. Is everything all right?'

'I'm not upset because she's dead,' I said, rising up from my chair. 'I'm upset because there's nothing I can do about it.'

I picked up my cereal bowl and carried it to the counter, dumping the dregs into the sink and rinsing it with a burst of water. I held the bowl for a moment, motionless, then placed it carefully on the counter. I set down the spoon next to it, stared at it, then pushed it slightly to the left until it sat parallel to the bowl. It was a perfect table-setting, like a photo from an ad.

'John?'

'It's not right,' I said. I adjusted the spoon again, scooting it closer to the bowl.

'The spoon?'

'The suicide. It's not right. Something's . . . not right.'

'What isn't right?'

'Do I look like I know?' I touched the spoon again, shifting it imperceptibly. I stared beyond it, at everything and nothing. 'It's too perfect.'

'Suicide is perfect?'

'She slit her wrists,' I said. 'Just like Allison Hill, and just like Jenny Zeller. Why?'

'It's a really common way to do it,' said Mom. 'It doesn't mean they're connected.'

I looked up sharply. 'But they are, aren't they?'

'I never said that.'

'But you know it's true. We all do, we just haven't admitted it yet. Too many suicides, and too similar.' I slammed my hand on the counter, suddenly angry. 'Dammit! It's a full-on killing spree right under our noses, and we didn't even think twice!'

'They're suicides, John; these girls are killing themselves.'

'No, they're not,' I said, my mind suddenly alive and racing with the possibilities. *It's so obvious!* 'We're supposed to think they're killing themselves, but they're not. The Handyman is not the only killer in town.'

'You think the police haven't already considered that?' asked Mom. 'If there's any evidence of murder in any of these deaths I guarantee they're following it up.'

'But there's not any evidence,' I said, 'at least not any that the police can recognise. It's a demon.'

She stared at me, silent. I felt my heart pounding with a blend of fear and excitement. *This has to be it! Last night at the dance I knew there had to be another, I knew it couldn't be*

185

the Handyman – and now here it's been, right in plain sight all along.

'Don't tell me you don't see it,' I started, but she cut me off.

'I see it,' she said. Her face was pale. 'I don't want to see it, but I do. It's like an optical illusion: you stare at it and stare at it, and once you finally see it you can't ever not see it again.'

'We're the only ones who can stop it,' I said. 'We're the only ones who know enough to do anything about it.' I ran into the hall. 'I've gotta get dressed and go to Marci's.'

'Wait!' shouted Mom. 'Let's talk about this.'

'That's what I'm going to do.'

'No,' she said, 'I mean you and me, here, together.' Mom followed me into the hall. 'You don't have to bring Marci into it. I'm trying to help you, and I'm right here.'

'Yeah,' I said, 'I know.' I went into my room and closed the door.

'Marci, John's here.'

I was standing in the Jensens' hallway, while Marci's mom knocked on her bedroom door. *Déjà vu.* There was no answer, and her mom knocked again.

'Marci, are you in there?'

'I don't want to see anyone,' said Marci. Her voice was cracked and feeble.

'Not even John?'

'Nobody,' said Marci, and her mom looked at me helplessly.

'I'm sorry, John; she's been like this all morning. Don't worry, she'll come out soon enough. You want a piece of bread?'

'No, thanks,' I said, being careful not to make a face. 'Just tell her to . . .' I paused, desperate to talk about the killers. *There's two!* I wanted to shout. *There's been two all along and we didn't see it!* But her mom was right there beside me, so I couldn't say anything crazy. 'Marci! We need to talk.'

'Not today, John,' she called back. 'Can't you give it a rest?'

Her mom smiled at me sadly. 'I'm sorry, John. You know how she gets.'

I took a deep breath. 'Yeah, I know. Tell her to call me. I don't know.'

'She needs some time alone,' said her mom, leading me back downstairs, 'but it won't be long until she needs you again. Don't worry; she'll call you whether I tell her to or not.' We reached the kitchen, and she picked up a pair of dirty leather gloves. 'I need to get the compost tilled in before it gets too much colder. You sure you don't want a snack or a drink or anything?'

'I'm fine,' I assured her. 'I can show myself out.'

She nodded and went out the back door, and I walked slowly down their dark hall towards the front. It was cold enough now that the front door was finally closed – the first time I'd actually seen it shut. I put my hand on the knob, then froze as I heard a burst of static from the nearest room.

'Officer Jensen, you there?' It was his police radio. I heard the creak of a chair and a rustle of newspaper, then Marci's dad spoke.

'Yeah, Steph, I'm here.' *Stephanie*, I thought, *from the police station*.

'We just got a call from another searcher, out by the lake.

They found another old firepit with some bones in it, and some burned-up gloves – sounds like a bigger glove remnant than we got with Coleman. Moore wants you to go check it out.'

Interesting, I thought. I crept closer.

'How old?' asked Officer Jensen.

'Pretty old,' said Stephanie. 'More likely Pastor Olsen than the Sheriff, assuming it's even legit. Anyway, bag it all and bring it, and we'll see if we get a match.'

'Will do, Steph. See ya.'

'See ya.'

I heard the faint clink of buckles, probably Officer Jensen pulling on his police belt. I couldn't open the front door without him hearing, and I didn't want him to know that I'd been listening, so I slipped out of the hallway and waited in another room, holding my breath. Jensen's footsteps creaked across the floor, into the hall, and then the front door squealed on its hinges. He stepped outside, and the door slammed shut behind him. I took a breath, waited for several seconds, then went to a window and watched him; he walked to his car, got in, and drove away.

Why is the Handyman destroying the hands? I wondered.

I opened the door and walked to my Chevy. It was cold and I shivered, wishing I'd brought a jacket. I turned to look up at Marci's window, where the blinds were closed tightly. *I told Marci that everything was lost, that our whole profile was worthless, but I was wrong. We were right about the religious messages, and we were right about Astrup being next. We just didn't take it seriously enough – we didn't realise that the Handyman would fight back when we messed with her plan. Meier didn't die because we built the wrong profile; he died because the profile was right, and we used it wrong.* I turned away from the house, still shivering, and got into my car.

Two killers: the Handyman and the suicides. I breathed deeply, trying to focus. *Two demons; it makes perfect sense for Nobody to bring back-up. I told her I was going to kill her – she'd be stupid to come alone. So instead she grabbed her friend the Handyman and brought him along, so he could distract me while Nobody hunted. Why didn't I see this before?*

I shook my head. *Everything I thought I knew about Nobody – the entire profile – was actually the Handyman. That puts me back to square one on Nobody, but the profile of the Handyman is still good. If I can find him, he'll lead me to her. I just need to focus.*

The doorbell rang three times before I got up to answer it. I opened the door and froze.

It was Father Erikson.

'Hello, John.'

He found me! My heart jumped into my throat, and I looked desperately at the window as if expecting to be tackled by a swarm of police. There was nothing. I took a step back, poised to bolt.

'That was quite a scene at the dance,' he said. 'I'm told you saved the day.'

So that was it: my big show at the dance. The whole school saw me talking to Ashley. Of course it would get out onto the news. I hadn't even thought to watch it, I was too distracted with Brooke and Rachel and Marci. I glanced at the blank TV, eager to turn it on and see what they were saying, but it was mid-afternoon; the noon show was over, and the evening news wouldn't be on for a few more hours. I sighed.

'You put that together, huh? There's a lot of kids named John, you know. It wasn't necessarily me.'

'Not necessarily,' he said, 'but more likely than not. I took a guess and came over.'

Then he didn't know for sure until I—

'Don't worry,' he said, as if reading my thoughts. 'I recognised the car outside. I would have known it was you whether you opened the door or not.'

I nodded, keeping my face calm, but inside I was terrified. *If the news story is enough for Erikson to put it together and find me, who else is going to find me? Will Nobody put it together as well? The police have tried so hard to keep my involvement with Forman quiet. Will this blow my cover?*

I pushed those thoughts away and looked at the Pastor. *Deal with him first.* 'What do you want?'

'You lied about talking to a counsellor. There's only one at the hospital, and she's never heard of you.'

I shrugged. 'It got you off my back. And it's a good thing. What would have happened at the dance last night if you'd called the police and I wasn't there to help?'

'Technically nothing, from what I hear,' he said. 'The bomb was fake. That doesn't make you any less brave, of course, but it made your attempt to defuse it a lot less vital.'

I smiled thinly. 'Fair enough. You gonna turn me in now? The Homecoming Hero?'

'I don't . . .' He didn't finish the sentence. 'Is your father here?'

'Nope.'

'When will he be back?'

'I've been wondering the same thing for nine years.'

The pastor nodded, as if that explained something important. 'And your mother?'

'Grocery shopping.'

He nodded again. 'You know, I'm not sure I understand you, John. I talk to a lot of troubled cases at the church, and all of them lie now and then, and all of them break promises, but you . . . you're the only one I've met who'll lie to my face and scare me to death and then turn around and risk his own life to help somebody.'

'I'm full of surprises.'

'That you are,' he said. 'Your theory about the Handyman, at the very least, seems to have been proven entirely accurate.' He shifted on his feet, looking over my shoulder at the room beyond.

'Why are you here?' I asked.

'Same thing as before,' he told me. 'I want you to talk to my friend.'

'Because you think I'm going to hurt someone.'

'I think you would benefit from a talk with a therapist.'

I laughed, thin and hollow. 'How many lives do I have to save before you stop thinking I'm a bad guy?'

'We had a deal, John—'

'The deal is off,' I said firmly. *It's time to end this,* I thought. *Act forceful – don't leave any room for argument.* 'You go to the police, and you tell them I talked about killing someone two weeks ago. They'll ask why you didn't report this earlier, and you'll sound like an idiot when all you can say is, "He asked me not to". They'll ask if you have any evidence beyond your own word, and you won't. They'll ask if you're aware that John Cleaver risked his life to save a building full of people, and you'll be officially out of options.' I folded my arms. 'The police like me a lot. But you go ahead and try, if it makes you feel better.'

I watched him carefully, keeping my own face impassive. *Did it work? Did he buy it? If he calls my bluff and goes to the police, I could actually get in a lot of trouble.* I had to hope my confidence convinced him.

He stood on the landing, not speaking. After a moment, he sighed and said, 'I see.' He looked me in the eye, the corners of his mouth turned down, his own eyes dull. *Sadness.* 'Just . . . be careful, John. You're getting into something very dangerous, probably more dangerous than I'm even aware of. If you need anything, please call me.'

I said nothing.

He turned and left.

Chapter 17

Sheriff Meier's body arrived at the mortuary a few days later, on Monday afternoon, and I got home from school just as Mom and Margaret were getting started. I washed up and joined them, cleaning the body and setting the features, smearing the wounds with Vaseline. While we worked I thought about Nobody, trying to piece together what little clues I had about her. *She kills young girls. She makes it look like suicide.*

That was it. That was all I knew. There had been no fingerprints at the scene but the girls' own; no sign of a struggle; no evidence that any of the deaths had been anything but suicide. I supposed it was possible the police knew something they weren't making public, but any secret evidence they had probably still pointed to suicide, or Officer Jensen would be a lot more protective of his daughter.

As I worked on the body I tried several times to roll it over and work on the back, but every time Mom found something else to do first: there was still dirt in his hair, and we had to wash it again; the string in his jaw was too tight, and it was making the nose looked pinched and unnatural. None of it was true – he looked fine. She was stalling.

'We're going to have to roll him over eventually,' I said. 'We can't embalm him until we seal up the back.'

'I know,' she said, grimacing. 'I just don't know if I can handle it. I'm pretty desensitised to this stuff, but still – David Coleman had how many wounds in his back? And how many more is this one going to have?'

I shrugged. 'There's no getting around it.'

She sighed and said, 'Let's do it, then.' We stood on the body's left and lifted it up, flopping it gently down onto its face. We stopped in surprise, mouths open, then bent over the back to look more closely: it was still heavily mangled, but not nearly as bad as Coleman's had been. I started counting, and Mom grabbed the file from the side counter.

'Twenty-two, twenty-three . . .'

'Thirty-four,' she said, looking up from the folder. 'That's even less than Mayor Robinson.'

'And Pastor Olsen had thirty-two,' I said. 'They were all pretty much the same, except Coleman. Why was he different?'

'That's not our concern,' said Mom quickly, snapping the folder closed and setting it aside. 'We're here to make sure Sheriff Meier looks as good for his viewing as he did in life – that's it. We are not investigating this.'

'But it's important.'

'Not for us,' she said again, picking up a jar of Vaseline. 'Let's just be grateful it's not as bad as we thought, and we won't speak of it any more.'

I started to protest again, but she glared at me and I stopped. Margaret glanced at us from her side table, said nothing, then turned back to her work on the organs. I closed my mouth and went to work on the lacerated back.

Three victims, all nearly identical, with a victim in the middle that breaks the pattern. It wasn't just the eyes, it was the back wounds as well. They weren't part of a rising trend, they were an anomalous spike. How does it fit?

What does it mean?

I reviewed the facts as I packed the stab wounds with cotton, struggling to make sense of the chaos. *The Handyman kills, he gets angry, he takes it out on his victims' backs. Something about Coleman made him far more angry than any of the others. So what made him angry?*

The obvious first guess was Coleman's sin. He was the only one killed for looking at porn, underage porn specifically, and that might have a special significance for the killer. Was he traumatised in his youth? Was he abused or molested? But this was an ageless demon we were talking about, not a human. Did they have a youth to be traumatised in? Could they even be traumatised at all?

But the more I thought about it, the less likely it seemed. The Handyman had already reacted to the porn by taking Coleman's eyes, and he had done it as coldly and clinically as he had the hands and tongue. The rage in evidence on Coleman's back was separate, and was sparked by something else. As odd as it seemed, I had to consider the possibility that the two anomalies in Coleman's corpse were unrelated. Something made the Handyman so mad that he lost control more than he ever had before. *An external force? Something in his personal life?* I felt completely bewildered. I didn't even know if he had a personal life.

We finished packing the stab wounds and smeared them with Vaseline, covering them tightly with bandaging tape and rolling the body back over. Mom began to prepare the embalming fluid, and I used a scalpel and hook to open the corpse's collar and pull out a vein. We slit it open, inserted the tubes, and turned on the pump.

Marci and I had already talked about the back wounds weeks ago, sitting in the office during the Mayor's funeral; we'd hypothesised that the cause of the anger was the killing itself. Something about the act of killing enrages him. But then why kill at all?

We know why he kills, I thought. *He wants to punish the guilty. But what prompts that desire? What mechanism clicks inside of his head and says, 'Now is the time to kill'?* Each victim had been fifteen days apart, except for the last one: Sunday, Monday, Tuesday, and Tuesday. Did the days mean anything, or just the time between them? Was the most recent killing a day early, or was the daily pattern simply a coincidence?

I looked at the calendar on the wall, a large poster of a beach resort with all twelve months printed in tiny blocks at the bottom. Mom watched me, probably guessing that I was thinking about the killings, but I ignored her and stepped up to the wall, pulling off my rubber gloves and tapping each death date with my finger: *8 August, 23 August, 7 September, 21 September.* That didn't tell me anything I didn't already know, so I began looking for other dates, grabbing a pen off the counter and marking everything I could think of. *Here's the attack at the dance. Here's when Coleman was fired. This is when they found the pastor's hands, and this is when they found the Mayor's . . .*

Saturday, 4 September. He burned the Mayor's hands, and was almost caught doing it, just three days before he turned

Coleman's back into hamburger. It was the closest relationship between any of the dates I'd marked.

I stared at the calendar, my mind racing, kicking myself for not seeing it before. *He was almost caught – is that what made him mad?* But no – the Handyman had written letters to the paper, and then forced Ashley to read another letter at the dance. It wasn't the revelation of evidence that made him angry, so it had to be something else. Some other aspect of the burning. *What did he do that he didn't have to do?* He didn't have to run. He could have stayed by the fire and waved as the hikers went past, and no one would have suspected a thing. They only saw the lumps because they got up close and poked through the fire, and they only got close because his running made them suspicious. He didn't have to run, but he did. Why?

It all came back to guilt: he ran because he didn't want anyone to see what he'd done. He felt guilty; he felt ashamed. He killed because his victims were sinners, but killing was also a sin, and he knew it. That's what made him angry enough to stab the bodies more than thirty times, and that's what made him go out and burn the hands in a ritual cleansing . . .

A ritual.

What if he wasn't finished?

The Handyman's attacks showed strong signs of ritual behaviour – the way he planned them so carefully, the way he killed so precisely, and the way he posed and displayed the bodies. What if this ritual extended long after the kill, to a ceremonial destruction of the victim's last remaining pieces? He'd done it with the pastor and with Coleman, and he'd tried to do it with Mayor Robinson, but the hikers had stumbled in and scared him away before he could finish. He used that ritual to absolve his guilt and diffuse his rage, and without that emotional release all his rage would have continued building and building until it exploded on Mr Coleman in an animalistic fury. Sixty-four stab wounds. It made sense.

It *almost* made sense. From what Officer Jensen had said, the Mayor's hands and tongue had still been destroyed by the fire; there was no real flesh left, just charred bones and lumps of what used to be meat. What else was there to do? A prayer he hadn't said? A curse he hadn't spoken? What was different about that day's ritual?

The gloves.

Stephanie had talked about gloves – remnants of burned gloves that had been in the fire with Coleman's hands, and now in the fire with the pastor's hands. There had been no gloves in the fire with Mayor Robinson's. That was the missing piece – that was the difference that had made his next attack so violent: *he hadn't been able to burn his gloves.*

But what did the gloves mean? He wore gloves when he killed, so they were evidence, but a ritual like this implied far more than simply burning evidence. He destroyed his victims' hands because they represented the sins that made his victims guilty; if he was equating hands with sin, it was no great stretch to think that the gloves represented his own hands, and his own sins. Over and over, kill after kill. What had he said at the end of his letter? *The city will be purified by fire.* He was using the fire to burn away his sins, and that one time he hadn't been able to do it. For all his bluster, for all his talk of righteous judgment, he knew deep down that he was just as guilty as we were. Maybe more so.

And that is the gap in his armour.

I stepped back from the calendar, looking quickly around the room. Margaret was still in the corner, cleaning the removed organs, and Mom was fidgeting with the pump. She looked up, met my eyes, then turned back to the pump with her lips pressed together. The sound of the embalming pump filled the room, a rhythmic heartbeat, and I breathed deeply. *I have him,* I thought. *I've cracked his code, and I know how he thinks.*

I still didn't know what this demon's powers were, though his reliance on mundane weapons made me suspect that he didn't have claws or super-strength or anything like that. Nobody still might – I knew virtually nothing about her so I needed to be careful of her. They were probably working together: he'd make a spectacle of himself to draw my attention, and as soon as I thought I had him, Nobody would jump out and attack me from behind.

I needed to find a way to separate them. *I need to lay a trap,* I thought. *I know the Handyman now; I can lure him somewhere and trap him like a rat.* Once he was contained, I'd only have to deal with one demon at a time.

Phase One: I need to make him really, really mad.

Chapter 18

Dear Editor

The Handyman killer has announced to our community that he has come to purify our town; to save Clayton from the evil men who would lead her into temptation and sin.

Forgive me if I call his bluff: nothing could be further from the truth! Are we to believe that this cold-blooded killer is a paragon of virtue? Are we to accept this unrepentant sinner as our spiritual guide? The Scriptures tell us, 'By their fruits ye shall know them,' and the Handyman's fruits are unmistakably evil. He is a monster, a sinner more vile than the righteous men he claims to have punished, and we would do well to ignore him.

To the Handyman himself, I have this to say: 'Come back to the fold. The sins you have committed can be washed away; the heavy burdens that weigh you down can be lifted. Your hands can be made clean. It will be long, and it will be difficult, but under the guidance of the Lord's servants you can be purified again.

'Look not to false prophets. Trust in the Church, and in its leaders. We will not lead you astray.'

Sincerely,
Father Brian Erikson

'You ready?'

Marci opened the door. 'You better believe it. What do you think of the shirt?' She was wearing a black shirt with short, kind of puffy sleeves.

'Yeah, it looks great. You've shown me that one before.'

'I've got so many,' she laughed, 'it's hard to keep track.'

'I'm glad you're feeling better.'

'I feel great,' she said. 'I feel perfect.' She smiled. 'Where we going?'

'We don't have to go anywhere,' I said, shrugging. It was getting too cold to go biking, or hiking, or any of the other things Marci typically liked to do. We'd spent the last couple of days hanging out at her house, watching TV or playing cards, and that was fine with me. The paper hadn't run my letter yet, and I was too on edge to do much of anything else.

'I can't stand it in here any more,' she said. 'I need to get out – I need to see the world again.'

'Sounds good to me. Any part of the world in particular?'

'Food first,' she said, following me out to the car. 'Something greasy and disgusting. The food in this house is almost too healthy to eat.' I chuckled, and we got in my car. 'Friendly Burger,' she said, buckling her belt. 'I haven't been there in a while.'

I nodded, and pulled out from the kerb. Friendly Burger was one of those places you only ever see in small towns: a burger joint owned, operated and patronised purely by the locals. The sign was a giant wooden cut-out of a smiling cheeseburger with two little arms, giving a thumbs-up; you could see it for blocks.

'You know what I love about this place?' asked Marci, as the sign came into view. 'It doesn't have any franchises.'

'And that makes you love it?'

'It means it's the only one,' she said. 'You go anywhere in the world and you'll find a McDonald's. But there's only one Friendly Burger, and it's only here. It's completely unique.'

'So it's only awesome because nobody else wants one?'

'Oh, I think everybody wants one; everyone who's been there, at least. What makes it awesome is that they refuse to sell out.'

We pulled into the lot and parked under the sign.

'You know what I always wonder about this place?' I said, pointing up. 'It's that sign. Would a hamburger really give a thumbs-up if he knew you were going to eat him?'

'Maybe being eaten is the culmination of all a hamburger's desires. It's like their heaven.'

'But what if there was something that ate humans? And what if they started a chain of restaurants where you could buy people-burgers? Would you pose for a sign and smile and wave about how happy you were to get eaten?'

'Not if it was a franchise,' she said, grinning slyly. 'I only pose for the one-of-a-kind people-burger places.'

'At least you have standards.'

'Now let's stop anthropomorphising our food and start

202

eating it. I've got six whole grains like a rock in my stomach, and I need some grease and ketchup to break it down.'

We went inside and waited in line; it was fairly crowded, even on a Tuesday night, and we stood chatting with various people Marci knew. She chatted; I just stood there, holding her hand. We didn't need to read the menu, because it hadn't changed in five years.

'Hey, John.'

I looked up in surprise and saw Brooke standing behind the counter, wearing a little paper Friendly Burger hat. It was our turn, and we stepped up to the counter.

'Hey, Marci,' she said, 'how's it going?'

'Great,' said Marci, her mouth hanging slightly open. 'I didn't know you worked here.'

'It's only been a couple of weeks,' said Brooke, 'since school started, I guess. I was at the parks all summer, on the water crew, so when fall came I needed something new.'

'Cool,' said Marci. 'You like it here?'

'Depends what I'm doing,' said Brooke, laughing and rolling her eyes. 'The counter's not so bad, but sooner or later somebody's got to clean the pop machines.' Her eyes went wide. 'I mean, they get cleaned every day, of course, I just don't like to be the one who does it. Sorry, that sounded gross.'

'No problem,' said Marci, and leaned in privately. 'Anything we should stay away from?'

'Of course not,' Brooke said loudly, glancing over her shoulder, then tapped the paper menu on the counter, pointing at the chicken nuggets. Marci raised her eyebrows, and Brooke nodded.

'Two Friendly Burgers, then,' said Marci. 'You want cheese, John?'

'Actually, can I get the fish fillet?'

She stared at me, then laughed and said, 'Of course, sorry – the meat thing. One Friendly Burger, one Friendly Fish. We'll share a fry and a drink.'

Brooke wrote the order on a small spiral notebook, ripped out the page, and started punching it into the cash register. I dug out my wallet and reached inside it for bills. She gave me the total, I handed her the money, and she opened the register to make change.

'Kind of funny, isn't it?' she said, counting out coins.

'Huh?'

'Last time we were here,' said Brooke, 'we were on that side of the counter, and now here am I on this side.'

Marci took my hand again, slightly tighter than before, and rested our balled-up hands on the counter. 'You guys had a date here?'

'Not really anywhere else to go,' I said.

'Yeah,' said Brooke. 'It was . . .' Her face fell. 'The night Forman took . . .' She looked around at the crowded room. 'Well, you know, I guess.' She handed me my change, suddenly quiet. 'Number 78.'

Marci and I stepped away from the counter to wait for our order, and Brooke smiled broadly at the next couple in line. She looked bright and happy, eager to talk to people, and beautiful even in her hideous Friendly Burger shirt.

Marci grabbed me in a hug, wrapping her arms tightly around my waist. I looked at her in surprise and saw her staring across the counter at Brooke. 'Kind of weird of her to mention her last date with you.'

'That's just how she is,' I said. 'She talks without thinking. If she knew you were upset about it she'd feel horrible.'

'Maybe,' said Marci, and then she turned and smiled up at me, filling my vision. 'I've got you now, though, don't I?'

I smiled back down, enjoying her closeness. Absolutely.'

Our food came, and we found the cleanest table we could. Marci filled the centre of our tray with a huge blob of ketchup, and stirred it idly with a cluster of fries.

'What was he like?' she asked, staring at her ketchup.

'Who?'

'Clark Forman. I saw him a few times, of course, but I didn't really know him. Not like you did. Not like Brooke.'

'Brooke was only there for a few hours,' I said, watching the ketchup as she played with it – deep and red, like thick blood. 'Forman was dead for most of that time, anyway. And I was there two days, I guess, but I still don't think I "knew" him. I knew "about" him, though; enough to get away from him.'

'He was horrible,' she said, spitting out the words like they tasted vile. 'He was a monster, and he deserves whatever death he got.' She looked up, meeting my eyes. 'I still can't believe you had to go through that.'

I stared back at her, trying to read her face: bitterness, and anger, but also tenderness. She lifted her hand from where it rested on the table, and reached across to hold my arm. *Is this affection, or is she being possessive?* I glanced back at the far side of the room, to the counter where Brooke was talking; just a tiny glance, a fraction of a second. Marci tightened her grip.

'When we were in Forman's house,' I said, trying to move her thoughts away from Brooke, 'I spent most of the time locked up – alone, for the first night, then in the basement for another day and a night.'

'It must have been horrifying.'

'I suppose,' I said. 'I think I was more angry than scared. I'm not as emotional as most people. When everyone else was traumatised, I was able to think it through and find a way out.'

'That's what makes you better than them,' she said firmly.

'Better?'

'You're the one that saved everyone, right?'

'Yeah.'

She nodded, and looked back down at her ketchup. She stirred it again, then put the fries in her mouth, chewed, and swallowed. 'So, how are the plans to save everyone from the Handyman?'

I cocked my head to the side, confused. *I guess she's gotten over whatever was bugging her about it at the dance.*

'Not bad,' I said. 'If all goes well, he might not ever kill anyone else.'

She looked up. 'Does it usually go well?'

I shook my head. 'It never has before.'

On Wednesday morning I got up early again and watched out the window for the paperboy. He came at 6 a.m., tossing the newspaper in the general direction of the mortuary, and I raced outside in the cold to get it. Back inside, I ripped off the rubber band and spread the paper out on the kitchen table, searching for the editorial page. There it was, right at the top of the *Letters to the Editor* section: my letter to the Handyman, attributed to Father Erikson. *They actually printed it.* I was worried they would hold it back as too controversial, or call and check with Erikson before they ran it, but they didn't. They took the name at face value, thought it was a message of hope in troubled times, and printed it.

Everyone would read it that way, except for the Handyman. To him, this was practically a dinner bell.

I need to call Erikson, I thought, but I forced myself to be patient. This had to look convincing or he'd never believe me. If I called too soon he might suspect that I was the one who wrote the letter, and then he'd never go along with my plan. I sat on my hands, then paced the room, then turned on the TV, flipped through the channels, and turned it off. *What if the Handyman sees the letter as early as I did, and decides to kill him now instead of waiting for nightfall?* The two weeks was up – if he waited fifteen days, like he usually did, the Handyman would strike that very night: Wednesday. If he got back on his old schedule, he might wait until Thursday – *and if he struck early, like he had before, then I'm already too late, and he killed somebody last night.*

I turned the TV back on, combed through it for news, but there was nothing about another body. I turned it back off and started pacing again.

Waiting was agony.

Finally, when Mom started to get up at eight o'clock, I took the phone into my room, locked the door and dialed the priest's home number. He picked it up on the second ring.

'Hello?'

Showtime. 'Father Erikson? You're okay?'

'Who is this?'

'It's me,' I said, 'John Cleaver – the kid who talks about demons all the time.'

'Oh.' Pause. 'Do you need something?'

'I need to see if you were okay,' I said, trying to sound urgent. 'I just read your letter in the paper, and I thought something might have happened.'

'What letter?'

'Your letter to the editor – I just read it. I don't know what you were thinking when you wrote it, but the Handyman is going to be seriously pissed off.'

'I didn't write a letter to the editor.'

'Sure you did,' I said. 'It's right here: "The Handyman killer has announced to our community that he has come to purify our town". I'm sure the paper thought it was innocent enough, but—'

'I didn't write that,' he said. 'Does it have my name on it?'

' "Father Brian Erikson",' I said. 'Isn't that you?'

'That's my name, but I didn't write it.' Pause. 'What else does it say?'

'Who do you think wrote it, then?' I asked.

'I have no idea,' he said, and I heard a door close over the phone. 'What else does it say?'

'A whole bunch of stuff tailor-made to enrage the Handyman,' I said, 'including his hatred of authority and his focus on religion. You know how mad that's going to make him. You even called him out as a sinner.'

'I told you, it's not me.' I heard another door close.

'Let me read it to you—'

'Never mind, I've got mine right here.' I heard the rustling of paper, followed by a long silence. After a minute or two he spoke again: 'I have to hang up, John. I need to call the paper and—'

'No!' I said. 'You have to get out of here.'

'Out?'

'Don't you see what this means? Whether you wrote that letter or not, the Handyman thinks you did, and that almost guarantees you'll be his next target.'

'But—'

'And if you didn't write it, that means someone else did it in your name to make you a target. That means there's two people who want you dead.'

Pause. 'How can you be so sure?'

'Read it again,' I said, looking over my own copy. 'The Handyman is obsessed with religion, and with authority figures. By his own admission, in the letter he sent to the Homecoming Dance, he's here to purify the town by killing the people who lead us astray. That suggests a very strong sense of buried guilt stemming from a religious background – that's Criminal Profiling 101. This letter throws that sense of guilt right back in his face, and from a religious leader, which makes it even worse. Then you've got the way the letter flaunts your own superiority, and tells the town to ignore his message. The Handyman's message is so important to him that he threatened an entire school with a bomb. Telling people to ignore it, and to follow you instead, is like asking to be killed.'

Silence.

'This letter uses the Handyman's own words against him,' I continued, 'with phrases like "you can be purified", and "we will not lead you astray".' *It also talks about the killer's hands*, I thought; that would probably set him off more than anything else in the letter, but I didn't want to mention that to Erikson. There was no way to explain the significance of it without revealing how much I knew, and that would only make me look suspicious.

'Basically,' I went on, 'you attack everything he believes in, you insult what he's trying to do, and you dredge up the same emotional wounds that probably made him into a killer in the first place.'

'But I didn't write the letter—'

'It doesn't matter who wrote it!' I shouted, a little too loudly; I was trying to sound desperate, and I hoped it was working. 'It doesn't matter who wrote it,' I repeated more quietly. 'What matters is that your name is on it, and that's all the killer is going to see. You're the next target, whether you like it or not.'

Silence.

'What if he doesn't read the paper?'

'He's written two letters to the editor; he reads the paper.'

More silence. 'Okay,' he said at last. 'You're right. But if the paper can print a retraction—'

'Then you'll look like a guilty coward, trying to go back on what you said.'

'Then I need to call the police.'

'So another one of them can die?' I asked. 'I tried to warn the police two weeks ago, after you and I figured out the religious connection, and they tried to protect William Astrup;

210

the killer found out about it and killed the Sheriff in retribution. For all we know, the killer *is* one of the police. Do you really want someone to die trying to protect you?'

'What else am I supposed to do? I can't just sit around and wait for him to kill me.'

This is it. 'You can leave,' I said. 'You can pack some things and get out of town – visit some family in the city, or go on a vacation you've been meaning to take – anything. If you're gone he can't kill you, and if there's no police protecting you then he can't kill them either.'

'What about my neighbours?'

'As long as you don't tell them anything, they're innocent,' I said, 'and the Handyman goes out of his way to keep innocents safe. Look at the Homecoming Dance – the bomb was fake and his gun wasn't even loaded.'

'He protects them until he gets into a rage,' the pastor said. 'Then they just become targets of opportunity. He attacked the Mayor's assistant, and he was just a bystander.'

'But he didn't kill him,' I said, 'and he only attacked him because it was part of his plan. He's too meticulous for targets of opportunity. If he can't kill you, on the terrain he's scoped out and prepared for, he won't kill anybody at all.'

'You really think so?'

No. 'Of course,' I lied. 'This is a very careful, very organised man.'

'Then he'll follow me,' the pastor said, 'and catch me while I'm leaving town.'

'Not if you leave now. It's only eight o'clock – he may not have even read the paper yet. Get out while you can, and come back in a week when it's safe.'

Pause. 'I won't be safe until he's caught,' said the pastor. 'I'm going to leave, but tonight I'm going to call the police and ask them to patrol the neighbourhood. If he's there, looking for me, they might pick him up, and if I don't tell them until late they won't have time to tip their hand with a stakeout.'

No! I was going to use your house as the trap. But his suggestion made sense, and I couldn't think of any way to talk him out of it without sounding suspicious. 'That's a good idea.' *Maybe I can use the mortuary – it's on the edge of town, in a neighbourhood with no streetlights. I'll have to get rid of Mom.*

'And you, John,' he said. 'I want you to promise me you won't get involved.'

'Of course.'

'Of course you'll promise me, or of course you'll get involved?'

Tricky guy, this pastor. 'I promise I won't get involved,' I lied. *If I had a nickel for every time I broke a solemn promise . . .*

'Good,' he said. 'I'll tell the police to watch for you, too, just in case.'

'You don't trust me?'

'I'm leaving town on your recommendation,' he said. 'I think that speaks for itself. I'm grateful that you called to warn me, but I want to make sure you're safe.'

'Thank you,' I said, tapping my notebook with the early drafts of the letter. 'I promise I'll stay away.'

We hung up, and I scouted around the mortuary a bit, looking for good places to hold someone. All of the obvious choices were *too* obvious – I couldn't just tell him to get into the closet and expect him to comply. It had to be somewhere he would naturally go anyway, and that meant the entry – but our main doors had glass, and it would be far too easy to escape.

Our side door, on the other hand, was perfect. There was a solid wooden door that led into a small stairway; from there you could go through another solid wooden door into the mortuary, or up to a third wooden door that led into our apartment. I'd need to barricade those doors even further, to stop a desperate demon armed with a hatchet, but I could do it, and it could work.

Time for Phase Two.

Chapter 19

Half an hour later I said goodbye to my mom and left the house, but instead of driving to school I parked a half a block from Father Erikson's house and waited, watching. True to his word, he emerged a while later with a suitcase, got in his car, and drove away. I waited a few minutes, just to be sure, then pulled into his driveway and slipped into the backyard. Normally I'd try to sneak in more subtly, but his call to the police tonight would take care of that – anything I did to the house would be blamed on the Handyman. I put my foot through a basement window, reached in carefully to unlatch it, and climbed inside.

The priest's house was surprisingly mundane – no basement full of weird religious paraphernalia, just stacks of old furniture and boxes full of airplane magazines. I went upstairs and found the priest's home to be just as neat and well-kept as it had been the other night.

If the Handyman was going to attack the priest, he wouldn't leave anything to chance: he needed to know his victim would be here when he came, and he needed assurance that he'd trust him enough to let him inside. In other words, he needed to call ahead and make an appointment. All I had to do was make sure that call came to me. Wearing gloves, I picked up the phone and hit the button for voicemail. The system asked for a password, and I typed in the standard default of 1234. It didn't work. *Crap.* I needed the Handyman to talk to me directly so I could set everything up. *Do I dare stay here all day? I don't want to be seen here, by him or by the police. What will he do if he calls and gets voicemail instead? No,* I decided, *he won't dare leave a recording of his voice. There's something about it – an accent, maybe, like I'd thought before – that scares him so much he didn't say a word at the dance.* He'd look for another number, and call the church. Maybe I'd have more luck there.

Hanging on a row of nails in the kitchen were a series of keys – spare keys to the church building, I assumed. I took them all and drove to St Mary's. The parking lot was empty, and I went around to the back and started trying keys. One of them worked, and I put it into a separate pocket so I could remember which one it was. The church was large and empty and quiet, lit with a vaguely yellow light from the wavy, tinted windows. I wandered around, peeking into classrooms and storage closets, until at last I found the pastor's office and tried more of the keys. Another one worked, so I dropped it into the same pocket as the first and let myself in.

The office was sparse, with various pictures and statues of Jesus the only real decoration, though there was a calendar on the wall with more airplane photos. I thought about simply waiting in the chapel, but I didn't know who else might have a key and show up during the day. I didn't want any interruptions or bystanders. I picked up the office phone, hit the voicemail button, and tried the 1234 password again. It worked this time, and I almost laughed. *I guess he doesn't expect anyone to break into a church.* I listened carefully to the voicemail options, found the one for call forwarding, and entered the number for Forman's cellphone. I confirmed the forward and left the church.

I was ready for the demon's call, but I still didn't know how the demon worked. I needed to be ready for anything. I got in my car and drove to Max's house for Phase Three: steal a gun.

While I was driving, the phone rang.

I looked at the caller ID – it was nothing I recognised, and it wasn't in the phone's memory. Probably a local number. I answered carefully.

'Hello?'

Silence. 'I'm sorry,' said an elderly female voice, 'I thought this was the number for Saint Mary's.'

Is this really an old lady, or is it a fake-out from the Handyman? Is it Nobody, calling on his behalf?

'This is Saint Mary's,' I said quickly. *I have to keep him talking.* 'Can I help you?'

'Well,' she said slowly, 'is Father Erikson there?'

'May I ask who's calling?'

'It's Fran from the sewing circle; he knows me.'

Do I trust her? Would the Handyman disguise himself as Fran from the sewing circle? How would he do it – how would he even know about her? I shook my head. *This is probably a real call.*

'I'll let him know you called,' I said. 'Thanks.' I hung up and pulled onto Max's street. His car was still in his driveway, and I stopped to think. I couldn't very well break into his house with him still in it.

I looked at the clock on the dash: 10.30 a.m. There wasn't any reason for him to be home this time of day unless he was sick, and that meant he wouldn't be leaving any time soon. If I wanted to get in, I'd need to talk to him. I parked by the kerb, walked up to the door and knocked.

He opened it, saw me and frowned; he was wearing a long black coat, slightly too long in the sleeves so that it hid his hands. 'What do you want?'

'How you doing?' I asked.

'Where's your girlfriend?'

'School, I guess. I'm ditching today.'

'Yeah,' he said, then repeated, 'What do you want?'

'I'm just saying hi. Why aren't you at school?'

'Why aren't you?'

'No reason.'

He looked past me, out to my car at the street. 'Is Marci with you?'

'No.'

'Why not?'

I glanced back at the street. 'Is that good or bad?'

He half-shrugged, half-shook his head; his eyes were blank. 'Can I come in?'

He sneered, or tried to, but he sighed halfway through and stepped back, opening the door wider. I stepped in, and he walked to the couch, leaving the door open. I closed it.

'You okay?' I asked.

'Like you care.'

'I just thought you'd be happier to see me. We haven't hung out in a couple of months.'

217

'Yippee,' he said, falling onto the couch. 'My best friend's not ignoring me any more.'

'I wasn't ignoring you.'

'Thank you, oh great and wonderful John, for descending from your place among the gods to speak to me. I apologise for failing to leap with joy upon seeing you.'

'You don't have to be that way about it.'

'Excuse me, then.'

'Look, I just thought I'd drop by and say hi. You don't have to make a huge deal out of it.'

'Where have you been for two months? What have you been doing?'

'I've been hanging out with Marci—'

'You've been hanging out with a huge group of hot girls, and it never occurred to you, even once, that I might like to hang out with some hot girls too. We've eaten lunch together every day for six fracking years, and then Marci shakes her boobs at you and I get dropped like a hot rock.'

'So this is about Marci?'

'Yeah,' he said, sneering properly this time. 'It's about Marci.' It was a face and voice he made a lot, though it was harsher now than usual, and I recognised it as sarcasm. That meant there was something else, but I had no idea what it might be.

'Sure,' I said, leaning against the front door. 'Like you wouldn't have done the same thing.'

'Whatever.' He stared at the TV for a moment – some action movie full of guns and shouting – then stood up abruptly. 'I need to take a dump.' He walked into the bathroom, turned on the fan, and locked the door.

I counted to five, waiting for him to open the door and yell something else, but nothing happened; I crept silently down the hall to his mom's bedroom and started looking for guns. I knew his dad used to keep one in the closet, but there was nothing on the top shelf, and the small dresser shoved in under the hanging clothes was filled with nothing but socks and underwear. I went quickly to the end table by the bed, found nothing, and then started digging under the bed. There was nothing.

The front door clicked open, and I froze.

'Max, are you home?'

It was his little sister, Audrey; she was eight, and I had assumed she'd be in school too. Max was still in the bathroom, and didn't answer her; with the fan running, he might not have heard her. I took a step towards the hall, but jumped back lightly when I heard Audrey's footsteps coming towards me. I slipped behind the door and held my breath; she walked past me down the hall, went into her own room and closed the door. I hurried back out to the living room, jogging on my toes to stay silent, and reached the door just as Max came out of the bathroom.

He looked at me, almost expressionless. 'You just been standing there the whole time?' I tried to think of a response, but he noticed Audrey's backpack on the floor and shouted loudly, 'Audrey!'

'What!' Her voice was muffled by the closed door.

'What are you doing home?'

'What are *you* doing home?'

'We're ditching, and you'd better not tell.'

'You and who else?'

219

Max looked at me, then back down the hall, puzzled. 'Me and John, stupid. What are you doing home?'

'I'm sick; the nurse sent me home.'

'Shut up, liar, the nurse calls Mom.'

'Mom told me to wait here.'

'Is she coming home early?'

'No.'

Max stared down the hall, like he was trying to think of something else to say, then kicked his bag and stalked into the kitchen. 'There's never any food in this stupid house.'

What can I do now? I thought. I can't look for guns with him standing right next to me, and I can't just leave him here and start wandering through his house. I followed Max into the kitchen and sat at the table, but he walked past me back into the living room, holding a bag of corn chips.

'Come on,' he grumbled.

I weighed my options – the basement stairs were right there, and he couldn't see me from his spot on the couch; I could slip down and look, but how long would it take before he came looking for me? I hesitated, not sure what to do, when I heard Audrey's door open and her footsteps in the hall. She went in the bathroom and closed the door.

I smiled. *Perfect.* I walked into the living room. 'Hey Max, can I use your bathroom?'

'Fine with me.'

'But Audrey's in it.'

'So use the downstairs one; I'm not your jail warden.'

I nodded and walked slowly to the stairs, trying not to appear excited. Once I was downstairs I started opening doors – there was Max's room, there was the bathroom, there was the furnace, there was a storage room . . .

Wait; back in the furnace room. I opened the door again and clicked on a light that hung from the ceiling, but it was faint and pale; giant blocks and cylinders rose up in the blackness, a furnace and a boiler and a water softener, all capped with a network of twisting pipes and ducts. A tall black shape loomed in the back corner, gleaming metallically in the dim light. A gun safe.

I walked back to it, ducking under the pipes that ran overhead. It was black and thick, like cast iron, though I was sure it was hardened steel. Blood-red lines ran around the borders, and a bright silver handle sat in the centre of the door. Above, encased in some kind of metal ring, was a number pad.

Crap.

I wiggled the handle, but it was locked. I peered closely at the number pad, as if it held some clue to breaking its own security, but of course there was nothing. *It was Max's dad who was the gun nut, not his mom,* I thought. *I've got to put myself into his mind, like a mini-profile.* I paused. *No, I've got to put myself into hers – she's the one in charge now. Does she care about the guns? No, she cares about her children. She doesn't lock this up because she's worried about burglars, she locks it up to make sure Audrey doesn't accidentally shoot herself. She doesn't have time to deal with guns she never uses, which means she doesn't have the combination memorised, which means it's written down somewhere. It might be somewhere nearby.* I looked behind it on the floor, up on the shelves that flanked the wall, but there was nothing to help me. *Where would I hide a safe combination from an eight year old?* Realisation hit me. *On top of a very tall safe.* I pulled over a bucket, being careful to be as quiet as possible, and stood on it to reach the top—

The cellphone rang, startling me, and I stumbled backwards off the bucket. I braced myself against the wall, caught my breath, and the phone rang again. I pulled it out, but the phone didn't recognise the number. *Another old lady.* I ignored it, but it rang again, and I started to worry that Max would hear. I pulled it out and answered it.

'Hello?'

'Hi,' said a man's voice. 'Is this the Saint Mary's Cathedral?'

'Yeah, about that,' I said, but stopped. There was something about his voice – it was friendly and cheerful, that was easy enough to tell, but there was something else. What was it? *I hate trying to read voices over the phone.*

'Yes,' I said slowly. I needed to hear him talk again. 'Can I help you?'

'I'm sure you can,' he said, and I recognised an East Coast accent – Boston, maybe, or New York. I didn't really know accents, but he definitely had one. *Exactly like I'd predicted when the Handyman refused to talk to Ashley.* 'I'm looking for Father Erikson.'

It's not a Georgia accent, I thought, *but that makes sense. It explains why no one got suspicious when they heard it.*

No one but me. Am I being paranoid, or is the profile I created actually turning out to be accurate?

'I'm afraid he's unavailable at the moment,' I said, trying to think of some way to keep him talking. 'I'm his assistant, though. Is there anything I can help you with?' *Do Catholic priests even have assistants?*

'He has an assistant?' asked the voice. *Crap, I guess they don't.*

'It's a big congregation,' I said. 'He asked me to help coordinate stuff and make appointments and so on.' I'm such a better liar when I have time to prepare.

'I see,' said the man. 'You wouldn't happen to know when I'd be able to talk to him, would you?'

'That depends on what you want to talk to him about,' I said, climbing back up on the bucket. 'Why don't you tell me what you want, and I'll see if I can help you.' I got a better look at the top of the safe this time, and was pleased to see a yellow piece of paper, lined, like from a legal pad, stuck down with clear plastic tape. There was a series of numbers written on it in flowing, feminine handwriting.

Yes!

'I see,' he said again. 'Well, it just so happens I'm a reporter; I was in Georgia covering the Handyman killings, and when he came here I followed him to stay on top of the story. I was real taken by Pastor Erikson's letter in the paper today, and I wonder if he might consent to an interview.'

A reporter, I thought. *It could be perfectly true – or it could be the ideal cover for a killer. It would give him the ideal excuse to talk to all four victims, and it would earn him their instant trust: he asks for an interview, they let him in, and the first time they turn around he shoots them in the back.*

More than that, his cover as a reporter would give him a foot in the door when it came time to publicise his message. The Handyman had mentioned in his letter at the dance that he'd tried to contact a reporter when his first letter failed to see print.

Was it a real reporter, or did he simply take his letter to the paper personally and claim that the killer had contacted him?

I needed to learn more about him, and it was worth a shot. 'Have you been working with the local paper?' I asked.

'I have indeed, sir.'

'Do you happen to know which reporter the Handyman contacted?'

The voice coughed. 'As a matter of fact, it was myself that he contacted. Musta thought I had more pull with the paper than I did, I guess.'

'I guess so,' I said. *This had to be the Handyman – it seemed so obvious! But no, it was only obvious to me because I'd spent two months getting inside his head. Nothing he'd said so far would seem suspicious to anyone else.*

This was my demon; it was time to set the trap. I read the numbers on the piece of paper, typed them into the keypad on the safe, and breathed a sigh of relief when the door clicked open.

'I think the pastor would be delighted to speak with you,' I said, stepping down to the floor and pulling open the safe. It was filled with rifles, pistols and shotguns, and with plenty of ammunition for each. *Jackpot.* 'Is tonight too early?'

'Not at all,' he said, 'though I'm afraid I'm not available until fairly late. Say, around nine o'clock?'

After dark, naturally. 'That should be fine,' I said. 'There's only one problem: the pastor's gotten several similar calls today, and all the attention has him worried that the Handyman might try to attack him in reprisal for his note. If it's all right with you, he'd like to meet in private at a place where no one else will find him.' *That should excite this guy.*

224

Pause. 'That seems like a very good idea.'

Yeah, I thought you'd like that. 'The pastor has a key to the local mortuary,' I said, 'to help maintain the chapel. The mortician and her family will be gone tonight, so if you'd like to meet him there, that will be the most private location.'

'I suppose that's okay.' I tried to read his voice: was he upset? Suspicious? Pleased? I wished I could see his face.

'Just remember,' I said, 'do not tell anyone. At all. The only people who know this right now are you, the pastor, and me. He's really trying to lay low, and we don't want anyone else to know where he is.' *Now we'll see if he's concerned about me, as the only potential witness.*

'I understand,' he said. 'That makes a lot of sense – I won't tell anybody. Are you going to be there tonight as well?'

I can read you like a book, I thought, smiling. *You have no idea what you're getting into.*

'I wasn't planning on it,' I said carefully. 'Do you think you'll need me?'

'I think it will be best,' said the reporter. 'Why don't you come too?'

'Sure thing. I'll see you tonight at nine o'clock.'

'See you—'

'Wait,' I said, before he hung up. 'I'm afraid I still didn't catch your name.'

'Uh, Harry,' said the reporter. 'Harry Poole.'

'Wonderful. I'll see you tonight, Mr Poole.'

I'd been downstairs too long, and Max would be getting suspicious. There was a silencer in a little case in the door of the safe, and I tried it in each gun until I found one it fit. I screwed them together and shoved them under my belt, then filled my pockets with a variety of bullets to make sure I got the right kind. My pants sagged with the weight, but my T-shirt was long and covered it pretty well. I closed the safe, closed the furnace-room door, and flushed the toilet on my way upstairs, just in case Max was listening.

'You were down there a while,' said Max, eyes glued to the TV.

'Yeah.' I leaned against the wall, trying to hide the bulge of the gun. 'I need to go.'

He kept his eyes on the TV, ate another chip, chewed and swallowed. 'Figures,' he said.

'I'll see you around.'

'Sure you will.'

I opened the door, stepped out, then paused and looked back. The living room was dark, lit by the dull blue-grey light of the TV; it washed out Max's features, making him look drained and gaunt. Already half a corpse. His jaw moved mechanically, his eyes dark and indifferent. I closed the door.

Max was done with life; he'd given up. It wasn't that much of a stretch, any more, to imagine someone ending their own life.

Chapter 20

Phase Four: get Mom out of the house. She was vacuuming the mortuary chapel when I got home, so I hid the gun in my car, slipped into the office and closed the door.

'Hey, Lauren.'

She looked up from the office computer, surprised, and smiled. 'Hey, John. You're home early.'

'Half-day,' I said, flopping into a chair. 'The teachers have some kind of training or something. I don't know what it is.'

'Man, I loved those days,' said Lauren, going back to her typing.

'Me too,' I said. *I wonder when we'll have a real one?* 'So, how's it going?'

'Another day in the mortuary,' she said, keeping her eyes on the screen. The keys clacked furiously under her fingers. 'Just finishing up some paperwork for your friend Rachel, actually. Looks like she comes in tomorrow.'

I let out a long breath. 'For all the good it does me. Mom didn't even let me help with the last girl.'

Lauren made a face. 'These are your friends, right? Doesn't that totally creep you out?'

'It's not creepy,' I said, 'it's just a job. We respect the dead, and we give them the best send-off we can. Besides, Mom's not keeping me out because it's a dead friend, she's keeping me out because it's a dead sixteen-year-old girl with no clothes on.'

'And that's officially the creepiest thing you've ever said,' said Lauren. She stopped typing, and then grimaced and shivered, like she'd just eaten something disgusting. 'Seriously – yuck.'

I smiled. 'I've got a live girlfriend – what do I need dead ones for?'

Lauren plugged her ears. 'I'm not listening.' I smiled wider, enjoying the torment. I stayed silent, and eventually Lauren uncovered her ears.

'I'm actually more worried about Mom than me,' I said. 'I think all this is really getting to her.'

'I know what you mean,' said Lauren. 'She's been really down lately.'

'I think it's time we did something about that.'

'I'm intrigued,' Lauren said. 'What do you have in mind?'

'I think you should take her to a movie.'

Lauren rolled her head back and stuck out her tongue. 'Gag me.'

'I'm serious. She's always trying to do stuff with you – even just asking her to hang out with you is going to make her cry.'

'That's not sweetening the deal.'

'She needs a break,' I said. 'You know it's a good idea.'

'She loves doing stuff with you, too,' said Lauren. 'Why don't *you* take her somewhere?'

'She sees me every day, which not only means that a night with you would be more special, it means you owe me. I need a break too.'

Lauren folded her arms. 'How do I know you're not just trying to get her out of the house for your own nefarious purposes?'

I smiled. 'What kind of trouble am I going to get into? The dead girl doesn't get here until tomorrow.'

'Ew!' she said, and threw a pen at me. 'I told you to stop that!'

'There's a movie in the theatre right now that she's wanted to see for a long time,' I said. 'The historical one. Go out to eat, go see the movie: it's easy.'

'You forgot to mention all the talking,' said Lauren. 'How long do you think we'll last before one of us picks a fight?'

'That's why a movie's so great – you're actually supposed to *not* talk.'

Lauren put her head down and rubbed her temples. 'Okay,' she said. 'Okay, you're right, it's a good idea; I'll do it. But now you owe me.'

'How about I promise not to make any more necrophilia jokes?'

She looked up, like she was adding numbers in her head, then made a face. *She just figured out what necrophilia means.* 'All right,' she said, 'but I'll hold you to it.'

'You're awesome.'

'I know,' she said. 'Now get out of here so I can finish this.'

I couldn't start my preparations until the women left, so I used my time to research Harry Poole on the Internet.

There was no record of a journalist by that name.

Margaret left at four, and then Mom and Lauren finally left at 6.30 p.m. They were going to El Toro, one of the only sit-down restaurants in town, followed by some huge historical romance movie about foreign people with personal problems. They'd be gone until midnight at least.

The first thing I had to do was block all the exits to the stairwell; once the Handyman got in, he wouldn't be getting back out. I took my bedroom door off its hinges, and Mom's door, and leaned them up against the door in our living room. Then I unplugged the fridge and shoved it over to hold them in place, followed by the couch on one side and the sofa on the other. It was seven o'clock when I climbed out of my mom's bedroom window onto the roof of the mortuary, then dropped down from the edge of the roof to the ground.

The inner door at the bottom of the stairs was at the end of a narrow hallway to the back of the mortuary, maybe twenty feet long, and I spent half an hour filling it with heavy oak caskets from our sample room. I wedged them in tightly – no one was getting that door open. It was 7.30 p.m.

I could still get in and out through the back door in the embalming room, so I wrote a quick note directing Harry Poole to the side door, and stuck it on the main glass entryway in the front. Then I backed my car into the driveway, maybe thirty yards past the door, and turned everything off. I twisted the rearview mirror upside down, giving me a kind of periscope view of the driveway that let me watch the whole area while staying completely hidden, and lay down on the floor. It was 7.45 p.m.

All I had to do now was wait.

The sky grew dark, and the air turned cold, and I began to shiver in my hiding-place below the dashboard. 8 p.m. I was hungry and uncomfortable. Nothing was happening, but I didn't dare to move for fear the Handyman was out there, watching, scoping out the house before getting himself into an unknown situation. The lights were on upstairs, and the exterior of the house looked completely normal. There was nothing suspicious about my car in the driveway. There was nothing to send the demon away.

It was 8.15 p.m.

I stared up at the mirror, watching. My phone was turned off, the neighbourhood was empty; everything was silent. I breathed slowly, trying not fidget or make a noise. Next to me on the floor were my weapons: Max's dad's gun, fully loaded and ready for combat, along with a roll of duct tape and the weathered green hose from our garden. I was all set.

8.20 p.m.

Time passed with agonising slowness, and I turned my thoughts to Marci. I thought about the way she looked, the way she smelled, the way she had felt when she moved against me at the dance. I closed my eyes and remembered her lips, soft and firm at once, pressed eagerly and wonderfully into my own. What did she mean to me? What, if anything, did I feel for her?

Everyone always talked about love, but I didn't have any idea what it really meant.

I wanted to kiss Marci again, to hold her again, to touch her and feel her near me, but that wasn't love. Lust, if anything. But I enjoyed talking to her, too, and there was nothing lustful about that. She was smart, and funny, and interested in the things that interested me. I liked to watch her, to listen to her, to know what she thought about the world around her. Was that friendship? Was it love? I spent a lot of time with her, and I enjoyed it, but when I was away I didn't really miss her – unless you counted dreams about embalming her. She was nice, but she wasn't necessary. I could have her in my life when I wanted her, and then forget her completely when I was doing something else. I could turn her on and off, like a TV.

But even as I thought it, I knew it wasn't entirely true. I did miss her – I missed dancing. There was something about that one dance at City Hall – not the kiss, but the dance – that I couldn't get out of my head. Something about the way she moved, or about the way I moved. Something about the way we moved together, perfectly synced, like we both knew the steps. It wasn't that it was a difficult dance – we just stepped back and forth, back and forth – but we were . . . together. We were unified. It wasn't the hot, raging connection of violence or fear, but it was there, strong and resilient. *Connection.*

Something moved in the corner of my eye, and I looked up at my mirror: a car had pulled up to the kerb. It was driving with its lights off, and no one was getting out. I looked at my watch: ten minutes to nine. *Was this him?* I glanced quickly around at my own car windows, suddenly conscious of my extremely limited field of vision. There was nothing there. I looked back at the mirror, watching the car, waiting for something to happen. The minutes ticked by, the newcomer and I as motionless as statues. At one minute to nine, the car door opened and a black shape stepped out, barely visible against the Crowleys' house beyond. The silhouette opened its trunk, pulled out a large duffel bag, then walked to the front of the mortuary.

Hello, Handyman.

The shape disappeared around the corner of the mortuary, and I held my breath, imagining him reading the note on the front door, terrified that he would turn tail and run, but he appeared again, walking down the driveway to the side door. I let my breath out quietly and readied the key to my car. He looked around, knocked, waited; no one answered. The lights were on upstairs; the note had told him to knock on the inside door. He looked around one more time before opening the door and going in. I sat up quickly and shoved the key into the ignition. *Give him time to reach the top. Four, three, two, one . . .*

I turned the key, the engine roared to life, and I slammed on the gas. The car leaped forward like a predator, eager to pounce and kill, and I steered close into the side of the mortuary, aiming for the door that hung half-open into the driveway. The side mirror broke off against the brick wall, flying away behind me, and then the front fender crashed into the open door and threw it closed with a bang. I stood on the brakes with both feet, keeping the wheel straight as the car skidded to a stop. I looked back – the door was pinned tightly shut by the trunk.

The other demon will be here any minute. I threw the car into park, grabbed the gun, the hose and the duct tape, and ran back to the trunk. Nothing attacked me. There was a shout from inside, and a thud against the door. I dropped to my knees, shoved the end of the garden hose into the exhaust pipe, and sealed it tightly around with duct tape.

'Hey! Open up!' The voice was muffled by the wooden door. I dropped to my stomach and slithered under the car, trying not to touch the heavy metal frame as it vibrated above me, pressed the free end of the hose against the gap at the base of the door, and attached it firmly in place. Ignoring his shouting, I pulled out another piece of tape, ripping it free with my teeth and sealing up the rest of the gap. *There*. Then I dropped the tape and shimmied back out, grabbing my gun and looking wildly around.

There was nothing.

Where is she?

Chapter 21

The thing trapped behind the door was pounding louder now, the door rattling against the unmoving car. I crouched down, cursing the lack of streetlights. *I can't see – the second demon could be anywhere.*

There was a pause in the pounding, then a loud metallic ping. I ducked behind the car, my heart pounding, and heard another one: *ping!* It was coming from my car. I peeked up and saw two bright metal craters in the trunk: bullet-holes. I looked back at the door to the house and saw two bullet-holes there as well, punching out through the doorknob as if he'd been trying to shoot it off. *I didn't hear the shot, just the impact – he must have a silencer as well.* The doorknob rattled, the door shook, but the car didn't budge. The thing inside swore, and a moment later I heard a loud thunk as something heavy slammed into the door. His hatchet. We were right about everything. We had predicted him perfectly, down to the last detail.

He's completely in my power.

I stayed down, straining my ears to hear any other sound, any other clue that might tell me where the second demon was. The neighbourhood was silent; even my car, the engine rumbling hungrily, was louder than the muffled hatchet strikes. The rhythm of the hatchet faltered, and I heard a loud, hacking cough. Something thudded against the inside of the door, large and heavy, then the hatchet began again. It was weaker now. I leaned in cautiously, sniffing at the bullet-holes near the doorknob; the smell was strong and acrid, like smoke. *It must be nearly impossible to breathe in there.*

I looked around at the neighbourhood again, confused, and muttered under my breath, 'Where are you?'

The pounding stopped. 'What's that? Who's there?' a voice said.

'Where's the other one?' I demanded.

'Let me out of here!'

'Where is she?' I asked again, turning to face the door. 'Where's Nobody?'

'That . . .' Cough. 'That doesn't even make sense.'

'Did anyone come with you?'

'Of course,' he said. 'I . . . I come with the Lord.' He pounded once more, feebly, then I heard the metal hatchet clatter to the floor, followed by the sound of loud retching and coughing. 'You're killing me,' he said. 'Satan's . . . servant. Let me out.'

'It's carbon-monoxide poisoning,' I said. It was deadly to humans, but I had no idea what it would do to a demon. 'Can that kill you?'

'Nothing can kill me.' He retched again. 'I am the Chosen of the Lord.'

'You're dying,' I said. 'If you want to get out, tell me where the other demon is.'

'I thought he was here,' he said, so weakly I could barely

hear him. 'Father Erikson, destroying the people. I thought he was here.'

'I'm not talking about your victims,' I said, 'I'm talking about the person you're working with. I know she's here, because I'm the one who called her. Now stop pretending and tell me.'

'No one . . . else.'

'Listen,' I said, leaning closer. 'I killed Forman, and I killed the one before him. I will kill you too, in a heartbeat, if I think you're not going to tell me what I want to know.'

'Clark Forman? The Torture House Killer?'

I hadn't heard that label before, but it was accurate enough. 'Yes. And the Clayton Killer.'

'But that's why I came,' he said, and his voice sounded closer to the door now. 'I came to save you from them. If you're the one who killed them, then you're on my side.'

His side. 'No,' I hissed, 'not your side at all. You kill any random idiot that you decide is evil. I kill real demons; real evil. They've been killing for thousands of years, maybe more, feeding on humans like predators. Like parasites. I am not just killing people, I am saving us.'

He retched again. 'Yes,' he croaked, 'you've seen them.' He started crying. 'No one else would believe me – they thought I was a common murderer. But you know. You know what they really are, and you know what *we* really are.' He collapsed in a fit of coughing so severe that I thought he might die. Then the coughing slowed, stopped, and his voice sounded closer than ever, as if he was pressing his face against the door.

'We're saviours.'

He's insane, I told myself. *He's crazy. He's a psychopathic serial killer saying anything he can to justify his actions . . .*

. . . just like I'm doing now.

I pulled back, lowering the gun. I'd speculated that there might be other demon hunters in the world, and that the Handyman might have killed one. *I never thought he might be one.* I scanned the darkness again, half-hoping I'd see a demon flying out at me from behind a shadow. At least then I'd know what to do with it. This one in the trap: was he a demon who hunted other demons? Was he even a demon at all? Maybe he was a normal human, like me, who'd seen too much and sworn to stop it by any means necessary.

And now he'd killed ten people, maybe more. Had any of them really been demons?

'You've seen the demons,' I said. 'Describe them to me.'

Silence.

'Describe them!' I said, leaning in towards the door. There was no answer but the stench of exhaust.

Damn. I stared at the door, trying to remember what I'd heard. Had he fallen? Was he still standing? Had the exhaust knocked him out, or was this a trick? I glanced down at the gun in my hand, trying to decide if I dared to move the car. *He can't die yet,* I thought. *I still have too many questions.*

For one brief moment I saw him in my mind's eye, a hulking demon in a cloud of black smoke, waiting silently to eviscerate me when I opened the door. I hesitated, suddenly wary, but then I saw something else: me, trapped in Forman's closet, beating uselessly at the fortified walls while he stood outside with a gun. I looked down at the gun in my hand, glaring as if it had betrayed me somehow.

I threw my weight against the back of the car, but it was heavy – far heavier than any car had a right to be. All the weight that had pinned the door closed was now working against me, and even with the wheels to help I only budged it an inch. *It's still in park*, I thought, and stepped back. *I have to get into the car to move it, but that will take me away from the door. If he makes a run for it, I'll lose him.* I stared at the door, at the hose running out from the exhaust, and swore. *I have to do it.* I pulled on the hose, ripping it away from the pipe, and aimed my gun at the door. Nothing moved, and there was still no sound from inside. Slowly I walked to the driver's open door, leaned in, and shoved the gear shift into neutral. I jumped back out immediately, aiming the gun at the door.

Nothing.

Setting the gun carefully on the roof of the car, I braced my hands and shoulder against the inside of the door and pushed forward. Even out of park, the car was fiendishly heavy, but I strained hard against it and started to overcome its inertia, creeping it forward inch by inch, foot by foot, until the side door of the house was exposed. Grabbing the gun again, I walked back, keeping the barrel trained on the door. Nothing moved, and I reached forward cautiously; the doorknob was shattered and twisted freely without pulling open the latch. I tugged on it, yanked it, and finally kicked it with my foot, hearing the wood crunch in around the broken latch. I held the gun in front of me like it was a holy symbol, as if its mere presence would ward away danger, and pulled the door open.

On the floor inside lay a man in a worn brown suit and

black leather gloves, draped across the stairs like a sack of cement. At his feet was a black pistol and an open duffel bag full of clear plastic sheets; in the corner was a small hatchet. Thin, poisonous smoke poured out of the stairwell and I stepped back, coughing.

'Are you dead?'

He didn't answer, and I crept forward far enough to reach out and nudge him with my toe. His eyes stayed closed, but he groaned and coughed, rolling onto his side.

'Hey,' I said, 'can you hear me?' He moved again, and I remembered his gun; I jumped over and stepped on it, dragging it out into the driveway with my foot. 'Hey,' I said louder. 'Just answer my questions.'

The Handyman coughed and tried to sit up, only to fall back down and tumble to the bottom of the stairs. He moaned and squeezed his eyes shut, then reached out his hand and crawled a few inches into the driveway.

I stepped back. 'Stay there. Can you talk?'

'Yeh,' he said, his voice ragged. He coughed again, more purposefully. 'Yes.'

'You said you've seen the demons,' I said. 'Describe them.'

'Evil.' He spoke without moving, his face down in the asphalt, sucking in clean air with each breath. 'They abuse their power; they lead innocents into sin. They have to be destroyed.'

'Describe them physically,' I said. 'Did you see claws? Fangs? You stab your victims with poles to give them wings – did you see wings? What *did* you see?'

'No wings,' he gasped, 'only in the world beyond.'

'What world?'

'Heaven and hell. There we will take our forms and live forever in peace, or forever in torment.'

I stared at him, feeling my rage grow. My finger tightened on the trigger. 'Is that it? Is that really all this is? You haven't seen anything – you're not a demon, you're not a demon hunter, you're just another lunatic serial killer.'

'I'm a—'

'Shut up!' I shouted, irrationally desperate. 'You're nothing; you're delusional. The things I've seen are real – they're real!' I waved the gun. 'If you're not hunting demons, why are you even here?'

'Too many deaths here,' he said, reaching out weakly. 'You were being punished for your sins. I came to save you; I came to cut out the corruption.'

His arm was stretched towards me and I saw his glove, black leather barely visible in the darkness. My pulse quickened, and I felt a surge of hope. 'Your hands,' I said quickly. 'You wear gloves because you hate your hands. Show me why.'

'No.'

'Take them off!' *What would it be – claws? Scales? It has to be something; he has to be a demon.* He rolled on his back, staring up at me with a scowl of pure hatred. I pushed the gun closer and he raised his hands up, growling deep in his throat.

Slowly he took off one glove, revealing a pale white hand covered in tattoos – symbols, words, horned skulls, even a swastika. I stared, trying to fit the hand into my profile, and he whimpered softly. He pulled off his second glove, and as he did so, he broke down – another soft whimper, a slackening of the shoulders, a droop in his face and a long, prolonged sob. His second hand was just as tattooed as the first.

'Forgive me, for I have sinned,' he said, rolling onto his side and covering his face with his hands. 'Forgive me, for I have sinned.'

It's the source of guilt, I thought, stepping back. *Those tattooed hands are why he kills – the sign of a sin he can never remove. Each kill pays for the last one, ridding the world of another sinner, but in killing he sins again. It's a chain he can never escape, leading back to . . .*

'Who was the first?' I asked, my voice hushed.

'No,' he moaned, rolling slowly back and forth.

'The first one you killed,' I asked. 'Who was it? It was a priest, wasn't it? A religious leader, probably one who punished you too harshly; maybe one who abused you.'

'No,' he said again, sobbing. 'No, no, no – I didn't mean to.'

'It doesn't matter,' I said, standing up straighter. The gun was firm and powerful in my hand – a magic wand that would make this killer go away. 'You've killed too many people, and for too long. This is my town, and I set out to save it from parasites like you – demon or not.' I aimed the gun at his head and he cowered under his arms, crying pathetically. He was a perfect picture of weakness and evil – a misguided killer living from lie to lie, reduced to a quivering wreck because he couldn't find another victim bad enough to justify the others. All his crimes, all his horror, all his sins, were crushing him to nothing. This wasn't even my choice; I was simply the mechanism by which the world as a whole chose to rid itself of his cancer.

I held the gun, but I didn't fire.

He needs to die, I told myself. *There are a million reasons for him to die and not a single one for him to live. Who will be better off with this wretch in the world? Who will cry over his grave? Who will even care where his grave is? I've killed two others, and he's no better than they were – he might even be worse. Mr Crowley killed to stay alive. This worm can't even say that.*

My finger on the trigger didn't move.

I gritted my teeth, willing myself to see him as a demon, as an object I could break at will, but instead I saw him as something else – not just as a human, but as me. *He's me. If I keep going down this path, this is how I'll end – scared and weak and guilty, always running from what I've done, always desperate to do it again and again and again.* I saw Crowley and Forman, both in the same position – helpless on the ground, looking up as I ended their lives. *Two down, and one more makes three.* Three was a charm. Three was a pattern. By legal definition, three victims made you a serial killer.

And I am not a serial killer.

I lowered the gun. 'I'm calling the police.'

'No.'

I pulled out Forman's phone and flipped it open. 'I won't kill you,' I said. 'I'm not a killer. The police will take you, they'll find all the evidence they need, and they'll put you in jail for the rest of your life.'

'They'll kill me!'

'I didn't say the rest of your life would be long.' I dialed 911 and looked around, at the car and the gun and the hose and the whole elaborate trap I'd set. 'And I'll have a hell of a lot of explaining to do.'

The phone rang, and I held it up to my ear. *What would I say? 'I trapped the Handyman in my house; come pick him up before I kill him'?* The phone rang again –

– and the Handyman lunged for my leg. I stumbled back and lost my footing, realising as I fell that I'd dropped both the phone and the gun in a reflexive move to break my fall. I stretched my hands back out, trying to catch the gun; it hung in the air as if time was frozen, spinning just beyond my reach, and then I landed heavily on my back and cracked my head against the driveway. I grunted, screwing my eyes shut as bolts of pain and light flashed through them. Something clattered in front of me, and my mind screamed *gun!* just in time to make me roll over, then over again, each time hearing the horrifying whisper of a silencer and the grating clang of metal on asphalt. I rolled over something cold and metal, grabbed it, and pointed it at him.

It was the cellphone.

'You think you can threaten me with that?' sneered the Handyman. All trace of weakness was gone. He loomed over me like a nightmare, hair skewed, eyes wild, teeth bared. He held his gun with both hands, shaky but level, pointed straight at my head. 'It looks like I'm going to slay a demon after all.'

I have one chance to scare him off. 'Harry Poole,' I said. 'Out-of-town reporter. The man who claimed several weeks ago to have a message from the Handyman turns out to be the Handyman himself.'

'I'm not the Handyman,' he said, lips curled in rage. 'I am the arm of the Lord; the arrow in His quiver, the lightning of His wrath.'

'Clayton Mortuary,' I said. 'Seven-two-four Jefferson.' Very slowly, I pulled the phone back and held it to my ear. 'You get all that?'

The Handyman's eyes went wide, and I held out the phone again. 'They got it. What's your next move?'

He stepped back, then forward, then charged towards me, knocking the phone out of my hand. It flew to the ground and he stomped on it violently, grinding it under his heel. Then, he stepped back and shot it, twice.

'They already know who you are,' I said, sitting up painfully, 'and they already know where. I figure you have maybe two minutes to get out of here. When I called the cops for the Clayton Killer last year, they had the entire neighbourhood blocked off in under four minutes.'

'They'll kill me,' he said, looking up slowly from the shattered phone. His face was pale, his eyes still wide with fear. 'They'll kill me.'

'It's worse than that,' I said, forcing myself to ignore the gun and remember his profile. *I have to attack his weak spots.* 'They'll judge you. A whole parade of cops and lawyers and witnesses and judges – even your fellow prisoners in whatever jail they put you in. They're going to look at you, and laugh at you, and call you evil.'

'Shut up.'

'Psychologists will interview you and call you a schizophrenic – not enough for an insanity defence, but enough to tell a jury that you justified your crimes with a delusion of God. Priests will testify in court that your divine message is the raving of a sinner—'

'Shut up!' he screamed, sticking the gun in my face.

'They will punish you,' I said, forcing myself to stay calm. 'Leave now and you can get away. I'll throw them off your trail, one demon hunter to another, but you have to go now. They'll come after you, and they'll post your name and your face all over the country, but if you're careful you can stay hidden. Run.'

'The whole country,' he said, eyes focused on nothing – on some memory, perhaps. 'She'll know.'

I frowned, not sure what to say next. I nodded. 'She will.'

'I will not be judged of man.' He raised the gun to his chin, a spout of red flew up from the top of his head, and he crumpled to the ground like a broken doll.

Chapter 22

'Hello, John,' said Officer Jensen, sitting across the table. 'You've met Officer Moore, and this is Cathy Ostler from the FBI. I know you've answered a lot of questions already, but they just want to ask a few more.'

The Handyman's body never disintegrated, I thought. *He was never a demon at all. There had to be a real demon in town somewhere – but where?*

'Hi,' I said. The woman sat down, and Officer Moore leaned against the table.

'So,' said the woman – Agent Ostler. 'Sounds like you've had quite a night.'

'You could say that.'

'Yes, I certainly could,' she said. 'At ten o'clock at night we get a phone call from a dead serial killer, we hear the confession of another serial killer, and when we arrive on the scene we find a wanted fugitive from ten states away dead at the feet of a teenage boy who's been previously involved in the deaths of one-two-three-four other people. "Quite a night" seems to be putting it pretty mildly.'

'Are you accusing me of something?'

'Have you done anything?'

'Well, I've apparently witnessed too many crimes. How often can I almost get killed before you assume I'm guilty of something? Is there a specific legal limit, or do you guys play it by ear?'

'Nobody is accusing you of anything,' said Officer Jensen, scowling at me. *He's warning me to watch my mouth.* 'But even you have to admit that your involvement in this most recent attack is a lot harder to explain away than the last two.'

'Not really,' I said, hoping my confidence would make my story seem stronger. 'The Handyman thought that certain community figures were leading the others into sin, so he killed them. He admitted that much in his letter. Then every news outlet in town made me look like a hero for saving the kids at the dance, and he came to the conclusion that I was one of the "bad" community figures. He came after me. End of story.'

'And the barricade in your living room?' asked Officer Moore.

I'd had just enough time to hide the gun and the exhaust hose before the police showed up; there hadn't been time to hide the barricades, so I tried to explain them away. 'I was home alone,' I said, 'and I saw a man sitting in his car in front of my house. I got scared – "Stranger Danger" and all that. It seemed like a good idea at the time.'

'If you were so scared,' asked Agent Ostler, 'why did you crawl out the window to confront him?'

'I crawled out the window to escape,' I said. 'He just kept knocking and knocking, and I thought he was going to get in. I thought I could drive away before he found me, but he must have heard the car.'

248

'He must have,' said Agent Ostler. 'He also must have the fastest pistol in the world, to have hit your moving car with two shots so close together. The bullet-holes were less than an inch apart.'

'I was going very slowly. I thought if I just put it in neutral and pushed it into the street, he wouldn't hear me.'

'But he did.'

'Turns out it's hard to steer while running alongside and pushing, so I hit the house. I've had an astonishing amount of bad luck over the last year.'

Agent Ostler stared at me, silent as a hawk, while Officer Jensen frowned at her. Officer Moore then spoke up. 'Everything you've told us makes a certain amount of sense,' he said, 'obviously pending a full forensic analysis. The only piece we're not sure of yet, and perhaps you can help us explain it, is—'

'How long were you going to keep Clark Forman's cellphone?' snapped Agent Ostler.

I was very good at feigning innocence. 'What?'

'The phone you used to call 911,' she said. 'Not only is it half a dozen felonies to hide the evidence from a previous case, but it calls that entire case – and your involvement in it – into question. What were you doing with his phone?'

'I'm afraid I don't know what you're talking about.'

'Don't make me get official on you,' she said, her face harsh, 'because I can put a stop to this friendly little meeting right now, and we can treat this like the federal case it is.'

Officer Jensen put out a hand to quiet her, then turned to me. 'Just tell us where you got the phone that you called us with tonight.'

'I didn't call you tonight,' I said. 'He did. Why, was it Forman's phone?'

They stared at me.

'Because that's pretty scary,' I said. 'Do you think this is the mystery accomplice you've been looking for?'

'He called the police on himself?' asked Agent Ostler, folding her arms.

'I guess he wanted to turn himself in,' I said. 'Or at least to confess to someone official, before he shot himself.'

Officer Jensen sighed, and Officer Moore leaned forward. 'You said he set out tonight to kill you, and now you say that he killed himself instead. What happened to change his mind?'

'I don't know,' I said, keeping my face blank. 'Maybe I just have that effect on people.'

Agent Ostler scowled. 'I am authorised to place you in protective custody if I have reason to believe you're in danger. Believe me when I say that the kind of custody I'm talking about would be largely indistinguishable from prison.'

'He won't run,' said Officer Jensen, closing his eyes and rubbing his temples. 'I can vouch for him.'

'You're sure?' she asked.

'He'll stay in town, he'll participate in every interview, and he'll facilitate the investigation in every way he can.' He looked at me pointedly. 'Is that right, John?'

'Of course,' I nodded. 'Anything you need.'

'All right then,' said Agent Ostler, 'you can go. But I assure you that we will be watching you very closely.'

*

'John, you're okay!' Mom ran across the police station lobby and grabbed me in a hug, crushing me with the force of it. I flailed my arms, patted her on the back, and pulled away just far enough to breathe.

'I was so worried about you,' she went on. 'I can't believe you're okay.'

'I'm fine,' I said, pulling further away. 'Just give me some air.'

'I never should have gone out tonight,' she said. 'I'll never do it again.'

'Please, no,' I said. 'Don't let one crazy killer justify any more smothering; I'll go insane.'

'This is the third crazy killer, as I'm sure you're well aware.' She stooped to look straight into my eyes, though she didn't have to stoop far. 'Tell me you had nothing to do with this,' she said. 'Tell me right now, right here, that this was an unprovoked attack.'

I looked back, my face still blank and innocent. 'I have never seen that man before tonight. I didn't even know he existed.'

'You swear?'

'I swear.' I looked past her and saw Lauren beyond, arms folded, face pale and tight; she was scared, but she was angry, too. *She knows I planned this, and she knows I tricked her into getting Mom out of the way. Will she tell the police?*

It was nearly two in the morning when we left the police station, and even later when my mom finally fell asleep. I lay awake all night, turning restlessly in bed. At three in the morning, still wide awake, I crept outside and into the forest, searching in the dark for Max's gun. It was still there, a good fifty feet into the trees, untouched and unsuspected. I wiped a streak of dirt from it with my hand, hefting it, then bent back down and buried it deeper. Agent Ostler was still too suspicious; I couldn't let her find me with a gun, even an unfired one.

I walked back to the mortuary, let myself in the back door and spent the next hour putting all the coffins away and imagining a hundred different killers – silent, invisible, unstoppable. *Where is Nobody?*

By four thirty I couldn't stand the waiting and called Marci's cell on our kitchen phone. It rang seven times before her voicemail picked up; I hung up, counted to three, and dialled the number again. She answered on the sixth ring.

'John?'

'Are you okay?'

'John, it's four thirty in the morning.'

'Are you okay?'

'Yeah, I'm fine. What's wrong?'

'Hold very still, and listen very closely. Do you hear anything?'

'What are you talking about?'

'Just do it.'

Pause. 'I can hear the water softener cycling in the basement.'

'That's it? Are you sure?'

'That's it,' she said, more awake, 'now tell me what's wrong. Is there something in my house?'

'I don't know,' I said. 'I don't know if you'd even be able to tell.'

'John, are you drunk? You're not making any sense.'

'I'm worried about you,' I said. 'That's a new thing for me, and I'm not very good at it. Look out your window.'

'You're freaking me out, John. Just tell me what's wrong.'

I took a deep breath. 'I think she's coming for you.'

'The Handyman?'

'The Handyman died last night; he came to my house, ranted for a while, and shot himself in the head.'

'Holy crap—'

'But I think there's another one,' I interrupted. 'One that we haven't talked about.'

'You said he came to your house?'

'I'm fine,' I told her. 'Now listen – you're the one who needs to be worried. Turn on your light, turn on all the lights in the house, and then go into your parents' room.'

'How's that going to help?'

'This killer won't touch you if there are any witnesses – or maybe it *can't* touch you around witnesses – I don't know. It makes everything look like suicide.'

She gasped.

'And I think . . .' *I'd never told her about the demons – out of everything I'd shared with Marci, that was the one secret I'd kept. Did I dare tell her now?*

I honestly don't think I have a choice.

'This is going to sound weird,' I said, 'but you have to trust me. I think this new killer might be supernatural.' I waited for her to laugh, or scoff, but she was completely silent. I continued, 'The Clayton Killer and Agent Forman were both . . . something. Creatures, demons, I don't know. I'm telling you this because I think the new killer is the same thing. I don't know if it's coming after you or . . . well, I don't know. I just want you to be safe.'

There was silence for a long time.

'Marci?'

'You were there,' she said slowly, 'in his house.'

'Yeah,' I said. 'That's how I know. I know it sounds insane but you have to trust me.'

'Brooke was there too.'

That was a weird thing to say. 'Yeah, she was.'

'Did she see it?'

'The demon? I don't know. I don't think so.'

'She wouldn't be scared now. Not after what she's gone through, and with you to help her.'

'Marci, are . . .' I paused. 'Are you okay? Did you turn on all the lights like I told you?'

'I'm sorry,' she said, 'I was just thinking. Sometimes I wish I could be . . .' Pause. 'Okay, my lights are on.'

'Go into your parents' room,' I said, 'and stay there until everyone else wakes up; it's the safest place right now. I'll be there at seven.'

'Thanks.' Pause. 'I love you, John.'

Love. Somehow it always comes back to love.

Do I love her too?

'I'll be there at seven,' I repeated, and hung up the phone.

When I got to her house at 6.50 a.m. she was already dead.

Chapter 23

Marci's body was curled up in the corner of the upstairs bathroom, her legs pulled into her chest, her arms draped over the edge of the bathtub. Blood was everywhere – on the walls, the mirror, the floor and ceiling; the tub was filled with a long, thick river of it, and the sink was full of tepid pink water. I stepped in carefully, avoiding the biggest pools and splashes.

'Hurry!' Marci's father shouted into his radio, his voice echoing through the hall. 'I want every paramedic in town in my house in the next five minutes, or so help me I'll start—' His radio crackled. 'Don't talk back to me! It's not your daughter lying in a pool of blood!'

Mrs Jensen was in another part of the house, wailing softly. I assumed the other kids were with her.

I reached across and touched Marci's arm; it was cold and limp. I turned it slightly, saw the wide red gash, and let go. Her joints had just enough resistance in them to catch my attention. Rigor mortis didn't begin until three hours after death, at the earliest, and I'd spoken to her barely two and a half hours before; she shouldn't have started to stiffen yet unless she'd died just minutes after we'd hung up – and even that was pushing it. I straightened up and stepped back, looking around at the blood on the walls; there was a crack on the mirror that hadn't been there two days ago. *You can't say there were no signs of a struggle this time.*

Good for you, Marci.

I took another step back and stood in the hall, looking in on the scene silently. I felt like a stone, cold and hard. *Does it affect me? Should it?* I'd never been squeamish around blood or death, but I'd never felt . . . *this* before. *I'm tired, maybe. Or angry.* But it wasn't that. I was hollow and empty, like I hadn't been in ages. I was a statue; I was a gargoyle. I was a piece of the wall, a part of the landscape, a clump of dirt. I was dead. *I am nothing.*

'It,' I said softly. The thing on the floor wasn't Marci any more. Marci was life and energy; Marci was a whirlwind of activity and words and light. She was a smile and a joke, a telling insight or a flash of ingenious logic. This thing on the floor was . . . meat and hair. It was a body no one would ever hold, wrapped in clothing no one would ever wear again. The part of her that had been Marci was gone, and nothing was left but death and silence.

I heard footsteps in the hall; felt a hand rest on my shoulder. *Officer Jensen.*

'They're on their way.'

'Is it you?' I asked.

'Huh?'

I turned to face him, pulling away from his hand.

'Just tell me straight out – are you Nobody? Because if you are, we can end this right now.'

'Hey,' he said, reaching again for my shoulder. 'Just calm

down, John. I know this is hard, but you gotta calm down. We can get through—'

'I don't want to get through this, I want to finish it. Now tell me, because I am not in the mood for any more games: are you Nobody?'

'You're not making sense, John; let's go sit down.'

'Nothing is making sense.' I stared at him, studying his face for any sign – any reaction that might tell me what I needed to know. 'If it's you, you can just tell me. You can say it right out loud because I already know. I already know everything.' He was silent. 'Tell me, dammit!'

'Easy,' he said, holding out his other hand. 'Easy. Just take a deep breath. Nice and deep.' His eyes were big and open, his mouth straight, the corners just slightly turned down. *Concern. Worry. Sadness. Perfectly normal reactions from a perfectly normal human. He doesn't know what I'm talking about. He's not a demon.* I took a deep breath and he nodded, watching me carefully. 'You say you "already know". What do you know about Marci?'

'About Marci?' I looked at the Marci-shaped thing in the corner, tiny and broken. *What had broken it? Where was it now? And how could I break it back?* 'I don't know a damn thing. But I'm going to find out.'

I raced towards home, barely slowing the car at each intersection, and turned wildly into our driveway, almost hitting the house before screeching to a halt by the back door. The embalming-room door. I stumbled out of the car, leaving the door hanging open, and shoved my key into the lock on the mortuary. Mom and Margaret looked up as I threw open the door, perfect twins in their blue masks and aprons, setting Rachel's features like two girls playing with a doll.

'Out,' said Mom curtly. 'You know I said you couldn't help with girls.' I ignored her, stepped in and locked the door behind me.

Margaret shook her head. 'She said no, John. We've talked about this.' I walked straight to the table, Rachel's body laid out before me like a giant doll, and picked up a scalpel.

'John,' said Mom, 'I just said—'

'Shut up.'

'John!'

'*Shut up!*' I roared. Then, more quietly: 'Marci's dead.'

They froze, speechless.

'Marci is dead,' I said again, more forcefully, 'and whatever killed Rachel killed her the same way. Now you can yell and scream all you want – you can call the cops for all I care – but this body has answers, and I am going to find them.' I stared at them defiantly, daring them to argue. Mom began to cry.

'We hadn't heard about Marci,' said Margaret, stepping towards me. 'We're very sorry. I don't think any of us are really in the right state to be here now, so let's just wait.'

'Step back,' I said, putting my hand on the table.

'No,' said Mom, coming around the table. 'Please don't, John, please let's just go upstairs—'

I caught her wrist, squeezing until my knuckles turned white. 'Get. Out. Of my way.' I shoved her to the side.

'Please, John,' she cried. 'Don't do it. Don't hurt her!'

'It is an *it*!' I shouted, slamming the table. 'This is not a

person, it is not a human being, it is not even an animal!
It is evidence! It is—'

'It is worthy of your respect,' said Mom. I looked at her
rabidly, wells of hatred boiling up inside me, but she stared
back without flinching. *You're not mad at her,* I told myself,
just the demon. Find the demon, and nothing else matters.

I nodded, and took a deep breath. 'Okay. With respect.
But don't try to stop me.'

Margaret glanced at Mom, eyes creased with worry. I ignored
them and looked down at the body. It was pale, almost bluish;
if Rachel had bled out as much as Marci had, this corpse
would be even more bloodless than usual. It was a stark contrast
to the old, butchered men we'd seen so much of lately –
instead of yellowed, wrinkly flesh, this body was smooth and
white, and virtually unharmed. The breasts and hips were
covered with blue privacy towels, but the belly between was
flat and clear. There had been no autopsy, no Y-incision, no
wounds of any kind. If not for the wide slits in her wrists, and
the embalming tubes Mom and Margaret had already attached
to the veins in the neck, the corpse would be pristine.

I picked up one of its arms, looking closer at the wound,
and was surprised to feel the joint resist the movement –
just like Marci's had. *Rachel's been dead too long for rigor
mortis, and Marci hadn't been dead long enough. Why are they
stiff?* I moved the arm, testing the motion in the shoulder,
the elbow, the wrist. It was slow, but not solid; it moved,
but with just enough resistance to feel odd. I moved the legs
and they felt the same, but I didn't know what to do beyond
that. I set the legs down, picked one up again, then swore
and set it back down. *I don't know what to do.*

I looked at the wounds again, picking up each hand in turn and peering into them, poking at them with the scalpel. They had been well-cleaned by the Coroner, and I saw nothing out of the ordinary: a long, clean cut down the length of each forearm, opening the artery in a lateral gash nearly eight inches long. It ended just past the wrists. *You take someone's pulse in their wrist,* I thought. A wound like this would have bled uncontrollably, spilling out her life in seconds.

She bled to death, just like Marci. Why does Nobody kill them this way? What does she get out of it? What does it mean?

I forced myself to slow down, to consider the situation more clearly. *What did the killer do that she didn't have to do?* If she wanted to kill, all she really had to do was find someone and kill them: instead she chose to focus on teenage girls, all of them fairly pretty, all of them generally well-liked. It was almost a progression, really, from the wallflower Jenny to the more active Allison and Rachel, to the social dynamo of Marci. Each victim was a step closer to me, but I wondered if it might be more than that; whether the lifestyle of the victims themselves – their looks and clothes and lives – was also a factor. *What would make someone want to kill young, attractive, popular girls? Was it desire? Was it jealousy?*

Then there was the wound itself to consider: why make it look like suicide? And *how* did she make it look like suicide? I examined the rest of Rachel's body, looking for defensive wounds, but there was nothing: her hands were free of nicks and cuts, her arms had no bruises from an attack or a solid grip; there were no abrasions or rope burns to suggest that she was bound or tied. Everything pointed to the idea that she was a willing participant in the death. Even the wrist slits were too clean to have been done without stillness and precision. *Does Nobody incapacitate them some other way? She's a demon, so she can do anything. Does she put them to sleep, or control their minds?* Yet Marci, judging by the sprays of blood around the room, had struggled. *But she hadn't struggled* against *anybody. It doesn't make sense.*

I picked up a comb and went through the hair, checking the scalp for any kind of bruises or wounds. *Nothing.* The base of the skull was clear, too – no cuts, no puncture wounds. Not even the pinprick of a hypodermic needle.

'Help me roll it over,' I said, waving my mom to the table. I put my hands under the shoulder, but Mom rested her hand on my arm, stopping me.

'We'll do it. You close your eyes.' She nodded to Margaret, who stepped away from the wall and approached the table slowly. They positioned themselves on the body's left and paused, watching me. I closed my eyes and listened to the rustle of clothes, the shuffle of feet, the faint click of fingernails on the metal table. 'Open.'

I opened my eyes and saw the body lying on its face, a privacy towel draped over the buttocks. The back was dark and discoloured, but that was common as the blood settled in a corpse. I poked at the back, ran my hands over it feeling for holes or cuts, but there was nothing. I sighed, leaning heavily on the table.

'There's only one place left to check,' I said, 'and I'm gonna bet you'll want to do it yourself.'

Mom looked at me, her eyes wet and red. 'You think she was raped?'

'I have no idea. Probably not.'

'Then we refuse,' said Mom. 'And you're not going to do it either.'

I looked up, calm and cold. 'I'm giving you one chance. Do it, or I will do it for you. There's probably nothing there, but I refuse to let any more people die because your sense of propriety made me miss a clue.' We stared at each other, testing the other's will, until finally she grumbled and stepped up to the table.

'What am I looking for?'

'Anything – damage, wounds, anything at all. Anything that might tell us who killed her, or why.'

'Fine. Close your eyes.'

I did, and listened for a few minutes as Mom and Margaret rustled the privacy towel, whispered lowly to each other, then rolled the body over and whispered further.

There's nothing here, I thought. *Maybe there really is no more evidence on the bodies; maybe it's just pure mind control with no physical evidence. Maybe we can never catch her at all.*

'Nothing,' said Mom. 'There's nothing there.'

I sighed and leaned against the wall, feeling my energy drain away. 'Then we've lost. I don't know what else to do.' I felt a hand on my shoulder, and opened my eyes to see Mom standing next to me.

'Just rest.' She pushed me gently towards a chair, and I collapsed into it. 'Your girlfriend died – your best friend – and you need to deal with it. It's completely understandable that you don't know how.' She smiled – a thin, painful smile. 'An amateur autopsy isn't how most people would choose to do it, obviously, but I know your heart's in the right place.'

'My heart has nothing to do with it.'

'Just rest,' she said again. 'Take a minute, then we'll go upstairs and eat. Margaret can finish this on her own. You left without any breakfast this morning, so it's no wonder you're feeling weak now.'

I stared at the body on the table, dull and lifeless, nearly bloodless, the embalming tubes hanging limply from its shoulder.

Nearly bloodless . . . Yet its back is just as bruised and blackened as any other corpse.

I stood up abruptly. 'Plug in the pump.' I crossed to the wall and pulled down the drain tube.

'It's okay,' said Mom, 'it can wait.'

'No, it can't.' I attached the drain pipe to the tube in Rachel's neck. 'The back is too bruised for the amount of blood she lost, and her limbs are stiff. There's something inside, and we need to get it out.' We normally dropped the tube down to a drain in the floor, but this time I put it in a bucket. I wanted to catch whatever dripped out.

'It's just rigor mortis,' said Margaret gently.

'It's been dead five days,' I said. 'It's not rigor mortis.' The two women looked at each other, and I walked to the shelf with the embalming chemicals. 'You can stand there or you can help; either way I'm embalming her right now.'

They hesitated a moment longer, then moved slowly into action: connecting the pump, mixing the coagulants and dyes, measuring out the formaldehyde. We attached everything, sealed off the wrist wounds with tight bandages, then turned on the pump. It was designed to use the body's own circulatory system, filling it with our chemical cocktail while pushing all the ichor out the other side. Mom adjusted it carefully, looking for a good rhythm to approximate the beating of a heart; she fiddled with it much longer than normal.

'There's something wrong,' she said. 'I can't get it to push through.'

'The arteries are mostly empty after this much blood loss,' said Margaret. 'They've probably collapsed.'

'There's something blocking them,' I said, my eyes fixed on the bucket. 'Just raise the pressure.' Mom twisted the dial and the pump hummed more loudly, its artificial heartbeats closer together. Soon the drain tube moved, twisting slightly to the side as it filled and pressurised, and then a thick, dark sludge began to drip out into the bucket.

Ashy and black, just like Crowley and Forman.

Mom gasped.

'What on earth is that?' muttered Margaret, leaning over the bucket with her jaw hanging open.

I looked up at Mom. She looked back silently, eyes wide. I breathed heavily, feeling suddenly exhausted. 'We were right.'

She stared a moment longer, then said feebly, 'What do we do?'

Margaret scooped up a fingerful with her gloved hand; the sludge was burned and greasy, like the charred residue from an uncleaned grill. 'How did Ron not notice that her body was filled with this crap?'

'Because they assumed it was a suicide, and they never looked any deeper. You didn't notice it with the other girls because you pumped it all straight into the sewer drain.'

'It looks like the stuff they used to find at all the Clayton Killer crime scenes,' said Margaret.

'Exactly,' I said.

She looked at me, then at Mom. 'What's going on?'

I reached down with my glove and dipped my finger in the muck, pulling it up and looking closer. *Exactly like Crowley and Forman.* 'It's a demon,' I said softly. 'Or the remains of one. It was living inside of her. It was controlling her.'

'A demon?' echoed Margaret. She opened her mouth to say something, then closed it. A moment later she spoke again. 'What do we do?'

'We call the police,' said Mom, turning off the pump. 'We call Agent Ostler –'

'We can't,' I said.

'– and we get her over here,' she continued firmly, 'and we show her everything.'

'We can't,' I said. 'I've told you before, we can't trust anyone in the FBI. If Forman was a demon, who's to say Ostler's not?'

'We have to warn them.'

'Who?' asked Margaret.

'Everyone,' said Mom. 'If we can't go to the police we go to the news.'

'And get laughed out of town,' I said.

'We can't just sit here!' Mom shouted.

I looked at the sludge again, imagining it inside of Marci's veins, controlling her movements, cutting her own wrists while Marci tried in vain to fight it off. *How did it get in there? And why?* Forman's confession rang in my mind: 'We are defined by what we lack.' *What does Nobody lack? A face, a name, an identity. A boyfriend. Cute clothes. She wants a normal life so she takes theirs, just like Crowley used to do, only Nobody doesn't kill them – she takes them over mind, body and soul.*

I searched back through my memories of the last few weeks, trying to remember any clues about what the demon did or said. *How long had it been there? What was really Marci, and what was the demon? Was the kiss real? Was the dance?* But Rachel hadn't died until a few hours after the dance, so it hadn't gotten to Marci until the next morning, at the earliest. And Rachel had been acting so weird that night, anyway, talking about . . . *about Marci.* She had talked about Marci all night, now that I thought about it, praising her and fawning over her. The last words I ever heard her speak were something about how she wanted to be – what? To be like Marci? To *be* Marci?

I froze. Marci had said the same thing just hours ago, before she died: 'I wish I could be . . .'

She'd been talking about Brooke.

Chapter 24

I ran for the door.

'John!'

'I have to go.'

'Look at yourself!'

I looked down – my finger was still covered in sludge, my gloves and apron pink with blood. I stripped everything off and threw it in the trash.

'Where are you going?' Mom asked, but I ignored her and bolted out the door in a sprint to Brooke's house.

Marci had been talking about Brooke ever since the dance: how brave she was, how strong she was, how close she was to me. When we'd seen her at Friendly Burger she'd almost fumed with jealousy; when I called her this morning and warned her about the demon, the first thing she'd thought of was Brooke.

How does it travel without being seen? How fast can it move? It's been four hours, maybe five, since Marci died. Am I too late?

I leaped up the steps to Brooke's porch and hammered on the door. 'Open up!' I heard footsteps inside, and banged again. Brooke's mom opened the door.

'Hello, John—'

'Did Brooke go to school this morning?'

'I . . .' She stopped in surprise. 'Um, no, no; she said she felt sick—'

I shoved her out of the way and ran through the door, charging down the hall and up the stairs to the first floor. The layout was different from the Crowleys' house, but it was easy enough to guess which door led to the back corner room. I swung around the edge of the banister, Brooke's mom shouting after me, and slammed my fist on the bedroom door. 'Brooke! Brooke, open up, it's John.'

'I don't want to see anybody today.' Her voice was weak. *No, please no.* I jiggled the knob, but it was locked. 'This is important, you have to let me in.' *I don't know how to save you if it's already inside.*

'John Cleaver!' shouted her mother, pounding up the stairs after me. 'What do you think you're doing!'

'Please, Brooke, there might still be time – you've got to open the door.' I slammed my hand on it, nearly breaking it. 'Open the door!'

Brooke's mom grabbed me from behind, pulling me back, and I fought to push her away. 'You don't understand,' I shouted. 'She's in danger!'

The lock clicked, and the door cracked open. I lunged forward, dragging her mom with me. Brooke's voice leaked through the open gap. 'It's okay, Mom.' The door swung wide, and there she was; the skin under her eyes was dark, like she hadn't slept in days, and she moved slowly, stiffly, like a zombie back from the dead. I stopped struggling and stared, mouth hanging open.

'No.' *I'm too late.*

'You look horrible,' said her mom, letting go and pushing past me to Brooke. 'Are you okay? I should call the doctor.'

'It's nothing, Mom, I'm just tired. I'll be fine in a few hours.'

'No,' I said again, stumbling against the banister. 'Please, no.'

'What's going on?' asked her mother.

'It's nothing, Mom,' said Brooke. 'He just heard I was sick and came to check on me. I must look pretty terrible to get this kind of reaction out of him.' She smiled, stiff and weak.

Her mom frowned. 'Whatever his problem is, I want him out of the house right now. I don't know what you think you're doing, John, but I have half a mind to call the police, the way you barged in here like that.'

I stared at Brooke, my mind numb. *What do I do? How can I stop her? If it's already inside, there's nothing I can do at all.*

'I'll go,' I said. Her mom let go of me, and I took a step back towards the stairs. 'I'm sorry.'

'I'm fine, John,' said Brooke. 'Really. Things were bad before, but now I feel . . . perfect.'

It's over.

I locked my bedroom door and flopped onto my bed, covering my eyes and gritting my teeth until my jaw hurt with the pain.

Nobody's inside Brooke now. Nobody is Brooke. I can't kill one without killing the other.

The phone rang, but I ignored it; Mom could check the

messages when she came upstairs later. I worked backwards through my memory, tracing Nobody's path from girl to girl. *There's got to be something I'm missing; some key piece that will unlock it and make it all work.* The demon started in . . . I didn't know. A body no one had found yet. From there she took over Jenny Zeller, spent some time in there, then in June she killed her and jumped to Allison Hill. She stayed in Allison for two months before jumping over to Rachel. *What had Rachel said the morning Allison died?* 'She called me five times last night.' Then it was the same with Rachel, obsessing over Marci all night at the dance; now Marci had grown obsessed with Brooke. I pulled a notebook from my backpack and wrote it down:

Intense focus on a new host right before killing the current one.

What prompted the obsession? Was it simply a slow hunt, with me as the prey? But that didn't make sense; if the demon knew who I was, it didn't have to spend months jumping from one girl to the next – it could have just come straight for me. And in the morning, when I'd told Marci about the demons, I was really talking to Nobody: I was telling the demon herself that I was the one she was looking for. The hunt was over, and all she had to do was kill me, but instead she killed her host and jumped into Brooke. If I wasn't her target, it had to be something else.

The phone rang again, loud and insistent. I let it ring. *What did I say to Marci this morning?* I thought. *What happened in our conversation that made Nobody want to leave Marci and take over Brooke?* I'd warned Marci about the killer; I'd told her I'd come over; I'd told her she'd be safe if she wasn't alone. Was that it? Maybe Nobody got spooked, and thought that if she didn't leave Marci right then, that she'd never get the chance, since Marci would never be alone again. Now that I'd visited Brooke, did Nobody know that I'd figured her out? Had I just put Brooke into danger?

Who am I kidding? Brooke will never leave this alive.

Maybe it was something else. Maybe it was the specific mention of the demons that had prompted Nobody to kill Marci and take Brooke. I'd told her about the demons, and her first response was something about Brooke. She'd asked me if I had been in Agent Forman's house. I'd said yes, and she'd said, 'Brooke was in there too.' Maybe she wanted to be Brooke because of Brooke's experience with Forman.

Or maybe it was our shared experience with Forman, Brooke and I together, that made it important. Even if she wasn't trying to kill me, she was definitely drawing closer and closer to me. Did she have some other plan, completely unrelated to killing?

She told me she loved me – those were her final words. Was that Marci, breaking through for one last message?

Or was it Nobody?

The phone rang again. I felt a sudden pit in my stomach, a swerve and plunge of vertigo. *Ring!* I crawled off of my bed and opened my bedroom door. *Ring!* I walked down the hall, step by step, and looked at the phone. The caller ID said Watson – Brooke's family. I picked it up. *Ring!* I hit the button.

'Hello?'

'Hey, John.' It was Brooke, her voice still soft and frail. 'How's it going?'

'Fine.' *Why was she calling? Did she know I'd figured her out? What was she doing?*

'Sorry about my mom,' said Brooke. 'You know how parents can be sometimes. So, what you doing?'

I had no idea how to answer. *I'm talking to a demon!* I looked at the walls, the windows, anything to spark some kind of active thought, but my brain wouldn't work. *This is the thing that killed Marci.*

'You there?' she asked.

I closed my eyes. 'It's you, isn't it?'

She coughed. 'Sorry about my voice, I'm kind of hoarse; it's Brooke.'

'No, it's not. It's Nobody, isn't it? You're Forman's friend.'

Silence. The phone crackled, slightly static; the clock ticked. She inhaled, a tiny intake of breath, so soft I could barely hear it. I shifted my feet.

Her voice was the shadow of a whisper. 'How did you know?'

'You killed Marci,' I said. 'You killed all of them.'

'No . . .'

'You're going to kill Brooke too. How long does she have?'

'No,' she whispered, 'never again.'

'What are you doing? Why are you killing these girls?'

'I didn't mean to. I never wanted to hurt anybody, but I couldn't take it any more. But it's okay now – that's all behind me.'

'What's behind you – killing? Why do you keep saying that?'

'I thought Marci would be the last one, I really did. She was prettier than Rachel, and smarter, and she had a boyfriend, and she looked so happy – but that wasn't real at all. She was a slob. She was fat. She was dumb—'

'She was brilliant,' I cut in, 'and she wasn't remotely fat.'

'Oh come on,' she hissed. It was Brooke's voice, but harsher and colder than Brooke had ever been. 'Marci was a cow. Rachel was a loser, but at least she was skinny. Now, Brooke, on the other hand, is perfect. She's tall, she's thin, it's like being a tree maybe, or a breeze. Her hair is long and flowing, not like Marci's tangled rat hair. She's clean, and her room is bright.'

'You're insane.'

'You were the final piece,' she said. 'I could tell, as soon as you saw Brooke in the Friendly Burger, that you loved her. I could—'

'I don't love anyone.'

'I could see it in your eyes,' she said, 'watching her, and in the things you'd shared together that Marci never had. I thought I could keep you, but it got worse and worse, and then this morning when you called to warn me, and you talked about her instead—'

'*You* talked about her, not me.'

'You talked about the demons,' said Brooke. 'I'd started to wonder if it might be you, with all of Marci's memories, but I wasn't sure until you said it this morning. You're the hunter, and that's what I wanted more than anything – that's why I came here.'

'To kill me?'

'No!' she insisted. 'I came to join you. That's why I knew it had to be Brooke, because she'd shared it all with you. They're horrible, John; they're evil, and awful, and we have

273

to destroy them. I can help you, John. I can lead you to them, and you can kill them, and we can be together.'

'But you're one of them.'

'No, I'm not!' she rasped, as loud as her weakened voice would let her. 'I am *not* one of Kanta's gods, or angels, or whatever he wants to call them. I am Brooke Watson. I am a regular, beautiful, perfect human girl.'

Kanta. It was Forman's other name, the one he used with his fellow demons. No one else knew it. If there was any doubt left that Brooke was Nobody, she'd abolished it with that single word.

'Don't you see how perfect this is?' she pleaded. 'I can help you, and we can stay together, and we can destroy them all. We can wipe them out, and get rid of them for good. You can have the girl you've always wanted, and I can have you. Forever.'

Someone to hunt with, I thought. *Someone to talk with.* It hit me like a brick, more tempting than I'd ever imagined: someone to be with forever, who would never leave me, who would always stay with me and always do the things I wanted to do. To be able to know that no matter what I did, no matter where I went, Brooke would always be there, always watching, always helping, always smiling and happy to see me . . .

. . . always trapped inside her own body, helpless and afraid. Every time I looked in her eyes I'd know it was a demon looking back, studying me, waiting for . . .

I'd always know, and so would Brooke.

And so would Nobody.

'It will never last,' I said. 'You'll just kill her again.'

'Never.'

'That's what you thought with Marci, too, and look what happened. How many times have you done it?'

Silence.

'How many?' I demanded. 'How many times have you killed an innocent girl because she was too short, or too tall, or her teeth were too crooked? How many times have you killed yourself, and some poor girl got in the way?'

'It's not me.'

'Yes, it is! You hate the demons, but that's what you are, so you hate yourself – and no matter how perfect these girls are, they will always be tainted, because *you* will always be there.'

'No!' Her voice was a roar, its weakness gone, its rawness terrifying. *I'm putting Brooke in danger,* I realised. *I have to calm her down – I have to keep her happy while I figure out what to do.*

'You don't know what it's like!' she shouted. 'You don't know what I have to go through every day, just being one of them!'

'I'm sorry,' I said, searching for a plan. 'You were right. It will be different this time, because you have me.'

She paused. 'I love you, John.'

I closed my eyes. *Just don't kill Brooke.* 'You're sick now, because you're still settling into the body, right?'

'Yes.'

'When will you be better?'

'Tomorrow sometime. It shouldn't take long.'

'Then I'll see you tomorrow. We'll go somewhere and talk.'

'A date?'

I breathed deep. 'Yes, a date. Does that sound good?'

'It sounds wonderful.'

'Okay then, I'll see you tomorrow. I . . .' *I can't say it.* 'I'll see you.'

Chapter 25

I have to kill her. It's the only choice. I paced back and forth in the hallway, head down, fingers clenched into fists. *She's going to kill herself anyway, sooner or later, so Brooke's already as good as dead. But if I kill her first, and find a way to kill Nobody too, then the chain will be broken and no one else will have to die. I can't save Brooke, but I can make her the last.*

I stopped, feeling my stomach roil and my throat grow cold as ice. I stumbled to the bathroom, knelt and threw up in the toilet. I threw up again, vomiting until my gut was empty and each heave was dry and painful. *I can't do it. I can't kill Brooke.* I wiped my mouth with the back of my hand and leaned against the wall, my strength drained and my body powerless. I felt like a husk, ready to crumple and blow away.

It lives in her blood. Anything I do to kill her will free the demon, and she'll spill out and live while Brooke's body dies behind her. I heaved again. *Maybe I could strangle her – there are plenty of ways to kill without blood. I could choke her to death, or tie her up and drop her in the lake . . .*

I beat my hands against the floor, crying. *Stop thinking about it!* But I couldn't stop. My mind kept going and going, filled with thoughts and images, imagining Brooke's dead body lurching back to life, forced into motion by the demon in her blood. *It's not enough to kill the host – I have to kill the demon inside.*

I curled up on the floor, squeezing my eyes shut and covering my ears, but the thoughts were inside my head and I couldn't block them out. *Fire would do it. Drop her in a big enough fire and the demon will burn to death before she can escape.*

Maybe there's a way to save her. A dialysis machine could pump the blood out, and the demon with it, and filter it all and put it back in. Or maybe not – the sludge is thick, and the pressure of pumping it out against its will would probably kill the host. And how could I possibly get access to a dialysis machine?

The front door opened, and footsteps came in. My heart sped up, irrationally certain it was the demon come to talk to me with Brooke's voice and face, but the cadence of the steps was my mom's; I let my muscles go slack, put my head on the cold tile floor, and tried to calm my breathing. The footsteps walked into the kitchen; the faucet turned on, then off. The footsteps wandered back into the hallway, disappearing with a creak into the softness of the carpet, and then Mom was gasping in the bathroom doorway.

'John!' She dropped her bag and knelt down, touching my shoulders, feeling my forehead, taking my pulse. I saw her glance into the toilet and grit her teeth, then she grabbed me under the arms and hauled me up. 'Come on,' she said softly. 'It's okay, come on up.' I held her arm with one hand, the wall with the other, and let her help me to my feet. Together we staggered into the living room, where she laid me down on the couch. She sat next to me, pulling my head onto her lap, and smoothed my hair with her hand.

'I'm so sorry, John. I'm so sorry about Marci.'

Had that really only been this morning? Not even seven hours had gone by since my call to Marci, and already she'd been dead so long it seemed like ages ago. I felt old and tired, like a weathered tyre cracking in the sun.

'I heard you come home, after you ran out,' said Mom. 'I thought I'd just let you be alone for a while. I should have come up.'

'It's not just Marci,' I said. 'You saw the demon sludge, right?'

Pause. 'Yes.'

I closed my eyes. 'It's been moving through them all, all the suicides, and now it's moved to someone else.'

She paused again. 'What are you going to do?'

'I don't know.' *I'm going to kill Brooke.* 'I don't know. I used to think I was trying to kill demons, and then I realised that killing wasn't enough, and I needed to save people, and now ... Now I can't do either one.' But I knew it wasn't true – I knew I could still find the strength to kill the demon. Saving Brooke wasn't an option any more, but I could always kill. Sometimes that seemed like the only thing I was ever good at. 'I don't want to be a killer.'

We sat in silence for a minute, then Mom spoke again. 'Lauren told me about last night. That you told her to get me out of the house.'

I pressed my fingertips against my forehead, rubbing away the beginning of a headache. It didn't work. 'She didn't know why. It's not her fault.'

'No, she didn't, but that's not making it any better. It's tearing her apart, thinking what could have happened to you.'

'That's a poor choice of words, given the circumstances.'

Mom sighed. 'Please, John. You can't just hide behind jokes and technicalities.' Pause. 'Did you kill that man?'

'No.'

'Were you planning to?'

'Yes.'

She sighed again, and I felt her arm tense on my shoulder; her leg tensed beneath my head, and I closed my eyes, bracing myself for a fight. Her next question was soft and quiet. 'Why didn't you?'

Not what I expected. 'I didn't want to. He was just a normal guy. Screwed up, but not a demon or anything.'

'He was a sociopath,' said Mom.

'He was me, twenty years from now; he was exactly what I was turning into. I decided I didn't want to.'

Her arm and leg relaxed, and I felt a drop of water on my head; a tear. 'So,' she said, 'what are you going to do now?'

'I don't know.'

'Do you know who the demon is in?'

'Yes.'

She stifled a small sob. 'Who?'

'No one.' *But she's already guessed,* I thought. 'It's no one you know.' I pulled away from her, sitting up and facing the wall. 'It doesn't matter.'

'I just want to—'

The phone rang. I felt cold again, dreading the call like it was my own death. Mom stood up, grabbed the phone and answered.

'Hello?' Pause. 'Oh, hello Brooke, it's nice to hear from you. Yes, he's right here, but . . .' She looked at me, frowned, and turned back to the phone. 'I'm afraid he's really not—'

'Wait!' I said, jumping up. 'I'll take it. I'll talk.'

'Are you sure?'

'Yes.'

She paused, holding the phone.

'Please,' I begged.

Mom lifted the phone to her face. 'Here he is.' She handed me the phone and I held it to my ear.

'Hello.'

'Hey, John.' Brooke's voice, Brooke's mouth, Brooke's body. It made me sick. 'I was thinking about tomorrow, trying to decide a good place to go. Do you have any specific plans?'

I took a deep breath before I replied, forcing myself to sound normal. *Just keep her happy – just one more day, maybe two. I'll figure something out but I've got to keep her happy.*

When I'd finished, Mom frowned. 'Are you sure you'll be okay?'

'Don't worry about it,' I said, walking slowly down the hall to my room. 'Don't worry about me.' *I'm not the one who's going to die.*

Fire was the only way. It was the only thing that could trap the demon and kill it for sure, with no mistakes and no chance for escape. *I have to do it – I have to stop Nobody from killing girl after girl after girl.* Brooke would die too, but she would be the last. Nobody would never again be able to sacrifice another girl's body to fuel her own impossible quest for perfection.

Fire would work. It was destruction embodied, and even if Nobody could regenerate, like Crowley, a good fire could keep up with her regeneration, and even surpass it. It would kill her before she could get clear of the body. All I had to do was find a good fire, or a good place to set one, and then get Brooke near enough to push her in. How could I do it without making her suspicious? Where could I do it without anyone seeing us, and trying to rescue her?

Maybe it wouldn't be so bad, living with Nobody. She might actually be happy – I could keep her happy forever, keep her in that body, and we could hunt the demons together just like she said. If I weighed the worth of lives in a pure, objective scale, Nobody and I could save hundreds, maybe thousands, if we killed just a handful of demons. The Formans of the world, the leaders of this hell community, were the biggest prize. Nobody herself might kill a few more times, but what was that compared to thousands of people, thousands of families?

I had no idea how many other demons were out there, how many of the deaths and murders and attacks that we heard about every day were the work of this tiny, sinister subset of the population. They never aged – they'd keep killing forever if we didn't stop them. I was willing to spend my life stopping them – wouldn't Nobody's host feel the same way? Wasn't it worth one girl's life, or two or five or even ten, to save millions?

I feel that way because I've made a choice, I thought. *The girls Nobody kills don't get that choice. Brooke never made that choice, and she never would.* She'd talked about saving people, not killing them; she'd said that the world needed more people who helped each other. But how could I make that choice when helping one person required me to kill someone else?

Brooke didn't get to choose, but what would she choose if she could? She wouldn't choose to be a killer. Certainly she wouldn't choose to be burned alive. I squeezed my palms against my eyes, pressing them until they hurt. I thought about Marci, dead and cold. I thought about Brooke, trapped and mute while a demon moved her body like a puppet; in a few weeks she'd be dead too. I thought about Forman and Crowley, dying on the ground; I thought about their victims, their families, about Max's lifeless eyes reflecting the hollow motion of a TV screen. I thought about my dad, gone more than half my life, perfectly alive and perfectly gone.

Why do people leave?

I'd spent a year hunting serial killers, getting into their heads and seeing what and how they thought; I'd entertained nearly every question imaginable, no matter how grisly, no matter how horrifying, and they had passed over me like harmless air. Yet this question was almost too much to think about.

Why do people leave?

The suicides had bothered me so much because they were voluntary – or so we'd all thought. Now we knew that the victims were being taken from us, instead of leaving on their own, it was easier to accept. It made sense, even if it still bothered me, and I could at least find a place for it in my head. It heartened me, in some strange way, to know that Marci had died fighting for her life; it made that life seem stronger, more worth living. If you could throw it away so easily, what good was it?

I looked at the phone, blessedly quiet. Brooke hadn't called in nearly an hour. I picked it up, stared at the numbers a moment, then dialled zero.

'What party would you like to reach?'

'Can I get a number in New York?' The last we'd heard from Dad was nearly a year ago, when he sent presents for Christmas. There was no return address, but the postmark was New York City.

'Please hold.' The line went dead, then music started – something brainless and peppy. I stared at the wall, ignoring the music, until a different voice cut it off.

'What party would you like to reach?'

'New York, please.'

'New York City?'

'Yeah.'

'Name?'

'Sam Cleaver,' I said, 'or maybe Samuel.'

Pause. 'I'm afraid I don't have anyone by that name.'

'No one?'

'No, sir.'

'No Sam Cleaver in the entire city of New York? There's like eight million people there.'

'None of them by that name, sir.'

Silence.

'Would you like to try another name, sir?'

'How about S. Cleaver?'

'I have a Sharon, that's it. Does your party have a middle name he might be listed under?'

'No.' I stared at the wall. 'Thanks.'

'Thank you for calling Information—'

I hung up the phone and dropped it on the bed next to me. I looked around, seeing the walls and windows and doors without comprehending any of them. My eyes fell on the phone, and I picked it up and hurled it at my closet door, bouncing it off the wood. The phone fell to the floor and I jumped up, grabbed it, and slammed it into the door again and again until the wood splintered and caved in. Shards stung my hand, and I hit the door one more time before throwing the phone against the opposite wall. My hand ached, speckled with drops of blood. I touched one of the drops with my hand, lightly, then smeared my whole hand across the wall. It left a faint bloody streak.

Fire. It was the only way.

Chapter 26

The phone rang twice before I picked it up.

'Good morning, John.'

'Hey, Brooke.' I winced at the name and put down my spoon.

'What's up?' *She sounds so cheerful, as if nothing's wrong at all.*

'Nothing,' I said. 'Are you feeling better?'

'A little bit. A few more hours and we can go do something together.'

'Yeah,' I said, running through my plan one last time. 'I thought it might be fun to head out to the lake and go fishing. Brooke always loved to go fishing.'

'I know,' she said coldly. 'I'm Brooke.'

'You're Brooke. I know. So anyway, does that sound good?'

'It sounds great!' she said. 'You want to go after school?'

'Terrific.' I paused, trying to sound as natural as possible, and pretended to remember something. 'Oh crap, I forgot I have to pick up a bunch of stuff for Mom. She's freaked out it's gonna snow soon, and wants me to get some gas for the snowblower, and salt for the walks, and that kind of stuff. It shouldn't take me long, but . . .'

'Oh no,' said Brooke. 'I really wanted to do something today!'

'Well . . .' I let her wait a bit, building suspense. 'I suppose I could meet you there. I'll come straight from the gas station. That could save us a lot of time if you bike out there and pick a good spot.'

'A good spot, huh?'

'Yeah. Someplace secluded.'

'John Cleaver,' she said, feigning shock. 'Whatever do you intend to do with me in a secluded spot by the lake?' I struggled to read her voice, though the general feeling was clear: she was eager, and thought I was planning something romantic.

'I'll see you there,' I said. *And you won't be the least bit suspicious when I show up with several cans of gas.*

'Awesome,' she said. 'I love you, John.'

'See ya.' I hung up the phone just as Mom stepped into the kitchen.

'Who was that?'

'Brooke.' There was no use hiding it; she could look it up in the caller ID history if she wanted to.

'You going somewhere with Brooke today?'

'Yeah.'

'Like, a date?' She was more suspicious than normal. *What is she thinking?*

'I guess so. Sort of.' She liked Brooke; she shouldn't have a problem with that, right?

'Huh,' she said, walking past me and pulling down a box of cereal. 'I realise you're not as emotional as most people, but still – your girlfriend died yesterday. Seems a little early, I think, don't you?'

Crap. 'That's why it's not really a date,' I said. 'We're just heading out to talk about it, try to come to terms with it. You know.'

'Yeah,' she said, nodding, though I could tell she didn't mean it. 'I know exactly what you're talking about.'

'What about you?' I asked, desperate to change the subject. 'You doing anything tonight?'

'Lauren and I are going shopping, actually.' She poured her cereal into a bowl, then opened the fridge to get the milk. I relaxed and tuned her out. 'We had a pretty good talk the other night, before the movie and the . . .' she waved her hand '. . . the police station. Turns out she hates buying groceries because she doesn't know where the good deals are. We're going to go together and see what we can find.'

'Great,' I said, only barely listening. 'I'll see you later then.'

'Not too late,' she said.

'Yeah.' I stood up. 'It won't take long.' I grabbed my jacket and backpack and headed for the door.

'Goodbye, John,' she said. 'Have a good day.'

I waved.

'I love you, John.'

'Yeah,' I said, walking out the door. *People keep saying that.*

School passed in a daze, an endless string of droning teachers and sad, consoling students. 'We're so sorry about Marci.' 'She was a wonderful person, and we all miss her.' 'You're very brave, coming back to school so soon.' I didn't feel brave, I felt numb. I felt cold. I felt tired.

I'd spent the whole night in my car with a screwdriver and a pair of bolt cutters, peeling back the panelling and cutting away the cables for each lock and window. The exterior handles worked, but if someone got stuck inside, they'd be trapped. I was lucky my car was that old; something with power locks and electric windows would have been nearly impossible to sabotage. *I guess that's a good safety feature on the new cars*, I thought. *If something happens to the doors, like on mine, these old cars can be a death trap.*

Bells rang, crowds buzzed, halls filled and emptied; filled and emptied. The sun in the sky was cold and white, like a disk of ice. I drifted through the school like a ghost, unnoticed by most, avoided by everyone else, silent and sombre and dead. When the final bell rang I trudged out to my car, drove to the gas station and filled four five-gallon cans with gas. *Twenty gallons.* Enough to run our huge riding snowblower through several major storms. *Enough to light a very, very big fire.* I pushed all thoughts and emotions away – all my nervousness, all my fear, all my sorrow. *I am a sociopath. I am a machine. I am a gust of wind: nameless, faceless – and blameless.*

I put three cans of gas in the back seat, lids off, next to box after box of old magazines I'd stolen from Father Erikson's house; the last can went in the trunk, next to a narrow funnel I'd stolen from our kitchen. I didn't need to steal any matches; I always had a book of them in my pocket. I sat down in the driver's seat and touched the underside of the roof with my finger, feeling the hole I'd put there with a single shot from Max's silenced gun.

I drove towards the lake, stopped halfway and poured two

289

cans of gas on the magazines and seat cushions in the back. The smell was terrible, but I ignored it.

I continued down the road, looking for Nobody, and found her almost at the farthest end, waving from a dirt turn-off. I slowed and pulled off, driving past her and parking behind a stand of trees. It was a good spot – the road kept going past the lake, but there was nothing out there for miles, and no one was likely to drive past or see us. I stepped out, locking the driver's door as I closed it. It would never open again. Nobody ran toward me, smiling with Brooke's mouth.

'You made it!' she said, then coughed and stepped back, waving her hand in front of her face. 'Wow, gas for the snowblower, huh?'

'They're pretty old cans; a lot of fumes get out.'

'At least it will have some time to air out while we fish,' she said. 'I've got the stuff right over here.' She pointed into the trees, and I saw her bike leaning against a trunk, two poles and a backpack propped up beside it.

'Wow,' I said, trying to sound alive. 'You carried those here on your bike?'

'I'm amazing,' she said. 'This isn't the first time I've biked out here to fish.' She drew closer. 'First time I've been out this far, though, with such a handsome young man.'

'Yeah,' I said, looking around. *This is it. Don't think, don't wait, just do it.* 'I was actually thinking of another spot; it's a little way back, but we can get a lot farther off the road. It's really nice.'

'Really?'

'Yeah. Very private.'

'Sounds great,' she said with a smile, 'but I'm not taking the poles this time.' She walked towards her bike. 'Race you there?'

'Why don't you just come with me? I can stick your bike in the trunk.'

'And we won't asphyxiate from the gas fumes first?'

'I made it here, didn't I? We'll roll down the windows; it'll be fine.'

She grinned. 'Let's do it.' She walked towards the car, and I followed. Nobody talked, and acted, as if she was half-Brooke – as if Brooke's memories were somehow mingled with her own. If that was true, she'd wait for me to open her door; Brooke was very old-fashioned that way. Sure enough, she stopped at the door, waiting, and I forced myself to smile. *Perfect.* I opened the door, she coughed and laughed and climbed in, and I closed it firmly behind her.

Goodbye, Brooke. I'm sorry.

Her hand went to the window roller, and I turned to walk back to the trunk. I opened it, listening to the silence as Nobody tried and failed to roll down the window. I pulled out the gas can and the funnel.

'John, I think your window's broken.' Its voice was muffled through the closed door. I heard a series of clicks as it tried the handle. 'The door's broken too. Wow, it smells awful in here.'

I closed the trunk and saw that Nobody had scooted across to the driver's side and was trying the handle there. It saw me, looked at me, saw the can in my hand.

'What are you doing?'

I set the gas can on the trunk, climbed up after it and

reached across to the hole in the roof. The funnel just barely fit.

'John!' it shouted. 'John, let me out! What are you doing up there?' The car shifted as she moved again, and when I reached back to lift the heavy gas can onto the roof I saw her scrambling over the seats to reach the back doors. She put a hand on the gas-soaked magazines and drew back in disgust. 'Is this gas?' She smelled her hand and her eyes went wide with terror. She stepped over the seats, her feet splashing down in the puddles of gas in the foot wells, and pounded on the rear window. 'John! What are you doing? Let me out!'

I hefted the gas can up onto the roof, unscrewed the cap, and tipped it lightly into the funnel. Gas streamed down, sending up a new wave of fumes, and Nobody screamed again. There was already plenty of gas in the car, but the fumes were the important part – that's what would ignite, mingling with the air to fill the entire car with flame. Nobody tried one door, then the other, banging on the windows.

'John, let me out! You're going to kill me! You're insane!'

I kept pouring, trying to keep the stream steady as the car jostled beneath me.

'John, this was all a joke!' she cried. 'I'm not a demon, I'm not Nobody, I'm just Brooke. It was a joke! You can't kill me!'

I closed my eyes and tipped the can upside down, pouring out the last few drops. Nobody hit the funnel from underneath, knocking it up and over, and the last slosh of gas poured out onto the roof. She was plugging the hole with her finger.

'Please, John, don't do this. Don't do this.' She was sobbing. 'You can't kill me. I am Nobody, I admit it, I am, but this is Brooke's body. She's still in here – you're killing her too! I know you want to kill demons – I want to kill them too, but you're killing Brooke! You're killing your friend! You love her! She loves you! Dammit, let me out!'

I threw the can aside, stood up and carefully wiped my hands as clean of gas as I could get them. I reached into my pocket for a book of matches, pulled it out, and tore the first match free.

Nobody was by the back window now, banging on the glass and snarling like an animal. Brooke's features were twisted into a mask of fury: lips curled up, teeth bared. Her hair and face were drenched in gasoline. 'I will kill you, John, I will eat your heart, you bastard!' She was screaming now, her voice an unrecognisable roar. 'You think this car can hold me in? You think this fire can hurt me?' She slammed her fist into the window. 'You can't kill me!'

I folded the matchbook around the match, pressing it tightly against the striking surface, and ripped it free. The match flared to life, a tiny flame hungry for fuel. I leaned forward, keeping clear of the gas, and reached out to drop the match into the hole in the roof. The car shook violently as Nobody slammed against the side door, and the flame caught on the puddle of spilled gas. The roof burst into flame and I stumbled back, falling onto the trunk. The fall knocked the wind out of my lungs, and the matchbook flew out of my hand.

I struggled for air as the burning gas began to run down the back window towards me. Nobody slammed into the door again, and I heard the side window crack. I rolled off the car, kneeling by the back wheel, and finally managed to draw a breath. The car shook again, the window shattered loudly, and a rain of broken glass exploded out from the car. Brooke's body crawled out through the window, soaked with sweat and gas; she scraped against the broken window, leaving long bloody gashes in her arms and legs. The body fell out in a heap, gasping for air and moaning with pain, and I backed away. *She's covered in gas. If I can find the matches, I can still kill her.*

'You,' she croaked, 'bastard.'

I turned wildly, looking for the matchbook; it was behind me, about ten feet away, and I lunged for it. Something caught my leg and I fell, landing on my wrist and bending it backwards. I screamed in pain.

'John Cleaver,' the demon hissed, Brooke's hand tight on my ankle. I rolled to the side and saw her crawling towards me, reaching out with her other hand and grasping my leg. Her eyes glared hellishly from behind long tangles of wet, bloody hair. 'I should have known you'd try to kill me. You never loved Brooke; she's weak, and stupid. You could never love a stupid blonde nothing like *her*.'

Her fingers – Brooke's fingers – dug into my leg like claws, and she pulled herself up further, letting go of my ankle and grabbing my chest. I tried to kick her off but she sat on my legs and slammed her fist into my gut, nearly doubling me over in pain. 'I should have known I could never be happy as Brooke, but you – you're something different altogether. Something powerful and driven. You're passionate.' She smiled wolfishly, baring her teeth. 'I love you.'

A drop of burning gas from the roof of the car finally dripped down through the hole, and the interior of the car roared into blazing life. Nobody sat firmly on my hips, pinning me to the ground, and picked up a fragment of glass. It was a small cube of safety glass, but it had a sharp edge.

'No,' I said, struggling to push her off. She brought up the glass, gripping it so tightly that her fingers ran red with smears of blood, and pressed it against her forearm. 'You'll kill her,' I croaked, but she smiled.

'I'm only finishing what you started. Soon we'll be together, more closely and more perfectly than you could ever be with Brooke. We'll be one. We'll be perfect.'

I grabbed her arms, trying to force them apart, but she brought them together with a terrifying, inhuman strength and plunged the glass shard into her arm. She dug it deep into the skin, raking it through muscle and artery and spraying hot red blood across my face. Blood pumped out in great spurts, covering me, and Brooke's body shook with pain. As the blood poured out she grew weaker, and I knocked the shard out of her hand. I gripped her ragged forearm with both fists, pressing it tightly, trying to stop the hot, sticky flow of blood

—and then something moved, thick and wet, against the palm of my hand.

I jerked back in an involuntary spasm of revulsion, as a dark black tendril reached out from inside of Brooke's arm. It was tentative, like a snake's tongue tasting the air. It grew longer, reaching towards me, and suddenly there were two, then three, then a vast web of black tentacles springing out of Brooke's body. I covered my face with one arm and flailed against them with the other, trying madly to knock them aside, gritting my teeth against the pain in my damaged wrist. I felt a wave of nausea as the wet tendrils touched my skin, and then they were everywhere – grasping, reaching, sticking. I tried to push them back, tried to free myself and run away, but Brooke's legs kept me pinned to the dirt while a sea of black tendrils grabbed my arms and forced them aside. Nobody loomed over me, a hideous mix of pain and triumph on Brooke's half-dead face.

'I love you, John. I've loved you since the day you called me, swearing to destroy us. It's what I always wanted, but never dared to do – but not you. You can actually do it. You have the strength I never had. Sometimes I wish I could be . . . *you*.'

Black slime oozed out of Brooke's jagged wound in great waves, undulating with some kind of hideous life. It seemed to hang in the air, a noxious blob frozen in time, then leaped suddenly at my face like a bolt of black lightning.

Chapter 27

I clamped my mouth shut, squeezed my eyes tightly closed, but it was everywhere – in my nose, in my ears, peeling back my lips and pressing in against my teeth. I pulled on my arms and legs, grunting with the effort to free them, trying to push back against the sludge with nothing but my tongue. My mouth was filled with the taste of ash and blood, the feel of grit and slime. It moved repugnantly inside me, pushing past my tongue, crawling up my nose, forcing itself into every crack and crevice. My head throbbed for want of air, my lungs burned; my ears buzzed with the sound of my own wild heartbeat and the sticky creep of sludge. I was blind and deaf, drowning in viscous evil, lost and alone.

I will not be taken, I thought. *I will not let this happen!* But there was no way to stop it – its grip was too tight, its tendrils too many, its darkness my entire world. I felt my chest bursting and caving in at once, desperate for air, and then abruptly the weight of Brooke's body fell backwards, its grip loosened, and I wrenched my hands free. My head was surrounded with black tar, warm and slimy, and I scrabbled at it like an animal.

I pulled the thing away from my head and opened my

eyes to blinding heat. The entire car was ablaze, the broken window spouting flame like a raging furnace. The sludge was on me, grasping at my hands, crawling back towards my head; Brooke lay on the ground in the spray of broken glass, bleeding and moving feebly. Her body was connected to mine by a black, pulsing web, snared together like flies. Hands were scraping at the sludge on my body, pulling and pushing it away. My hands and other hands, worn and familiar.

My mom loomed over me, teeth bared in a grimace of effort, real and alive, wrestling with the demon like charred, black taffy.

I tore at the sludge in my mouth, spitting it out, clawing it out of my nose and gums. 'Mom,' I croaked. My voice was thin and distant; hers was inaudible. I pulled at the sludge in my ears, struggling to free them, and suddenly the world burst with a rush of sound – the aural surface shock after a deepwater dive.

'Get off of him,' Mom raged, but it was no use. The demon had recovered from whatever initial attack had knocked it away, and it had adapted to face a new opponent. With a sweep of its tendrils it knocked Mom's feet out from under her, thick whips of black pinning her arms so she couldn't catch herself. She landed heavily, grunting with the impact, and the black sludge swarmed back to me like a mass of hungry worms.

'You can never stop us,' hissed Brooke's voice. Her eyes were closed, and she lay in a limp knot like a discarded puppet. The black sludge forced my arms to the sides and oozed slowly up my body to my head. Brooke's mouth moved unnaturally, as if independently of her body.

'John and I are one; I am John now, and we will never be apart.'

'Shut up,' I snarled, but it was a threatless cry; I was immobile and helpless.

'Get away from him, whatever you are.' The sludge was flowing away from Mom to focus on me, and she struggled free of its grip.

'I love him,' whispered Brooke's voice, 'and he loves me.' The sludge was up to my neck, hot and vile on my skin.

'Never,' said Mom, diving back towards the sludge. 'Brooke maybe, but never you.'

'He does,' said the voice, and the ashy black tendrils reached up to my face, prying at my mouth. I pressed my lips tightly together, flexing every muscle in my face, but still it started to open them, to crawl back inside.

Mom looked at me in desperation, her eyes wet with tears, her hands clawing at the flowing black sludge. She screamed helplessly and staggered back.

'John hates himself,' she said loudly, looking back and forth between Brooke and me as if unsure where to direct her voice. 'Become a part of him and he'll hate you too. He always will.'

The sludge slowed, tendrils pausing in mid-air. *What are you doing?* I thought.

Mom swallowed and went on, 'He didn't love Brooke either, or Marci, or anyone else, and they didn't love him.' She looked at me, eyes pleading. *She's sorry*, I thought. *I know that face; I know her better than anyone in the world. Why is she saying these things if she's sorry about them?* There was another look there, too, hidden behind the other. *What is she doing?*

'There's only one person he's ever loved,' she said, 'and only one person who's ever loved him back.'

The look in her eyes became clear, and suddenly I knew she was saying goodbye. *Don't do it!* I screamed, but my mouth was full of ash and I couldn't make a sound.

Mom stared into my eyes, intense and terrified. '*Me.*'

The sludge stopped moving completely.

'Who's been with him through everything?' Mom asked. 'Who's the only person who's never left him, and the only person he's never left? He even abandons himself sometimes, throwing his life away in one idiotic plan after another, but never his mother. Never me. I've been there since the beginning, helping him through every crisis, hiding the first demon's slime from the police, showing him how to control himself and his dark side. I'm the only person he's ever loved and the only person he'll ever love, and if you want him to love you, then . . .' She paused, eyes wide, and swallowed again. 'Then you have to take me.'

No! I shouted again, but it was too late; the demon was sliding off, oozing back, shooting out lines to Mom.

'I knew you were coming here,' she said, watching me as the demon surged up her legs, 'and I knew why.' It wrapped itself hungrily around her chest, dropping me painfully on the ground as it raced upwards to her face. 'I knew what you were planning, but I couldn't let you do it. I—' and then it was around her face and flowing into every orifice, her mouth, her nose, her ears, her eyes.

I struggled to my feet and dashed towards her, but a black tentacle jerked my leg to the side and I fell, landing on my hurt wrist again and crying out as it snapped audibly. I rolled on the ground, screaming, then forced myself to my knees and looked at Mom. The demon was on her fully now, an amorphous blob no longer connected to me or to Brooke. Her body stiffened as the ooze flowed in, the last black tendril disappearing inside just as I reached her.

'Mom,' I said. 'Fight it.' I grasped uselessly at her ears and mouth, as if I could pull the sludge back out by force of will. 'Fight back!' I shouted. 'Push it out! We can save you!'

Mom staggered to the side. I put out a hand to steady her, but she stumbled away. She grunted with effort: 'Not . . . in control . . . yet. Still . . . me.' She paused and fell to one knee, barely catching herself; she moved stiffly, like a mannequin coming to life. I tried to help her up, searching for anything I could do to save her, but she lurched away. I looked up, traced her path, and cried out.

'No!'

She was moving directly towards the burning car.

'The only . . . way . . .' She stopped abruptly, her head cranking harshly to the side; I leaped forward to pull her back, but she raised a stiff arm and managed to bat my broken wrist. I screamed and fell to my knees, my vision blurring with the pain.

She fell against the side of the burning car, then rolled to the side to look me in the face. 'I love you, John.' Her voice was thick and layered, in harmony with itself – two voices in one. I stood up, reaching for her, but she ducked into the raging fire of the broken side window. She howled in pain, flinching back and crawling forwards all at once, and then she was through the window and falling onto the floor of the car. The flames leaped wildly around her, dancing and roaring.

I stood in shock, staring at the fire, watching numbly as her body rose up in the midst of the flames, writhing and screaming, black tendrils fighting their way out of her body only to shrivel in the superheated air and burn against the scalding roof and windows. She struggled and flailed; she blackened and died; the human and the demon fuelling the fire until it sang with joy.

I couldn't move. I stared at the fire, at the spot in the middle where my mom's silhouette curled, faded, then disappeared, and couldn't budge an inch. There were a thousand thoughts in my head, crowding and jostling for attention until they became meaningless white noise, and my head was empty. I was a hole in the world, emptiness given form. I was nothing. I was nobody.

Brooke moved, and my head turned to follow the motion. She was lying on the ground, broken and bleeding. Her leg had twitched; it twitched again. I stooped down and felt her breath on my hand, felt her pulse pumping weakly in her uncut wrist. *She's alive.* I stared numbly, too surprised by this to think about anything else. Her leg twitched again, and I started to think, as if it were the first primordial thought, that it would be a good idea to pull her away from the burning car. I grabbed her forearms, raised them over her head, and dragged her to the side. Her cut wrist was still seeping blood, though slower than before, and I looked around for something to bandage it with. There was nothing. I took off my shirt, still soaked in gas and blood, and tied it tightly around the open gash.

Mom's car was just a few yards away, the engine still running, the door still open; she must have pulled up in a rush and leaped out to save me. *She saved me.* I straightened up, looked back at the burning car, then down at Brooke. *She came to stop me, she saw the demon, and she saved me.* I took a step towards the burning car, then Mom's car, then stopped again. *Mom's dead. The demon's dead.*

She saved me.

Brooke moaned. *I need to call an ambulance.* I bent down and searched Brooke's jacket, finding her cellphone in her pocket and pulling it out. I dialed 911, and heard sirens in the distance. *That's too soon. I haven't called yet.* I looked out at the road and saw lights flashing through the trees, red and blue, fire trucks and police cars and ambulances. Officer Jensen was running towards me, and then I was on the ground, kneeling by Brooke, clutching my arm to my chest. *What's wrong with my arm? I think it's broken.*

'John, are you okay?'

I was surrounded by uniforms – paramedics and police. I found a face that looked familiar and talked to it.

'My mom is dead.'

'She's the one who called us,' said the face. It was Officer Jensen. 'She said you were in trouble.'

'She's dead. She was in the car.'

'What happened?'

'She killed the girls,' I said. 'All the suicides, she killed them all.'

'Your mother?'

'No.' I shook my head, suddenly angry. 'Nobody.'

The face was pushed away and another face came into

303

view, checking my pulse and probing me with doctors' implements. 'We're taking you to the hospital,' it said, 'you're going into shock. Can you tell us how you feel?'

'I feel . . .' *What do I feel?*

I guess that's enough.

I feel.

Chapter 28

Brooke woke up late that night, just as the doctor finished setting my wrist in a cast. She asked for me immediately, and when I walked into her hospital room a nurse was setting down a vase of flowers; there were dozens of vases and flowerpots adorning the room. *No one got me flowers when I was in here last spring. Is that because I'm a guy, or because no one likes me?*

'Hey, John,' said Brooke. She was pale and worn, her hair limp and flat against her head. There were deep bags under her eyes, and her arms looked thinner than normal. The nurse left, closing the door behind her, and we were alone. Brooke lifted her bandaged arm. 'Looks like we're twins.'

I held up my cast and nodded. 'Great minds think alike.'

'And great wrists – I don't know,' she said. 'What happened to yours?'

'Broken,' I said. 'You tripped me, then Mom did. Or I suppose technically the . . . uh . . . demon tripped me twice.' *How much did she know?*

'The demon,' said Brooke, looking down. 'Is that what they are?'

So she at least remembers that much. 'I don't know,' I said.

'Forman called them gods. Crowley hated being one, and Nobody – the one who got you – hated them all.'

'Crowley,' whispered Brooke. 'Was he the first one? The Clayton Killer?'

'Yeah.'

'And you killed him?'

I didn't say anything for a long time, then nodded my head. 'Yeah.'

Brooke tapped her bandage. 'And now this.' She took a breath. 'It was horrifying, you know. All of it. I remember everything.'

'I wondered if you would.'

'It was like our minds merged together, but I didn't have any control; we saw the same things, and thought the same things, and remembered the same things, but she was in charge and I was just watching.' She closed her eyes. 'The things she thought, John. Pure darkness. Nothing good about anyone, ever, especially herself. All she did was hate and want, hate and want, over and over forever. I almost wanted you to kill me so I wouldn't have to hear it any more.'

'I'm sorry.'

She shook her head. 'Don't be. You did what you thought you had to do. If I'd known about them before, I probably would have helped you kill the first two.' She shuddered. 'Knowing what I know now, I'd definitely do it.'

I stared at her, and she stared back. 'What are you saying?' I asked.

Her voice was calm and even, her gaze unflinching. 'I'm saying we have to stop them,' she said. 'There's too many, and these three are nothing compared to what else is out there. We have to find them, and we have to stop them.'

'But I lost Forman's phone,' I said. 'That was our only link. That was the only way we could find them, and track them, and—'

'I don't think you understand,' said Brooke. 'We don't need Forman's phone. I told you, I remember *everything*.'

I stood silently, processing her words and their ramifications. *Everything*. I nodded. 'Okay. Now try to rest; it's over for now.'

She laid back in the bed, staring at the ceiling. 'No, John. It will never be over.'

Agent Ostler was waiting in the hall. She nodded as I stepped out.

'The doctor says you're released,' she said. 'You recover from trauma very quickly; the paramedics were impressed.'

'I've had a lot of practice.'

'That you have.' She fell into step beside me as we walked down the hall. 'Brooke will be in the hospital a few more days. Your mother, of course, is dead.'

'Thank you for breaking it to me so gently.'

'Perhaps you can tell me why there was a bullet-hole in the roof of your car?'

'I bought it used.'

'Preliminary evidence from the car suggests, very strongly, that someone set fire to it purposely. Any comment on that?'

'To be fair, it was a very ugly car.'

'Someone broke into Father Erikson's house a few days ago, then broke into his chapel and forwarded his phone to, believe it or not, Agent Forman's cellphone number.' She smiled humourlessly. 'That number seems to turn up in the strangest places, don't you think?'

'Or you may have just written it down wrong,' I said, shrugging. 'Don't feel bad; these things happen.'

Agent Ostler stepped in front of me and stopped, blocking my path. 'Maybe this will get a real answer. Your mother called me this afternoon; said she had something I'd want to see. Perhaps you can guess what she showed me.'

I blew out a long, slow breath, pretending to think. 'The shoe museum?'

'Black sludge,' she said. 'She had some interesting theories about it as well. And she was very worried that you were getting yourself into some kind of trouble.'

I spread my arms, gesturing at the hospital around us. 'How prophetic.'

Ostler watched me a moment longer, then scowled. 'You still don't want to talk; that's fine. But there's one more thing I don't understand.' She paused, seeming to prepare herself. 'If my theory is correct, you've taken down three of the damn things.' I looked up, and she held my gaze as she spoke. 'That's a better record than any of my people, and we've been hunting them for years. How'd you do it?'

I stared at her. *Did she really just say what I think she said?* I weighed my options, and decided to draw her out a little more. 'Three what?'

'You tell me. Nobody's figured that out yet.'

I smiled. 'As a matter of fact, Nobody has.' I glanced around; we were completely alone. 'All that stuff you talked about earlier – the fire and the break-ins and everything?

That all goes away.' I allowed her to think about this. Then: 'After that, Brooke and I have a little proposition for you.'

Marci's body was laid out on the embalming table, pale and still beneath the sheet. I pulled back the top with my good hand, exposing her head and shoulders. She was beautiful. I scratched the cast on my broken wrist, staring down at Marci's face – a face I'd seen a thousand times, ten thousand times, in the real world and in my dreams. I reached out a finger, gently, gingerly, and touched her cheek. It was cold.

'Hi,' I said, uncertain. 'I know you're not really there. This is just your body. Kind of funny, I guess, that the one guy who didn't want you for your body ended up getting it anyway, and losing everything else.' I rested my hand on the table, looking down. 'I don't mean funny. Ironic? You were the one who was good with words, not me.'

I pulled up the side of the sheet, exposing her arm, and stroked her fingers. 'My dad left when I was seven. He was a jerk, and he beat my mom, and he hit me and Lauren a few times, and we hated him – but we loved him too, you know? That's what you do; he's "Dad". I don't think you can help it. And then he left, and it broke my heart – broke it so hard I didn't think I even had one any more.' I held her fingers tightly in my own, staring at her lifeless face. 'I've never told this to anyone – not to Mom, not to Doctor Neblin, not to anybody. I suppose technically I still haven't, since you're not even here, but it feels good to say it, anyway.'

I looked back at her hand, feeling the ridges and bones of each knuckle, rubbing them between my fingers. 'Now my mom is gone too, and I know it sounds totally crazy, but

309

. . . it's one of the worst things that's ever happened to me, and one of the best. She died, and it broke my heart again, and that means . . .' I looked back at her face, then up at the ceiling, watching the ventilator fan turn slowly behind its hard metal grate. 'I think that means that I have a heart.' I huffed, half a laugh and half a cry. 'Who'd have guessed?'

There were tears on my cheek, cold and wet. I let go of Marci's hand to wipe them away, then pulled the sheet back down to cover her arm. 'Listen, I'm no good at this. I'm still a mess – I'm probably a bigger mess now that Mom's dead – and I can't just change overnight. You're the lucky one in this relationship, getting out before you had to know me any better and see how messed up I really am. But I wanted you to know – or I wanted to tell you, anyway – that you helped a lot. Mom's death showed me that I'm not as lost as I thought I was, and I can still have some kind of normal life, but you're the one who showed me how. How to live. I'm sorry you're not here for it, but . . . wherever you are, if you're anywhere, maybe it'll make you happy to know that you helped me.'

I paused, watching her, then leaned down and kissed her – a tiny brush of lips, almost nothing at all. 'I think I finally know, now that you're gone, that I really did love you. I just didn't know how.' I straightened up. 'I guess that isn't very funny either.'

I pulled the sheet back over her head, walked to the door. 'Goodnight, Marci.'

I paused. 'I love you.'

I turned out the light and closed the door.